THE TIGER CHASE

ANDY McD

THE TIGER CHASE
By ANDY M^CD
www.andymcd.com.au

Published in Australia by McDermott House 2022
P.O. Box 395 Coolangatta
Queensland 4225 Australia
info@andymcd.com.au

First published in the USA 2004 by The American
Book Publishing Group.

Copyright © ANDY M^CD 2022
All Rights Reserved

A catalogue record for this
book is available from the
National Library of Australia

ISBN: 978-0-6453709-4-2 (pbk)
ISBN: 978-0-6453709-5-9 (ebk)

Cover design by Media Max Design © 2010
Typesetting and design by McDermott House © 2022

All characters and events in this publication are fictitious, any resemblance to real persons, living or dead, or any events past or present are purely coincidental.

No part of this book may be reproduced in any form, by photocopying or by any electronic or mechanical means, including information storage or retrieval systems, without permission in writing from both the copyright owner and the publisher of this book.

For the tiger that lost its life to poachers ... today!

**Other titles by
ANDY McD**

**X
Flirting with The Moon**

**Quest of the New Templars series:
Book 1 – Resurrection**

**Children's books:
The Last Tiger**

1

A shaft of morning light slices through the canopy, igniting the golden head. A flame burns a trail through the undergrowth. The tiger is on the move.

He is the father of Xiao Gong Zhu, sent from Blue Tiger Mountain to summon the daughter of Yin. The future of his species depends on his success.

Something on the breeze brings him to a sudden halt. With the cloak of camouflage, he dissolves into the forest. Flickering eyes watch as nostrils flare. The scent of the evil ape is here. But beneath the stench lays the aroma of fresh meat. After his long journey, the mighty beast's instincts have dulled, so with the balance of hunger outweighing fear, he continues forward.

***

Lee Chong and his two associates smiled with greed when they heard the tiger's roar. They crept towards the snare set two days earlier, listening as the crazed animal thrashed and fought to free itself. A mournful groan was followed by a pitiful whimper then the tiger roared again in frustration.

Chong caught a glimpse of his prize through the trees. The trap had worked.

The tiger spotted the man and exploded forwards. *Thwack!* The wire snare attached to one of its back paws snatched its body backwards.

The exhausted beast dropped to its haunches; its blazing eyes fixed on its attacker.

Chong watched for over an hour as the doomed creature repeated its futile attempts at escape. He wanted to savour every moment of the animal's pain believing that its strength would transfer to him when he finally killed it.

A wild tiger had not been seen in the forest for almost fifty years. A purebred South China tiger would be sold to the highest bidder, and there'd be no shortage of takers.

Lee Chong remembered when he was a boy how his father would return from the forest with tiger pelts and sacks of bones. But his father was a hunter paid by the Chinese government to eradicate the tiger pest that supposedly threatened the surrounding villages. Chong was a poacher. The tiger was worth more dead than alive. It would be the answer to his prayers. He would squeeze the remnants of life from the mighty beast with his bare hands. Then, with his new power and wealth, he would leave his wife and Hunan for a better life in Hong Kong.

The three men circled the tiger with their rifles at the ready.

Chong watched his associates carefully. He trusted no one.

The beast, panting heavily, lowered itself to the ground in submission. Its energy was spent.

Chong grinned. Gesturing to Xia Lu and Zen Ming to stay where they were, he moved forward for the kill.

Xia and Zen stepped back and grinned at each other behind Chong's back.

Suddenly, the tiger reared up, yanked at the snare one more time and snapped it.

Lee Chong froze, as if suspended in time, staring into the tortured golden eyes of the cat. He saw his reflection surrounded by a blue light. The aura flickered. There was movement behind him. A shadow. A giant blue beast…

The Tiger Chase

Lee Chong was a boy again, seated on his mother's knee. 'Old hunters tell of the blue tiger,' his mother said, combing his hair, 'a mysterious spirit that roams and protects the forests. Some say it is the manifestation of the female force of Yin; others say it is the tiger god sent to devour the souls of hunters and poachers, returning them to the forest as tigers.'

The tiger pounced and swiped Chong across the side of his head. Its fully extended claws tore through the flesh of his face.
   BANG!
   BANG!
   Two shots rang out.

Lee Chong looked down at himself lying in a pool of blood. He was relaxed, drifting among the trees. He saw Xia and Zen struggling to carry the dead tiger away. But he no longer cared. Soon he was gazing down on the forest, the wind carrying him away.
   Blue stripes shimmered in the late afternoon and a cool northern breeze soothed the blistering heat of the day. The shoulders of the mighty beast seemed to rise and fall. Faint rumbles of thunder rolled above like a warning growl.
   Chong recognised the blue monolith spanning the horizons—it was the barrier between the real world and the mythical sanctuary, Blue Tiger Mountain.
   Tall, ancient trees and an impenetrable barrier of bamboo and thickets surrounded the base of the rock. Dense cloud enshrined its summit. A millennium of crosswinds had polished the ninety-degree rock face to a quartz-like texture, making it impossible to scale, while centuries of rain erosion had carved out strange vertical stripes along its length.
   Lee Chong had been here before, and so had his father. In fact, they had spent most of their lives trying to find the entrance to the

secret valley. Now, here he was effortlessly floating over the barrier. He wondered if he'd died and was travelling to paradise.

Soon he was standing at the edge of a clear stream. In the distance he could hear the soothing sound of a waterfall and the beautiful song of the nightingale. Something startled him. He instinctively reached for his gun, but it wasn't there. His eyes opened wide when a tiger emerged from the trees and padded towards him.

'This is Wang. He will not harm you.'

Chong swung round to see an old man sitting on a rock. 'Who are you?' he said, trying to control the quiver in his voice.

'You know who I am. Lee Chong. And you know why you are here.'

Chong glanced at the tiger, then back at the old man. 'You are Huan Loh? The Guardian?'

The old man smiled and gestured for his guest to sit by the edge of the stream. He pointed to the blue mountain in the distance and spoke into the air. 'It is said that the spirit of the blue tiger is omnipresent and roams the forest watching over all creatures. But here the physical beast lies dormant—waiting, watching and protecting the secret.' He looked down at Chong. 'It is also said there is a hidden entrance in the rock. Many have dedicated their lives to finding it, but all have failed. Only a select few know of its whereabouts.

'Tao is the single principle of the universe, and it is divided into two opposite, compromising principles—Yin and Yang—'

Lee Chong rolled his eyes. He was already bored.

The old man continued to speak in a slow, deliberate manner: 'Yin is everything female and is symbolised by the tiger, while Yang is everything male and is represented by the dragon. The flame of Yin burns low, almost as low as Yang. Since the demise of the dragon—Yang—the opposite forces of the universe are dangerously compromised, and the world's equilibrium disturbed. Now with the tiger—Yin—close to extinction, the world is approaching the time of rebirth. A time of rejuvenation will see the forces of Yin and Yang restored and together they will cleanse the earth and return it to its former glory.

The Tiger Chase

'In this paradise there is no place for man unless he can change his ways and reverse the destruction he has caused.' The old man fruitlessly searched Lee Chong's eyes for signs of empathy. He sighed before continuing: 'It is written that a fair tiger maiden of Yin and a dragon warrior of Yang will come from the west to protect Xiao Gong Zhu —The Little Princess.' He stood, strolled over to the tiger and stood by its side.

The tiger licked his hand.

'You have been given a choice, Lee Chong. You will return to the world, but you must change your ways. The fair one will come to you from the place of angels. She will seek your help. Tread carefully. If you choose not to help her, you will be condemned for eternity. Do you understand, Lee Chong?'

Lee Chong awoke in the forest alone. He remembered his experience but dismissed it as a dream. After making his way back to his village, he learned that Xia and Zen had disappeared. He knew they would be in Hong Kong by now.

That night, lying in a hospital bed with half his face heavily dressed, Chong watched a news report on TV. Anger raged inside him.

'Reports tonight of poachers allegedly killing what could possibly be the last wild South China tiger…' the young Chinese reporter said.

The major networks had picked up the report and beamed the story around the world. This would make the tiger carcass priceless.

Lee Chong shivered as a tiger looked back at him from the TV. A sense of infinite pity suddenly overwhelmed him when he stared into its golden eyes. But the pity, not for the tiger, was for himself.

Part One

Yin (The Tigress)

PART ONE

2

A crowd stood around the edge of the tiger enclosure at the Minnesota Zoo. They gasped and applauded as Toby, a four-year-old Bengal male, shimmied up a bare tree stump, retrieved a piece of meat, and dropped back to the ground. Then everyone laughed when he scurried away with his tail between his legs.

One of the older tigers had climbed from its favourite perch and was heading towards him.

'And this is Rajah. As you've probably realised, he is the dominant male. He is twelve years old and weighs in at 250 kilos,' Doctor Beth Smith said, speaking into a microphone and addressing the crowd.

'Is he a man-eater?' a young boy asked.

'In the wild, the tiger has been known to eat man, yes. The wild tiger is a solitary animal, a predator. One tiger's territory can stretch 160 kilometres, depending on the amount of prey available, but the forests are being destroyed at such a rate that he is forced to venture closer to civilisation in search of food. In desperation, he would kill and eat a human.'

'Is it true that people eat tigers?' a little girl seated on her father's shoulders, asked.

'Yes, that is also true. Some people believe that if they eat certain animals the strength of that animal will pass into them.'

'And does it?'

'No! There is no scientific proof to confirm this.'

Rajah stood at the edge of the enclosure peering back at the crowd across the moat. He lifted his chin and sniffed the air. The crowd gasped again when he opened his enormous mouth and yawned.

'Well, ladies and gentlemen, boys and girls, that brings us to the end of our presentation. If you are interested in the plight of the tiger and would like to learn more, you can check out the information and books in our bookstore or visit our website. I'm Doctor Elizabeth Smith. Thank you and enjoy the rest of your day.'

The crowd slowly dispersed except for a few children who stood by the fence chatting, giggling and eating ice cream.

Beth unplugged the microphone and smiled at Rajah. 'You big show-off!'

Rajah groaned.

Realising that he'd caught the scent of the ice cream, Beth reached into the cooler box by her feet, pulled out a frozen milk cube, and threw it to the tiger.

The children laughed when the large cube unintentionally hit the unsuspecting tiger on the side of the head, startling him into a half-roar and half-whimper.

Beth packed up the equipment and headed back to the zoo admin centre.

***

Andrew Conan of the Association of Zoos and Aquariums (AZA) sat in his office reading an email attachment sent by his superior:

Doctor Elizabeth Smith from LA holds a degree in veterinary medicine and reproductive physiology from the University of California, Davis.

During her time at Davis, she worked as a volunteer at the Sacramento Zoo with the Sumatran tigers and became interested in the tiger species. Focusing her studies and energies on the tiger's plight, she soon became a dedicated activist.

The Tiger Chase

She is a member of The Conservation Breeding Specialist Group (CBSG). She regularly attends meetings and mixes easily with experts whom she impresses with her knowledge and passion.

While still in her early twenties, she was chosen by the CBSG to visit zoos around the country to evaluate the health and individual requirements of the captive tigers. She then compiled a dossier including her professional opinions and recommendations to enhance the needs of the captive animals.

'Hmm ...' Andrew Conan said closing the attachment. 'Sounds like we've got our girl.' He pressed the intercom on his desk. 'Tanya, could you get me the number of Dr Elizabeth Smith at the Minnesota Zoo please?'

***

Beth returned home from a sixteen-hour day. All she wanted to do was have a hot bath, a glass of wine, and relax to her favourite music. When she entered her dull, one-bedroom apartment, she immediately felt depressed. Tom, her ginger cat, greeted her as usual rubbing his body along her legs and purring loudly until she picked him up. But even the genuine affection of her only friend couldn't quell the pangs of loneliness.

Later, when she lay in the hot bubble bath, she looked up at the dingy, damp ceiling and felt quite depressed. Sipping her wine, she suddenly realised she hadn't eaten for over eight hours—at least the wine tasted good. She took another sip then wondered, as she often did, what it would be like to be in a relationship. Before she knew it the self-pity had taken hold. It was just the wine she would tell herself later.

The next morning, Beth awoke to the sound of the phone ringing. Emerging, reluctantly, from beneath the bed sheets, she fumbled for the receiver.

'Hello.'

'Hello, Doctor Smith?'

'Yes.'

'Good morning, Doctor Smith, I do hope I didn't wake you.'

'You did.'

'Oh … so sorry. Doctor Smith, my name is Andrew Conan. I work for the Association of Zoos & Aquariums.' He cleared his throat but didn't wait for a response. 'You are probably aware that the International Union for Conservation of Nature (IUCN) held meetings over the last two weeks in Hong Kong with the Southeast Asian Zoos Association (SEAZA).'

'Uh huh.'

'The meetings went very well, but the most exciting and important outcome is that China has asked the United States to assist them in developing a Species Survival Plan for the South China tiger. The South China tiger is, as I'm sure you know, the antecedent of all the tiger subspecies and the closest to extinction. Well, Doctor Smith, I'll come straight to the point. We want to offer you a post in China. If you accept, you will leave in two weeks.'

Beth sat up in bed. 'Wow! This is a bit of a shock.'

'I'll bet.'

'What would my duties be?'

'Basically, you'll be in charge of setting up the program, examining the captive tigers and the facilities, and paving the way for future visits by our team.'

'Mr Conan, I'm deeply honoured that you thought of me, but I'll need some time to think about this.'

'Yes, of course. I don't expect a decision right away. I'll send you down more information. Talk it over with your husband and your family and let me know in a few days.'

'Thank you, I will.' She replaced the receiver, dropped back into bed and lay there thinking. *Husband indeed.* But her mind was abuzz with the thoughts of China and the South China tiger. What an opportunity. Then the negatives began to seep through. What about my work here? My family and friends?

She got up, fixed a bowl of cereal and automatically switched on the TV. Sitting at her small dining table eating breakfast, she needed to think. Her parents would understand. She only saw them at holidays anyway. In fact, they would insist she went. As for friends, the only friend she had, apart from work associates, was Tom her cat, and her parents would look after him until her return. She decided to talk to her boss as soon as she got to the zoo. If it was okay with him, she would consider it.

'Next up we have a disturbing report from China …'

Beth frowned at the TV.

'I'm talking to Doctor Li Pang at the Chonging Zoo. Doctor, is it true that poachers may have recently killed the last wild South China tiger?' the ABC foreign correspondent asked.

Doctor Pang waited for his interpreter to translate the question then shook his head dismissively.

'But the recent census, Doctor, reported no findings of tigers in the wild. So where did this one come from?'

Doctor Pang didn't wait for the translation; he pushed past the reporter and disappeared off camera.

Two weeks later Beth flew to LA to spend the weekend with her parents and drop off Tom.

'Of course you must go, Beth,' her boss had said. Her parents were sad and happy simultaneously, as only parents can be.

Tom curled up on the comfortable couch of his new LA pad and went to sleep.

Beth flew out of LAX on Monday morning, heading for China.

3

Beth had decided to start a blog covering her time in China. Her first post would be an introduction to her work, which she'd just finished on her laptop during the first leg of her journey. She would post it to her site when she arrived in China and hopefully create some interest in the South China tiger. As the plane approached Hanoi for a connection flight to Shanghai, she read silently through her words:

> *There are four living tiger subspecies found in China: the Siberian tiger (Panthera tigris altacia), found in the far northeast; the Indochinese tiger (Panthera tigris corbetti), found in the far southeast, bordering Vietnam and Lao PDR; the Bengal (Panthera tigris tigris) on the Nepal border; and the Southeast China tiger (Panthera tigris amoyenis), which is believed to be the evolutionary antecedent of all tigers and is found in the southern parts of China.*
>
> *Although the situations with other endangered species—the giant pandas, the African rhinos and elephants—are at critical levels, increased media focus has helped lift their profiles securing funding and placing pressure on the governments involved to ban hunting and the use of body parts for traditional Chinese medicines and trophies.*
>
> *Unfortunately, the South China tiger has received no such attention. Unbelievably, at this time there are fewer than one hundred left in captivity. None have been spotted in the wild for over thirty years.*

The Tiger Chase

Prior to the 1950s, there were reputed to be more than four thousand South China tigers roaming the mountainous ranges and dense forests of the Hunan, Guangdong, and Fujian provinces. Ironically, in 1959, when the Siberian tiger was declared a protected species, the South China tiger was declared a pest and hunted mercilessly after the Chinese government placed a bounty on its head. Since the 1960s, over three thousand pelts have been counted.

In 1981, the Chinese government became a member of The Convention on International Trade in Endangered Species (CITES) and introduced new laws and legislation banning the trade of tiger parts. They also set out to develop a program to preserve tiger habitat. Today tigers are protected by The Wildlife Protection Law of 1989.

The laws have proved ineffective and the trade, although now illegal, has flourished. The prices on the black market have rapidly increased offering great incentives to poachers who can earn as much as ten years' income for one kill. Add to this the growing population and the fact that 99 per cent of China's original forest has been destroyed, the future for the tiger looks bleak.

The remaining captive South China tigers have descended from only six founders because no wild animals have been captured for such a long time. Ideally, 120 tigers descended from thirty would ensure genetic diversity. Serious problems from years of uncontrolled inbreeding, the occurrence of ill health, and low fertility rates due to malnutrition and inadequate enclosures, have taken their toll. Hence, a future master plan is desperately needed. It is estimated that if the current trend is allowed to continue, there is a 50 per cent chance of the species becoming extinct in as little as five years' time.

Beth closed her laptop and wiped a tear from her cheek. The captain announced they would be landing at Hanoi in approximately ten minutes.

The sweltering humidity seemed to grab Beth when she stepped down from the plane and headed for the transit lounge. She was glad her only hand luggage was a manageable backpack. It was late afternoon. The airport was busy. Three flights had arrived simultaneously. Droves of tired travellers hastily followed the baggage collection signs. Beth had just over an hour until boarding her connecting flight, so she strolled freely through the crowd with her hands in her pockets.

Wandering into one of the airport bookstores, she picked up a book and flicked through the pages, but she had far too much on her mind. Replacing the book, she moved to the next shop, which sold duty free goods. Instead of entering, she peered through the window at the cameras and watches that adorned the glass shelves and she watched as people stuffed large bottles of whiskey and cigarette cartons into their bags.

There was a coffee bar farther along, so she slowly made her way towards it. As she did, she noticed a temporary looking store which was attracting a large crowd. She pushed her way through the entrance but could see very little. There seemed to be a commotion at the back of the shop. Beth found herself edging her way through the crowd.

A short, stout, Vietnamese man wearing a fez stood on a wooden box behind a large glass counter. He held up jars and bottles while shouting in his native tongue.

The crowd seemed to grow excited by his words and waved money in the air.

Beth assumed it was some kind of auction but as she didn't speak a word of Vietnamese, she couldn't understand the excitement. She slowly worked her way through the pulsating crowd. When she finally reached the counter, the salesman caught her eye.

'Ahh, lookie, lookie, Amelican lady come to buy medicine.'

Everyone turned to look at Beth.

'What would you like today, lady? Cure for headache? Toothache? Leplosy? Or lheumatism perhaps? Maybe would like aphlodisiac? Make a very happy lady.'

The Tiger Chase

The crowd laughed when the salesman thrust his hips backwards and forwards.

Beth looked away in disgust and her eyes fell on the labelled jars on the counter. 'Oh my God!' She lifted her hands to her mouth, reading the tiny English translation at the bottom of the label—Ground Tiger Bone Tonic. She quickly looked at the rest of the labels and felt an uncontrollable sense of panic and anger. Tiger penis soup, bottles of tiger wine, ground bone, claws, teeth, whiskers, and even eyeballs. There was almost every part of the tiger's anatomy ground or dried and sealed in different jars and bottles. Beth almost lost her balance when the crowd pushed and shoved.

The salesman's attention returned to his excited customers who were stuffing money into his hands and pointing at the jars they required.

If she'd listened to her immediate impulse, Beth would have gone berserk and smashed every jar before scratching out the man's eyes and throwing them to the crowd, but she remained calm. Instead, she picked up a small jar of tiger bone and asked, 'How much for this?'

The salesman looked at her and grinned. 'One-fifty Amelican dollar.'

A tiny piece of spit landed on Beth's cheek. She wiped her hand across her face then reached into her backpack for her wallet. Keeping it close to her chest, she counted out 150 dollars, then a realisation suddenly hit her. Was she really contemplating smuggling illegal contraband into China? No, of course not, but although her interest in the substance was purely scientific, she doubted the Chinese authorities would see it that way. And anyway, analysis of the substances would only prove what Beth already knew. They were fake. Unfortunately, once bone is ground into powder, it's almost impossible to determine which species it originated from. Most products on the illegal market are either dog bone, cow or pig. The real contraband would only be available to the super rich who were willing to pay whatever price the dealers demanded. It certainly wouldn't be for sale in a shabby makeshift store like this one.

Returning the wallet to her bag, Beth moved backwards through the crowd, feeling the need to get as far away from the shop as possible.

For the rest of the flight, Beth tried to snooze but the images of the frenzied buying of medicines occupied her mind. She wondered about the people who actually believed these remedies worked. Then she reminded herself that it wasn't just the Chinese that participated in this belief. Many countries, including the western ones, did also. She continued to write in her blog:

> *As history has shown, the American buffalo was wiped out because its tongue was regarded as a delicacy. Many other species have suffered a similar fate. There are animals on the verge of extinction, such as the English pine marten, and the Australian cassowary who have fallen prey to hunting, poaching and the destruction of their natural habitats. In all cases there is only one reason for their decline—man!*

4

The cool evening breeze blowing in from the East China Sea, was a welcome relief after the humidity of Hanoi.

The director of the Shanghai Zoo, Doctor Chan Jiang, was waiting in the arrivals lounge. He checked his watch for the fifth time. At his side was Yu Quan, an interpreter assigned by The American Embassy to accompany Beth during her stay in China.

Beth finally came through customs.

Yu Quan rushed to meet her, smiling and bowing. 'Welcome to China, Doctor Smith.'

'Thank you!' Beth said, shaking the young woman's hand.

Doctor Jiang bowed, shook Beth by the hand and, unceremoniously, led them out to his car.

Beth and Yu Quan spent the next few weeks travelling to the zoos across China which housed the remaining purebred tigers. First, they went to the Suzhou Zoo, which was the closest to Shanghai. Then they travelled to the Chongqing Zoo in the Sichuan province where Beth could inspect and possibly make new entries in *The South China Tiger Studbook,* which was kept there. Her plan was to use Chongqing as a base—from there she could travel out to the surrounding reserves. Chongqing was the closest to the forests where the last tiger habitat was believed to be, and where the last sightings and capture took place.

Beth worked closely with the staff at each zoo, teaching them new techniques in reproductive management, dietary requirements and correct animal husbandry. The most important part of her studies was to gather genetic data and DNA samples from each animal to eventually develop a genome resource bank to help improve genetic diversity. Each tiger was tattooed then fitted with a transponder under its skin between its shoulder blades. This would allow a barcode gun to scan the animal's identification from as far away as three metres away.

Beth's Chinese assignment lasted three months, which had passed far too quickly for there was still much work to be done. Her working visa was for twelve months so she applied for an extension from AZA.

After pressure from herself, the Chinese authorities and the American Consulate—who claimed this kind of program was invaluable in terms of American and Chinese relations—her superiors finally agreed to another three months. But she was placed on a strict budget. There would be no more flying around the country. They thought it better she stayed in Chongqing.

Beth was grateful for the extra time but didn't think it was nearly enough. She would press the issue again during the next three months.

Doctor Li Pang—whom Beth had seen on the news bulletin from her home back in Minnesota—was the leading authority on South China tigers at the Chongqing Zoo. Beth and Li got on well. They shared a passion for the welfare of the animals. Although he didn't speak English, Li was a great storyteller, so Beth was grateful for Yu Quan's translations.

While they worked, Li spoke of his family. 'My father was from a long line of hunters. During the 1950s, he became a wealthy man when the government declared the tiger a pest and placed a bounty on its head. Ironically, it was this wealth that put me through veterinarian school.'

'And now you're helping the animal your father almost destroyed,' Beth said.

Li waited for Yu's translation, nodded, then went on to explain how as a teenager he'd grown to resent the Chinese culture. He was sickened whenever he saw the hides and body parts his father used for trading, so he'd decided to learn as much as he could about traditional Chinese medicines in the hope that one day he could prove they were just placebos peddled by unscrupulous profiteers.

Beth enjoyed listening to Li's stories of the old days, how the forest-people lived in harmony with their surroundings, worshipping the much-revered tiger, which they looked upon as their guardian. He told her of the first European missionaries who had entered the provinces at the beginning of the last century, bullying the petrified villagers with their new religion and guns. 'The missionaries would shoot tigers and hang them in the centre of the village to ridicule the ancient beliefs and prove how powerful their god was.'

'Are there any tigers left in the wild, Li?' Beth asked.

'Probably not. The demand for tiger derivatives in the West is as great as in Asia now. There is a major export/import trade happening. Recently twenty sacks of tiger bones were confiscated at the Nepal–Tibet border on route to China. Between 1985 and 1990, Traffic Japan reported that 1,700 kilograms of tiger bones were imported into South Korea, representing the deaths of over fifty tigers. In the early 80s, Traffic International reported that a single brewery in Taiwan imported 2,000 kilograms of bone a year to produce 100,000 bottles of tiger wine.'

'But what about now?'

'Still happening, just underground and more organised.'

Beth found it hard to accept this kind of thing still taking place. 'But where are the bones coming from?'

Li shrugged. 'Poachers, illegal distribution.'

'But how can anyone be sure the genuine product is genuine if it's ground into powder?'

'Nobody can.'

'So the merchants are ripping off everyone—'

'And the tigers are still dying.'

5

Beth Smith, Doctor Li Pang and their interpreter, Yu Quan, stood at the edge of an extensive agricultural development at the threshold of a dense forest. Beyond this were the vast mountain ranges of the Simian Shan mountain reserve on the border of the Sichuan and Guizhou provinces.

Li told Beth, while Yu translated, that no tigers had been spotted in this area for over thirty years and even wild pig and deer were now scarce. They agreed that this would not be a suitable place to reintroduce the South China tiger if the possibility ever occurred. 'However, the Fanjinshan Biosphere reserve in the neighbouring province of Guizhou would be more suitable,' Li added.

'But what of the habitat of the existing tigers?' Beth said.

'The Tao Yuan Dong reserve in the Jiangnan Mountains on the Hunan eastern border is believed to hold an undocumented number of wild tigers,' Li said. 'Unfortunately, deforestation and illegal logging has taken its toll on all the provinces. The largest of the reserves now only cover 10,000 and 20,000 ha. This is inadequate to sustain a viable tiger population. But in the mountains, wild pig and sambar are plentiful and good habitat exists for approximately 2000 km². I believe, if anywhere, this is where the tiger still roams.'

'We have to go there,' Beth whispered.

Li looked at Yu for a translation. He smiled when she told him what Beth had said. 'I thought you might say that, sooner or later. But it would be a long journey, and in reality, we would only see forests and mountains just like the ones we have seen today.'

Beth was familiar with the recent census which had declared the South China tiger extinct in the wild, but this only made her more determined to prove the so-called experts wrong. Although it was likely she would never see a wild tiger, the mountains of the Hunan province seemed to be drawing her to them. Maybe there was a divine reason why she was in China. She wanted to go there as soon as possible.

Beth insisted on footing the cost of the trip. At first, she couldn't understand Yu's lack of enthusiasm when she instructed her to purchase three hard seats on the evening train from Chongqing. But when the train left Chengdu Station just after nine in the evening, she soon realised that *hard* seats meant exactly that. Squashed in with mainly backpackers and tourists, she regretted her stinginess. She didn't sleep a wink but in the morning she was glad for the window seat. Each hour, the landscape changed dramatically from sprawling flat plains to heavily wooded mountain ranges, plateaus torn in half by winding-muddy rivers, giant lakes, and steep gorges.

Beth took advantage of the time in the cramped train compartment to catch up with her blog journal while also listening to more of Li's anecdotes.

Li reminisced about his childhood in a small forest village nestled on one of the high plateaus overlooking the Ba Bao Shan reserve on the Guangdong and Hunan border. He was excited about going home.

Yu Quan also enjoyed talking about the local people and their traditions.

Beth found their stories fascinating.

When the train finally pulled into Guilin Station at 4.51 pm—almost twenty hours after leaving Chongqing—the trio was tired and cranky. They decided to find a place to stay, have dinner and enjoy an early night. Beth would have liked to have seen the town in the evening, but she was far too whacked.

Early the next morning they left their hotel to find the main street already busy. Swarms of workers on bicycles and mopeds, horse drawn carts laden with hay and market produce lumbering towards the marketplace, and old trucks with squeaky suspensions, spewing out diesel fumes.

The roads were divided into two—one side for bikes and carts, the other for trucks, buses and cars. The buses were crammed full of people spilling over onto the roofs and hanging on side rails.

Li hired a reasonably cheap four-wheel drive.

The trio headed south towards the Guangdong border.

Of all the landscapes Beth had witnessed, the giant limestone pinnacles jutting out of the earth at Guilin were among the most unusual. But even in this famous natural attraction, every piece of flat land between the giant dragon's teeth and the river slithering among them was cleared for agriculture. A patchwork of different coloured crops appeared as a stalemate between civilisation and nature.

Li's village was 2,000 metres above sea level and was the farthest southern township in the Hunan province.

Since tiger hunting was declared illegal, the villagers had reverted to an agricultural way of life. Logging had also been slowed and small hydroelectric plants were being built to relieve the pressure on the forests for fuel.

Li's immediate family no longer lived in the province; they'd moved to Shanghai some time ago to enjoy a wealthier capitalist lifestyle. Many of the villagers remembered Li though and welcomed him and his associates warmly.

They stayed at the home of Li's distant cousin, Lee Chong and his wife, who lived on the edge of the forest.

Lee Chong bowed his head impartially and shook Beth's hand.

Beth noticed he didn't seem so pleased to see his cousin. She tried not to stare at the large scar on the side of his face.

Lee Chong's wife was humble and quiet but welcoming.

That evening after dinner they sat outside around a small fire, talking and sharing stories. Lee Chong and his wife used the traditional Hunan dialect. Fortunately, Yu was able to translate.

The atmosphere changed when Beth asked Lee Chong, through Yu, 'Have you seen any wild tigers recently?'

The Tiger Chase

Lee Chong's expression changed from indifference to anger. 'There are no more tigers,' he growled. 'You are wasting your time travelling all this way. Perhaps you should go farther north in search of the panda or maybe tell the zoos to release our tigers back into the wild.' He stormed into the hut, followed by his wife.

Li read Beth's puzzled expression. 'Don't worry, people are sensitive in these parts. They don't like the outside world interfering. He'll calm down in the morning.'

As the evening wore on, Li told them about the legend of Huan Loh. 'Huan Loh was the people's champion, killing more tigers than any other hunter. It is said that at the height of his fame, the blue tiger visited him in a dream. The spirit ordered him to throw down his weapon and become the guardian of the tiger and its habitat or perish. It is believed Huan Loh still lives in the forest protecting the animals to this day. He would be one hundred and twenty years old now if this were true.'

Yu Quan had also heard the legend and told how the ancient people believed that a giant blue tiger roamed the mountains warding off evil spirits. 'They also believed that tigers had the power to turn into men and help their ancestors in times of need.'

Beth was enchanted by the tales and couldn't wait to explore the forest the next day.

6

The thick morning mist shrouded the valley below, making the air feel cold and damp. The trees echoed with a multitude of birdsong. The wilderness greeted the dawn with the clash of musk deer antlers, the screech of wild pigs and the far-off roar of a tiger—or was that Beth's imagination?

She scooped cold water from the tiny mountain stream with her hands, splashed it on her face and felt refreshed as a cool breeze wafted up the mountainside. The images of blue tigers, missionaries and hunters had dominated her dreams the night before. She was awake when the dawn broke so had decided to go for a walk.

Li and Yu were also awake and having breakfast when she returned to the hut. Mrs Lee busied herself in the kitchen while her husband chopped wood outside. Beth wasn't hungry, but she had breakfast anyway and graciously accepted the packed lunch that Mrs Lee had prepared for them.

Lee Chong didn't enter the hut or even wish them well before they left; instead, he stayed out of sight tending to his chickens.

The four-wheel drive easily handled the narrow tracks for the first few kilometres but slowed considerably as the forest grew denser. Li drove with a fixed determination. Suddenly, the vehicle bounced and veered to the left. Li fought to regain control of the wheel.

Beth's knuckles turned white as she grasped the overhead handle.

Every now and then they stopped and left the vehicle to view some significant landmark or to study the tell-tale signs of tiger prey. Wild pig and deer became more visible the farther they travelled.

They approached a large mountain range. As they came to a small clearing, Li stopped the four-wheel drive and turned off the engine.

Beth couldn't believe they'd been travelling for almost five hours.

'Time for lunch,' Li said.

'Where are we actually going, Li?' Beth asked.

'You'll see,' he replied, grinning.

After lunch, Li told them they would travel around the mountain for about another two hours, abandon the vehicle, then journey the rest of the way on foot.

Beth frowned after Yu's translation. 'Abandon the vehicle?'

Li didn't reply. He started the engine and pulled away tentatively.

After rounding the mountain and leaving it behind, it soon became apparent that the vehicle was no longer of use. Dense forest ahead swept away into deep gullies and rose over hills before ending abruptly in the far distance at an enormous, rectangular, blue monolith that stretched across the horizon like a giant fortress.

Beth, unable to estimate its height, could only muster the word, 'Awesome!'

'Lánlǎohǔ!' Li cried, turning in his seat. *'Lánlǎohǔ!'*

'Blue Tiger,' Yu translated, grinning at Beth. 'Blue Tiger!'

Beth looked at her watch. The time was 2.00 pm.

Li seemed to read her thoughts. 'Trust me, trust me,' he said, climbing from the four-wheel drive. He took the backpacks and Beth's aluminium instrument case from the back. 'Come, come, there is still a long way to go before nightfall, but there is a trail we can follow.'

'Nightfall?' Beth cried. 'I thought this was just a day excursion. You didn't say anything about staying overnight.'

Li giggled. 'Please. Just trust me. It will—'

'We're not going any farther, Doctor Pang, until you tell us where we're going,' Beth demanded, not waiting for the translation.

'Okay, but we need to reach the *secret place* before nightfall and make camp there.'

Beth's ears pricked up. *'Secret place?'*

Li passed Beth a drink canteen. 'Don't you see, Doctor Smith? This is why you are here.'

'No, I don't see. Tell him I *don't* see at all, Yu.'

'You will. Please, Beth, just trust me,' Li replied.

Ten minutes later, they were on their way through the forest on foot.

Beth realised Li had purposely triggered her curiosity. Her thoughts soon blotted out her worries. She imagined an ancient lost city waiting for them, or a magical hidden valley that nobody had entered for thousands of years. The excitement renewed her strength and she walked with more haste.

Later, as dusk descended, the trio neared the blue rock face. The air became still, and a strange silence enveloped the forest. The trees stood motionless as if waiting for something to happen. Even the birdcalls and distant animal cries had fallen silent. The only sound was the harsh wind whistling across the plateau of the distant summit.

Beth marvelled at the steep jagged cliff that rose from the forest at a ninety-degree angle. Its surface was smooth except for deep vertical gouges which looked like tiger stripes. The summit was shrouded in a slowly churning mist.

'We must keep moving,' Li announced, marching ahead.

Clumping bamboo and thick bushes strangulated by sharp twisting vines hid the base of the cliff face. Li seemed to be looking for something, peering into the thicket, as he increased his lead.

Beth was about to demand she rest when Li suddenly became excited.

'This is it … this is it!' Li shouted back to the girls.

Beth looked both ways along the length of impenetrable undergrowth. 'This is what? I don't see anything.'

Li paid no attention. He pushed his way through a thick clump of bamboo then disappeared.

Beth and Yu caught up to the spot where Li had vanished. Beth gazed up at the rock. She wasn't afraid of heights, but she wasn't prepared for rock climbing. In fact, she was exhausted. Throwing down her bag, she flopped to the ground and sat back against her instrument case.

The Tiger Chase

Yu offered Beth a drink from her water canteen and the two sat silently on the ground not knowing what to expect next.

Suddenly there was a loud, 'HA HAH!' followed by the *CLUNK, CLOMP* of bamboo stalks knocking together. Li appeared smiling widely. 'Come, come,' he shouted, excitedly pulling them to their feet and lifting their bags. 'This way. Quickly.'

The girls followed Li through the bamboo. Thorn-covered vines tore at their skin.

Beth tripped and cursed, struggling to lift her weary feet. All she could see beyond the bamboo was the cliff face that towered before them. She began to panic a little with the uncertainty of not knowing where they were going. Looking up at the rock once more, she frowned and shivered. Night was almost upon them, and they were about to reach a dead end. Beth began to wonder about Li. What did she really know about him? Why had she been so willing to trust him, letting him bring her all this way? He'd led her to believe they were venturing into the reserve on a day trip. She realised she didn't know anything about him at all. Now, here she was hundreds of kilometres from civilisation with a total stranger.

'Yahhh hooooo!' Li jumped in the air then disappeared.

The fading light made it impossible for Beth and Yu to see clearly as they stood speechless and frightened at the base of the rock. Behind them the curtain of bamboo and thorns had closed, and it was too dark to head back. Before them was a wall of solid unscalable rock—it seemed worse than any nightmare.

With the opposing forces of tiredness and adrenaline fighting for her attention, Beth thought she would pass out, but she was jolted back into awareness when the darkness suddenly exploded into flickering light.

Li mysteriously reappeared, jumping up and down with a flaming torch in his hand. The shadows danced on the rock face when Li darted from side to side. 'Come, quickly.'

Beth didn't need a translation; she knew exactly what he was saying. Forgetting her fear, she clumsily scrambled towards him with Yu behind her.

'Follow me,' Li yelled, disappearing into a small opening in the ground.

Beth looked down into a chamber illuminated by the torch.

Li grinned up at the girls, beckoning with his free hand for them to follow.

Beth stood negotiating the opening then, after deciding there was only one way to enter, she jumped into the hole feet first.

Yu followed.

'What's going on, Li?' Beth demanded after steadying herself.

Li, ignoring Beth, handed Yu the torch then grabbed a thick rope hanging from a large rock at the side of the entrance. He grunted, pulling the rope. After much effort, the rock slid across the opening and closed it off.

Yu didn't wait for Beth to speak. She launched into an attack in Mandarin that was aimed directly at Li.

Beth did the same in English.

Li absorbed the multilingual reprimand with sympathetic nods, grimaces and understanding headshakes in all the right places. When the girls finally calmed, he told them they would sleep in the cave overnight and he promised everything would be explained in the morning.

Beth squinted round the cave and noticed there was fresh straw at the edges. The air was dry and warm. The sound of the wind above and the flickering torch made her feel sleepy—she was too tired and angry to argue anymore. Dropping her bag and herself to the floor, she crawled over to the nearest pile of straw.

***

Beth couldn't believe how stupid she'd been. After worrying about scaling the giant rock monolith all day, she'd failed to notice the moving stairway rising from the trees towards the summit. She stepped aboard the stairway, leaned on the rail and rested her weary body. The stairway slowly carried her to the top of the mountain.

The Tiger Chase

The paddy fields below reminded Beth of the patchwork quilt she had made as a child with her mother. Then she noticed an old lady who looked vaguely familiar gathering rice in one of the fields.

Beth stepped from the staircase at the top and found herself back in the forest. She saw the man who had sold her the tiger bone at Hanoi Airport standing beneath a tree. He wore a tiger skin on his back and a golden rhinoceros horn on his head. He smiled and bowed his head. Beth hurried past.

But when the man raised his head, his face had changed. Instead of the salesman, the face of Li Pang now grinned at her. 'Don't worry, I'll look after you,' he said and laughed.

Beth looked away then ran along a deserted road towards a forest of yellow trees.

What sounded like a million cats meowing echoed through the canopy. A brass band played 'The Star-Spangled Banner' somewhere in the distance.

Trying to focus her eyes, she noticed a tall soldier with his back to her standing on the roof of an old station wagon.

The man stood erect holding a machine gun. He suddenly fired a volley of shots, sweeping from side to side through the trees. *JAGA—JAGA—JAGA—JAGA—JAGA.*

Beth lifted her hands to her ears and knelt as the deafening sound penetrated her head. 'Stop!' she cried. 'Stop!'

The ground shook, trees cracked and toppled, splinters of timber whistled overhead, and a cloud of dust rose into the air.

The gunfire stopped.

Beth heard the gun fall to the ground. Then silence. She looked up.

The soldier turned to face her. His frowning face seemed so familiar.

'GRRREARGH!' A deafening roar exploded. A giant blue tiger stood amid the devastation.

Two men were pinned under the front paws of the beast. They struggled and cursed in an attempt to break free. But it was all in vain.

An old Chinese man holding a glowing tiger cub, sat on the blue tiger's back.

Somewhere a bell like an alarm clock rang.

Beth looked up at the soldier, but he was gone.

The old man's movement was that of a time lapsed image. Every time Beth blinked, he was closer. She didn't see him climb from the tiger's back. All she knew was one moment he was there, and the next he was right in front of her.

The old man held up the tiger cub. 'Xiao Gong Zhu,' he whispered.

Beth reached out and took the cub. It glowed golden in her hands.

'GRRREARGH!' Another roar.

Beth blinked. The old man was seated on the blue tiger's back.

The mighty beast moved off, releasing the men from its grip.

One of the men jumped to his feet and demanded the blue tiger return and fight him.

The other man slowly crawled away whimpering.

Beth looked down at the frightened cub nestling passively in her hands.

The old man's voice whispered in the breeze. 'Xiao Gong Zhu … Xiao Gong Zhu …'

***

'Beth … Beth …'

Beth lay half asleep listening while Yu slowly repeated her name. She groaned and slowly opened her eyes.

The only light in the cave was from a small fire that Li had lit. Li was busy boiling rice for breakfast.

Beth sat up and touched Yu's arm. 'Yu … what does Xiao Gong Zhu mean?'

'Little Princess,' Yu replied.

'Little Princess?'

Li thrust a cup of green tea in her hand.

The wind howled high above as they sat on the ground eating the rice from small tin dishes which Li had produced from his backpack.

Li sat quietly, scooping rice into his mouth as if waiting for the inevitable 'WTF' question. When it finally came from Beth, he nodded and quickly swallowed his food. He explained that the reason he hadn't told them too much was for their own safety. 'There are still illegal hunters in these parts who wouldn't hesitate to kidnap and torture us to learn of our destination.' He sipped his tea. 'The route we are following is an ancient and secret one. Its whereabouts have been passed down to only a few chosen people. You will be the first westerner ever to lay eyes upon this place. You must protect its secrets always.'

Beth narrowed her eyes while Yu translated almost as quickly as Li spoke. She still hadn't made up her mind whether to trust him yet, but she had to admit, it all seemed very exciting. 'Where are we going, Li?'

'How about I show you?' Li said putting the breakfast dishes back in his bag. He rearranged the straw and checked around the floor. When he was satisfied, he lit the torch, extinguished the fire, then led the girls towards the back of the cave.

The darkness peeling back along the walls, being chased by the light, revealed the entrance to a tunnel.

Li led them, single file, into the passage.

Beth's calf muscles soon ached as the sandy ground began to incline.

The sound of the howling wind far above was almost hypnotic when they climbed higher into the rock.

Li's heavy breathing laboured loudly, losing its rhythm and echoing off the walls.

After almost two hours, Beth needed to rest.

Shortly after, they reached what seemed to be another dead end. The wind had died down.

Beth and Yu fell against the wall and slipped to the ground, sucking in as much oxygen as they could.

After a few moments rest, Li handed the torch to Yu. He searched the tunnel's end, running his fingers along the rock until he found a small recess. A strained grunt echoed down the passage as he jerked his head back and pulled using all his strength. The sand-covered floor quickly absorbed the large drops of sweat which fell from his forehead.

The rock moved slightly. Fingers of sunlight crept around the opening.

Li changed his grip and pulled harder.

The rock grated and groaned before slowly opening into the tunnel like the door of a huge vault.

The morning sun cascaded into the entrance.

Beth was forced to cover her eyes with her hands until they adjusted to the light.

Li took the torch from Yu, extinguished it and placed it on a small rock alcove just inside the cave. He then leapt through the exit and took a deep breath of fresh air.

The girls cautiously followed.

When her eyes finally adjusted to the sunlight, Beth couldn't believe what she saw. Was she still dreaming?

7

Below them, treetops of multi-shaded greens gently swirled and hissed like a calm ocean. Giant boulders randomly stood among the trees as if placed there by an ancient race of giants. A thin waterfall cascaded down the rock into a blue pool glistening from the morning sun.

'Welcome to the centre of the universe!' Li said with a huge smile and his arms wide.

'What is this place, Li?' Beth asked.

'This is the place where the spirits of our ancestors roam freely with the animals of heaven and earth. The forest thrives here as nature intended without the destructive hand of man.'

Beth was filled with exuberance while she absorbed the serenity of the enchanting forest.

'It has been many years since I have physically been here, but I travel here regularly in my dreams … as you have also.'

'Okay,' Beth mumbled. She'd grown tired of asking questions. She listened and scanned the view with wide eyes as Li continued, fuelled with excitement.

'From here we will travel through the forest for two days. No harm will befall us as long as we commit no harm to the forest.'

Beth frowned and was about to interrupt Yu's translation.

Li lifted his finger to his lips. 'When I said I was from the village, I wasn't completely telling the truth. I was adopted. My father searched all his life for the entrance to the mountain. One day, he found a baby boy abandoned in the forest close to the rock.

He took the child back to his village and he and his wife raised him as their own.'

'The child was you,' Beth said.

Li nodded. 'My parents never told me, but I knew. In my dreams I would travel home, and I was taught the ways of the ancients. I grew up with a love of the forest and the welfare of its animals.

'When I first met you, Beth Smith, I was not sure … then when we stayed overnight in Guilin, I travelled home to Blue Tiger Mountain on the wings of a dragon, and the teacher showed me that you were the one.'

'Wait a minute, you're losing me, Li … you're losing me,' Beth said.

Yu giggled at Beth's screwed-up expression.

Li understood. 'Your questions will be answered, but not by me. I am just a guide, here to serve you. There is one thing that puzzles me, however,' he added, furrowing his brow while surveying the rock door. 'In my dreams there is a man by your side … a tall, western man.'

Beth raked her hands through her hair. She didn't know what to make of all this. All she wanted to do was find some signs of wild tigers. She hadn't picked Li as a crackpot. She thought of going back, but when she looked down at the beautiful valley, she knew she had to go on. She spoke to Yu of her concerns while Li struggled to close the rock door.

Surprisingly, Yu dismissed her concerns. 'Look at this place, Beth.'

Beth's eyes followed the blue rock until it disappeared into the horizon. It did appear to be a barrier. Could this place really have been protected from the outside world as Li claimed?

'You cannot pass up a chance like this, Beth. You have to go on.'

'But what about Li?'

The veins in Li's face almost popped as he moved the rock a few centimetres.

'He is harmless,' Yu said.

Beth nodded but she wasn't too sure.

After twenty minutes of pushing, pulling, grunting, and growling,

The Tiger Chase

Li was finally satisfied that the rock was back in place. He placed his backpack over his shoulder and beckoned them to follow him.

Beth checked her watch. It said midnight. 'Hey, wait a minute.'

Yu checked hers. It had also stopped at midnight.

Li laughed. 'No time here but forest time,' he said. 'Forest time *all* the time.'

'Oh, right. That clears that up then. Li, is there anything else you want to tell us?' Beth said.

Yu didn't bother translating Beth's sarcasm.

The path was rather steep, but it was easy going on the long trek down.

When they reached the level of the canopy, Beth was surprised at the amount of sunlight filtering through to the forest floor. A strong fragrance reminded her of the rose bushes and jasmine in her parents' garden. Although the forest was beautiful on the other side of the wall—as Li called it—it seemed somewhat bland compared to the assortment of beautifully coloured bushes and smooth fruit-covered vines that harmoniously mingled and hugged the tall slender trees.

A beautiful birdsong danced on the warm breeze and the distant sound of cascading water made the surrounding haven an extravagance in sight, smell and sound.

The land of Oberon and Titania. The Garden of Eden. Beth pinched herself to make sure she wasn't dreaming.

'We'll make our way to the rock pool, there we can freshen up and fill our water canteens,' Li said, leading the way.

The soft undergrowth was a welcome relief on their sore feet after the rock path. It didn't take them long to reach the edge of the clear, blue pool. A cool mist from the waterfall added a welcome chill to the air.

If Beth had a choice of anything to drink in the whole world, it would definitely have been the pure water she'd just gulped down a little too quickly. She leaned forward to take another drink.

Suddenly there was a splash.

Beth gasped and jumped up as a chilling wave of water washed over her.

Li's head bobbed up from the centre of the pool. 'Waaaaa hoooooo!'

'Nice one, *Li*,' Beth said, playfully patting her wet clothes. She took off her boots and socks, sat at the edge of the pool and sighed when she dipped her feet into the cool water.

Yu's actions were identical to Beth's.

The mid-morning sun felt warm on their faces as they reluctantly left the pool and headed into the forest.

'Look!' Li pointed through the trees. There was a herd of wild deer in the distance. 'Tiger prey,' he said, smiling.

'Interesting,' Beth mumbled. Prey, a viable habitat and no humans. *Did this mean there could be tigers?*

Li pointed out the varieties of bird and fowl and small animals as they continued through the forest.

But it was the distant animal cries that excited Beth the most. She recognised some, but others eluded her. Once again, her imagination kicked in. *'GRRREARGH!'* The roar of the Yin tiger protecting its territory. Or the ancient dragon of Yang swooping the treetops.

During the trip, Yu had given Beth a brief explanation on the fundamental importance in Chinese philosophy of the two opposing yet complementary forces of the universe, Yin and Yang. 'According to the *I Ching* or *The Book of Changes*, they represent the positive and negative, the masculine and feminine, the light and dark, and good and evil. Sometimes these forces are symbolised as wind and water or as tiger and dragon.'

Finally, the long hot day was drawing to a close. The setting sun's scarlet rays sliced through the treetops, and long shadows lay across the ground like discarded branches from a woodcutter's axe.

Li led the girls to a small clearing. He placed his bag against a circular flat stone and turned to face Beth and Yu. 'We will be safe here for the night.'

Beth didn't ask any questions. She'd made her mind up while walking; Yu was right, this could be an amazing opportunity. From what she'd seen today—the abundance of prey, the untouched forest, and no signs of civilization—it was enough to keep her interest piqued. She had a nagging feeling though that it was all too good to be true, half-expecting to stumble into an 18–30 holiday resort at any time.

Li lit a fire on the circular stone then crept off into the shadows.

'Err ... where's he going?' Beth asked Yu.

'To get food.'

'Oh right ... a Quickie Mart? Great.'

Yu laughed politely.

When the darkness closed in around them, they moved closer to the fire. The moonlit treetops shimmered in the evening breeze and the hypnotic sound of crickets and cicadas reverberated through the air. A nocturnal beast groaned in the distance after waking from its daytime slumber. The insects fell into a unified silence. Suddenly the hush surrendered once more to the crescendo of a million pairs of hind legs rubbing together.

Beth and Yu's eyes lit up when Li returned carrying fruit and berries, the carcass of a pheasant tucked under his arm.

He silently handed a few berries to the girls then, after gutting and vigorously plucking the bird, he placed it on a homemade spit constructed from branches, stoked the fire then sat back, slowly turning the spit.

The irresistible smell of roast game soon filled the campsite, and all three sat eagerly yet very tiredly waiting for their dinner to cook.

While the bird rotated over the flames, Li began to sing a traditional Chinese song.

Yu joined in.

Beth sat unable to hide an embarrassed smile.

The white tender flesh was succulent and sweet. Not what Beth had expected at all. Li had prepared the berries in a special way, which complemented the meat perfectly. When they washed it all down with the cool fresh water from their canteens, their stomachs were full.

Li collected all the scraps and threw them on the fire, explaining the importance of leaving the place as they'd found it.

Beth lay back and looked up at the night sky. The stars seemed closer than usual on this enchanting evening. She remembered her seventh birthday. Her parents had painstakingly stuck hundreds of little luminous stars to her bedroom ceiling. She wished she could reach out, scoop up the constellations in her hands and throw them over her body. The twinkling night show relocated to the back of her eyelids.

***

Who was he? And why was he frowning at her? She knew him from somewhere, but she couldn't think where. The strange old man was there also. She wasn't quite sure where they were, but it definitely wasn't China. It was somewhere in America.

The old man stood staring at her, shaking his head.

Beth noticed a tear roll down his cheek. She felt an overwhelming sensation of failure. 'What have I done?' she asked, trying not to cry. She looked at the tall man standing next to her.

His familiar face scowled at her.

The old man's image was fading.

There was something warm against her feet. She looked down. There was a tiger lying there. Kneeling, she ran her fingers through its golden fur then she burst into tears.

The tiger was dead.

She looked for the old man, but he was gone. When her eyes returned to the tiger it had also gone. In its place stood a jar of ground tiger bone. Wrapped around the jar was a bloodstained American hundred-dollar bill.

***

Li gently shook her awake.

Beth threw her arms around his neck and sobbed.

Li's knowing expression told her that he understood and that everything would be okay.

8

The next day was much the same as the previous one. They didn't speak much. Instead, they pushed on in silence. The forest grew denser the farther they travelled.

Later, Li suddenly grew excited and pointed to a border of trees which seemed to blend forming a barrier. 'This way,' he shouted, marching off in front. He led them to an arched entrance through the trees. 'Through here. Quickly!'

The scenery changed dramatically when they passed through the thick border. An orchard of fruit trees, vines and exotic flowers reminded Beth of the botanical gardens in her hometown. This area had obviously been cultivated. The aromas of jasmine and roses reinstalled an aura of déjà vu as Beth absorbed the familiar surroundings. The ground was soft, so she took off her boots and socks. The warm grass tickled between her toes, soothing her sore feet.

The small wooden hut looked idyllic and inviting when they caught sight of it in the distance. Its shingled roof reflected the sun and shimmered, giving the impression of a glowing mirage. A thin plume of smoke twisted towards them from the tall stone chimney.

The girls struggled to keep up with Li's brisk stride.

Approaching the hut, Beth noticed a small figure standing in the doorway. Before she could even see his face, she knew it was Huan Lo.

The old man lowered his head, acknowledging Li who stood before him bowing.

Yu also bowed.

Beth stood awkwardly, not sure whether to bow or curtsy.

Huan Loh seemed to be avoiding Beth's eyes.

Li spoke to the old man.

Beth looked at Yu expecting a translation.

'They are speaking in an ancient dialect.'

'But you can understand it, right?'

Yu shook her head.

Huan Loh spoke to Li, Li translated to Yu, and Yu translated to Beth.

'I've heard of Chinese whispers, but this is ridiculous,' Beth said jokingly under her breath.

Yu explained that Huan Loh was welcoming them to his home.

'Thank you, thank you,' Beth replied, bowing.

It smelled good. It looked good. Yum. It tasted good. That's all Beth needed to know. It tasted like Mongolian lamb, which happened to be one of her favourite dishes, but she was far too hungry to ask what it was.

They sat around a small wooden table in silence. They ate with chopsticks from small porcelain bowls and drank fresh goats' milk from wooden cups.

Li broke the ice by asking Beth if she had any questions for Huan Loh.

'Yes, are there any tigers here?'

The old man laughed.

Beth was embarrassed by her eagerness. 'Sorry ... great place you got here,' she said, trying to make light of her rudeness.

There was a long thoughtful pause before the old man spoke. 'You have been here before, many times in fact. In this life you first came to me as the infant princess with the golden hair. You are the chosen one. In spirit your presence has contributed to the natural balance of the forest for thousands of years. The animals and trees are your servants, as am I.' He bowed his head and kept it low while Li then Yu translated his words.

'Alrighty, then ...' Beth exaggerated a glance at her watch—midnight. 'Goodness, is it that time already?'

The Tiger Chase

'The blood of greatness runs through your veins,' Huan Loh continued. 'In a past life you were the daughter of one of the wealthiest landowners in China. Your father was a cruel and greedy man who ordered the mass destruction of the forests. He was a mighty hunter and collected furs and skins as trophies. His appetite for blood sports was so great that he would organise massive nationwide hunting parties.

'They would venture out into the forest for months at a time destroying and killing as they went. He believed that with each powerful and majestic animal he killed the power would transfer into him. Unfortunately, even today this belief continues among those who practice the philosophies of so-called, traditional Chinese medicines.

'The hu long—dragon—was the most feared of all the creatures and, when it was hunted to near extinction, the sensitive balance between Yin and Yang was dangerously compromised.

'It is written that the wind, the rain and the earth joined forces and created an impenetrable sanctuary. A human keeper was appointed to watch over and protect the animals and the sacred habitat.'

'And that was you,' Beth said.

Huan Loh laughed. 'I am an old man, but I am not that old.'

Li laughed and translated Huan's words to Yu.

Yu laughed while she translated the words to Beth.

Beth blushed.

Li made green tea while Huan Loh continued.

'It is said that life is made of ironies. With each generation, a single hunter rises above his peers and becomes legendary with his feats of strength and cunning. Each century one of these men is taken from the outside world and placed in the sanctuary as penance. Once here, he must promise to honour and protect this sacred place and all its animals. If he cannot, he will be reincarnated as a tiger and hunted and killed by his successors.

'Almost one hundred years ago a twenty-year-old son of a nobleman earned the reputation of being the best hunter in the land.

I hang my head in shame when I confess to the hundreds of wealthy bounties earned from the slaughter of tiger and panda, for I was that young man.

'My journey started as dreams. I would find myself in a strange, yet somehow familiar, place where the errors of my life were played before my eyes. My conscience became so heavy that I prayed for forgiveness. One day I was brought here by a young guide, very much the same as you were. I buried my predecessor and have stayed here ever since as it is written. It is also written that when the dragon and the tiger return together the keeper will no longer be required. He will change into a tiger, father many cubs and live a long and prosperous life.'

'Oookay ... so let me see if I've got this right. You're telling me that you're one hundred and twenty years old, and—'

Without waiting for a translation, Huan Loh cut Beth off in mid-sentence. 'In your first of many lives you were the Yin tigress. Although opposites, you lived in harmony with the Yang dragon and jointly ruled over the forests and high grounds. You were everything feminine, he masculine. You ruled the wind, he the rain. It is also written that you will return when the forests need you most. You will bring the wind and destroy the habitats of the loggers and the poachers, and he will bring the rains and wash them away. Together you will replant the forests and release the animals from the sanctuary. In doing so, you will restore the balance of Yin and Yang, and the world will return to a peaceful equilibrium.'

'Phew ... well, that's enough about me then,' Beth said. 'Tell us a bit about yourself, Huan. Hobbies? Music? Fashion? I bet the TV reception's crap out here.' She normally hated sarcasm but couldn't help herself.

Yu Quan didn't translate Beth's words.

Beth was growing impatient. 'Oh, come on, please? Enough already. I'm a zoologist from LA and this is the first time I've ever even been to China, not to mention this place.'

Huan Loh sat quietly listening to Li.

The Tiger Chase

'And who's this dragon guy? Oh, don't tell me. Of course. It's Li. The hunter found him in the forest as a child. Bless. And he's been here in his dreams. And, and …' she waved her hand and left the sentence hanging. 'This is all getting a bit Hans-Christian-Andersony for me. I'm sorry, but this is the real world, folks, and I'm afraid I haven't got time for all this nonsense. All I wanted was to see some tigers in their natural habitat and if that's not going to happen it's a waste of time me being here.'

Li looked exasperated while he listened to Yu's translation.

Huan Loh simply nodded when he listened to Li. 'Li is not the dragon—he is merely a servant, as am I. The dragon is someone you already know. Your paths have crossed many times throughout your lives. Like you, he is a westerner. He is your opposite.'

'Well, I can honestly say I don't know anyone who would match that description. So, I think you might have got the wrong gal.'

'Shush.' The old man put his finger to his lips. 'You must have faith and listen … it is the one who comes to you in your dreams. Soon you will meet again.'

Beth was about to give up and go to bed when Huan Loh suddenly changed the subject.

'Tomorrow you will find what you have come here for.'

'What?'

The old man grinned a toothless grin.

'Tigers?' Beth's gaze searched the eyes of the other three. 'Well?'

Huan Loh whispered something to Li, stood up then left the room.

'What did he say?'

Li smiled. 'Lao hu!'

Beth looked at Yu.

Yu grinned and raised her eyebrows. 'Tigers!'

9

Beth awoke from a deep sleep when a beam of morning sunshine pierced through the crudely planked gable, landing across her face. She climbed out of bed, stretched, yawned, then dressed without waking Yu, who was sleeping on the feather mattress next to hers.

She crept through the small living area and out through the front door. Stepping off the porch she took a deep breath of fresh air and decided to go for a stroll. She instinctively checked her watch—midnight. She had no idea of the real time, but that didn't seem to matter. The morning mist was slowly dispersing. The warming sun lifted the damp shadows, leaving everything green and fresh. The dawn chorus was in harmony with the gentle breeze. The trees were whispering her name, inviting her into the forest.

When Beth wandered farther, she found it impossible not to exclaim out loud, 'Great day in the morning.' Suddenly, just as she was enjoying her relaxed and wonderful surroundings, she stopped and stood very still. Years of training had taught her not to panic but this was different. There was no assistant waiting outside the cage with a tranquilliser gun. There was nowhere to run. This was the real thing. Knowing it was important not to make eye contact, she held her breath and stood perfectly still, while under the scrutinising stare of a full-grown tiger crouching in the bushes to her left. If she blinked or moved it would probably pounce, but if she stood still, it might become bored and move on. It all depended on when it had last eaten. All she could do was pray and wait.

The Tiger Chase

The two-and-a-half-metre long tiger rose slowly to its feet and strolled in Beth's direction, licking its lips.

Beth wished this was just another of those weird dreams. The cool breeze blew through her hair and lifted it slightly, causing the tiger to flinch. She felt the fear drop through her diaphragm and down into her bowels. Looking slightly to the left she watched helplessly from the corners of her eyes.

The tiger approached with its body low. Its shoulders rose from the back of its neck like slow pistons and its claws spread beneath its weight. Instead of walking in a straight line, it stalked slowly from side to side with its tail swaying and its golden eyes fixed on its prey.

This is it, Beth thought. It's all over. Was she stupid or just unlucky? Maybe she should run for it anyway. Perhaps she could make it to the trees—and then to the hut—and then maybe she could ... who was she kidding? She was dead meat, and she knew it.

The tiger came closer.

Beth could feel the panic rising through her. She closed her eyes tight like a little girl at bedtime. If she couldn't see the Boogeyman, the Boogeyman couldn't see her. If he couldn't see her, he couldn't eat her. Eat her? Bad analogy.

She trembled when she heard heavy panting getting closer and the powerful claws treading the long grass. The tiger had moved behind her. Waiting for it to pounce, she prayed for it to be quick.

The heat from the animal's breath and the roughness of its abrasive tongue flicked across the back of her bare legs. The enormous head butted her thigh.

'Ahh.' It wasn't a scream, more of a whimper. She waited for the sharp teeth to penetrate.

The head pushed again. The warm nose, the stinging tongue.

The next shunt knocked her off her feet and she fell to her knees bracing herself for the inevitable strike that would snap her neck in two. Beth kept her eyes closed and she began to tremble with fear. Then ... *Ouch!* ... the rough tongue again, this time on her face.

The tiger was circling her. *Oh, my God, it's going to play with me like a cat with a mouse. Please, God, make it quick.*

Its head shoved again, this time from the side and harder. Beth fell over onto her side and felt a giant paw pulling at her, easily rolling her onto her back.

The tiger's head came down onto her chest, nestling from side to side, its paw pushing and pulling her backwards and forwards.

Beth could feel a fraction of its weight when it rested its heavy paw on her chest and nudged her with its head. She was pinned to the ground. The fear had overpowered her long before the beast. She felt like a helpless doe.

'Ouch!' The rough tongue again. Across her arm. Then her face. This time, when she yelled, she instinctively hit out. Her hand hit its solid forehead. A low growl rumbled above her.

The head came down again. It nuzzled its nose under her back as if trying to lift her. The growl grew louder. The tiger prodded, rubbed and rolled her like it was kneading bread.

Opening her eyes, she hit out once more. Hot saliva ran down her cheek.

Two golden eyes cocked from side to side. An enormous tongue flicked out between giant fangs.

'Ouch!' It scoured the side of her face. Beth lay frowning while the big cat continued to push its nose underneath her. She pushed its head with both her hands.

The tiger pressed harder with its nose.

'Oh my God!' She suddenly felt brave and put her hands on either side of its head.

The tiger reared its head. *'GRRREARGH!'*

Beth flinched and closed her eyes.

'Chuff.'

She knew that sound. She'd heard it many times in the zoos. It was the sound of affection. She opened her eyes and grabbed the paw that rested across her, before lifting herself to a seated position and stroking the tiger's head. 'You're a pussy cat,' she yelled. 'A big, beautiful pussy cat.' She couldn't help it. She was a kid again. She threw herself onto the big cat, dug her fingers into his fur and tickled him.

The tiger gave her another painful lick, rolled over onto his back and lifted his front paws beneath his chin.

Beth giggled and rubbed his white belly. The fear was gone. She frolicked with the beautiful gentle creature. She felt honoured and special, the same way she'd felt with the dolphins at the San Diego Zoo and the pandas at Minnesota. But this was different ... better. This was a purebred South China tiger, the kind that hadn't been spotted in the wild for over forty years. His plight suddenly returned to her thoughts. She knelt down and took his head in her arms.

He licked her cheek.

'Ouch!' At that moment, she decided to find out for herself why she was there and what she had to do.

'Wang!'

The tiger's head shot up at the sound of Huan Loh's voice. Its ears moved forward, and its forehead scrunched up.

'Hey!' Beth cried, when the beast sprang to its feet and pounced over her head.

The tiger padded up to the trees where Huan Loh stood. It gently licked and rubbed against his hand.

In return, Huan Loh stroked the animal's head.

The tiger sat beside the old man and casually looked in Beth's direction.

Beth pulled herself to her feet. 'Wang?'

Huan Loh nodded and turned back towards the hut.

The tiger followed.

Beth strolled behind, captivated by the tiger—the velvet texture of gold on black, the slow swing of its tail, the soft pad of its powerful paws. She thought of the captive South China tigers she'd examined in the zoos. None were as big and as healthy as this one. She couldn't wait to examine him. There were lots of questions she wanted to ask

Huan Loh, but she had to be patient. Even if she'd learned to speak Chinese, she'd still need Li to translate the ancient language Huan spoke. She realised she owed Li an awful lot and was thankful to him for bringing her here.

Li stood at the doorway smiling when Huan Loh, the tiger and Beth approached the hut.

Beth didn't need a translation while the two men spoke and laughed.

Yu pushed her way through the doorway. 'ARGHHHH!' She ducked behind Li. 'Lao hu —Tiger.' When she realised everyone was laughing and not scared, she blushed. 'Lao hu?'

The tiger pushed past and entered the house.

'Guess this is his home, huh?' Beth mumbled, following the tiger into the hut.

The tiger ignored them, casually lowered itself in front of the fire, yawned, lifted one of its hind legs, and licked its balls.

Beth and Li laughed.

Yu blushed.

Breakfast was bean sprouts and boiled vegetables washed down with green tea.

'Tell me about the tiger. What's his name? How old is he? And why is he so tame?' Beth asked Huan Loh.

'His name is Wang, which means King, due to the large Chinese symbol on his forehead. Most tigers have this mark, but they are not as prominent as this one. Like me, he is a very old man—about twenty. A tiger must be fast, cunning and strong to survive in the wild. Unfortunately, there are no small western girls here who would make easy prey.' He laughed, followed by Li and then Yu.

Beth smiled and nodded sarcastically.

Huan Loh continued: 'Although still cunning and strong, the speed of this once awesome hunter has diminished. Sometime ago my meat store was raided in the middle of the night. On another occasion my chickens were stolen. Apart from the tracks that he left, he had also quite visibly made this a part of his territory: torn bark, deeply scratched tree trunks and the stench of urine were all telltale signs to an old hunter.

The Tiger Chase

'One day I spotted him in the distance. He was monitoring me as he would all potential prey in his territory. I retreated to the safety of my hut. Over the following weeks I spotted him regularly. I saw him every day for a month—watching me from the trees. Then he didn't come. The next day he also failed to show. So, I followed the vultures that circled yonder and I found what I had suspected. Thankfully, there was still time.

'He had fallen sick and lay dying. The forest was moving in to reclaim him. I could not stand by and let this wonderful creature die. In the past I had saved many animals from death, but never a tiger. I hastily returned to my hut and mixed up a strong batch of medicine. My heart felt heavy when I forced the potion down his throat. As he looked up at me through dull eyes, the life force was seeping from his body, leaving him deflated and motionless. I lay with him and prayed to the forest.

'In our dream we travelled to the sacred place. At first, I was chastised for breaking the law of the forest, but I pleaded and begged. Finally, they gave him more years and we returned together ... as friends.'

Huan Loh agreed to let Beth examine Wang.

Beth grabbed her instrument case and immediately set to work. The examination was one big game for Wang. He rolled over and wiggled when Beth tried to take body fat ratios. He licked her on the end of her nose when she examined his teeth. He chuffed loudly and shook his head when she looked in his ears and eyes, and he playfully swiped her when she checked his claws. After a complete physical check-up, she took blood, urine, and faeces samples for future analysis then she lifted out the sperm sample extractor from her bag.

Wang groaned when he saw the ominous piece of equipment.

'Okay old man, I get the picture,' Beth said returning the extractor to her bag. She estimated his weight to be around 195 kilos, which was big for a South China tiger. But she found it impossible to estimate his age due to the perfect condition of his coat and teeth. Knowing that wild tigers on average live around ten years, she found it hard to believe he was twenty years old.

Beth found herself talking to and treating Wang the same as she did her cat, Tom. 'Who's a big, beautiful boy then?' she said, tickling his belly and stroking his head.

Wang obviously enjoyed the attention. He stayed by her side all day.

With all Beth's time spent either travelling or working, she couldn't remember when she last enjoyed a day as much as this one. She was like a child again, playing hide-and-seek, laughing and wrestling with Wang.

The sun slowly slid below the distant blue mountains and the cricket chorus gently gathered momentum. Beth couldn't believe how quickly the day had gone. When Wang finally left her side and disappeared into the trees, she felt sad. A feeling of selfishness fell over her when she returned to the hut and noticed Li and Yu sitting together outside. She'd completely forgotten about them. 'Hi guys, I'm so sorry, I think I got a bit carried away. What did you two do today?' she said.

Yu blushed as she translated to Li.

Li just smiled and shrugged.

Yu explained how they'd spent the day relaxing and hadn't ventured far from the hut.

Li rose to his feet. 'Okay we need to retire early.'

Beth looked confused after Yu's translation. 'Are we going back already?'

Li shook his head. 'No, but tomorrow will be a big day.'

'What's happening tomorrow?' Beth said.

Li grinned. 'Big day tomorrow. Early night tonight.'

After a light dinner, Beth went to bed but lay awake reliving the day in her mind.

***

'Why are you here? I don't like you … go away … don't pull my hair … I'll tell my momma on you. Get away from me, ya big bully!'

The Tiger Chase

Beth turned and burst through a set of double doors. She was in her dull, high school corridor now.

Students on either side jeered and pointed.

Beth gazed straight ahead and pushed forward.

The girls looked at her as if she was filth. 'Slut!' one of them called out.

The corridor became an endless kaleidoscope of faces. The laughing and the jeering grew louder. Finally, she looked down at herself and almost died of embarrassment. She was naked. The tiny schoolbook in her hand barely covered her. Wrapping her arms around herself, she crouched and began to sob.

The corridor suddenly fell silent.

A hand stroked her hair.

She looked up to see that face again. Although she was looking straight at him, she couldn't make out his features. But she knew it was him, and she knew she didn't like him. He meant something to her, something from her past maybe. 'Why are you here?' Then she noticed Wang by his side ... no, it wasn't Wang—it was a female tiger.

The man held out his hand.

Beth reluctantly took it.

The corridor dissolved. They were now standing in a forest.

The tigress ran towards the trees. Four cubs jumped out in ambush and licked and tugged at the tiger's fur. Then they vanished into golden dust.

***

Moments later, Beth was sitting up in bed trying to figure out the meaning to it all. She'd occasionally had the naked dreams as a child. 'It means you have something to prove, dear,' her mother had said. The dreams stopped after she graduated from Davis. Her qualifications validating her, or so she thought. But if that was the case, why did she just have another one? And why now?

She got up to get a drink of water.

Yu and Li were sitting at the table.

'You guys couldn't sleep either, eh?' she asked, pouring them all a drink.

Yu shook her head. 'Beth.' She swallowed and glanced at Li for support. 'I have to be honest with you. I am part of this ... I have listened and I have watched ... and I have also had dreams.'

Beth sat down and, with a mouthful of water, gestured for Yu to continue.

'I knew exactly what Huan Loh meant when he said he was a strategically placed pawn. Although my part is slowly being revealed to me, I still don't know what is going to happen, but I am sure something great is upon us. Fate has brought the four of us together in this place and I want you to know that whatever happens, you will have my support one hundred per cent.'

'Thank you. I really appreciate that and hey, don't talk to me about dreams. I've just had the weirdest yet. I can't make any sense of them whatsoever—'

Huan Loh entered the room. He sat cross-legged on the floor. Then, as if in a trance, he began to speak, 'At first, they will not understand you. You will have many battles to fight. In your hands will be entrusted the future. You must be strong for they will try to take it from you. You will be afraid, but your fear is within. The fear of failure and rejection may cloud your vision and you will temporarily lose your way.'

'Okay ...' Beth the sceptic was back.

Li whispered that Huan Loh was sharing his dream.

'What, kind of like an up-to-date news bulletin, you mean?' Beth said.

Yu didn't translate Beth's words. Instead, she sat solemn faced, waiting while Li translated the old man's vision.

'Danger lies ahead,' Yu continued when Li had finished. 'Alone you will not succeed. You will travel back to the place of angels a heroine. But you will be stripped naked. Then you must find him. From that moment on, fate lies in your hands for the outcome is not written.'

The Tiger Chase

Beth was trying to be blasé about it all. But a certain chord kept striking in her mind. Were she and Huan Loh having the same dreams? No, that's impossible. She took a large gulp of water.

The old man jolted when a beam of morning sunlight struck his forehead. He yawned and stretched as if waking from a deep sleep, and rose from the floor.

Li jumped up, gave the old man his seat, then made tea.

Breakfast was a quiet affair.

Beth departed for her morning bathe in the stream close by. When she returned, she was somewhat despondent.

'He is still wild,' Huan Loh said.

'Huh?' Beth looked puzzled after the translation, but she knew exactly what Huan Loh meant. She'd searched, unsuccessfully, for Wang. Even the cool freshness of the stream had failed to lift her disappointment.

'His territory calls to him. He must return regularly.'

How did the old guy know what she was thinking?

Li noticed Beth's anxiety and nodded at Yu. 'Cheer up, Beth, because today …' she glanced at Li, 'today we're going searching for wild tigers.'

'Yesss!' Beth hissed. Finally. She couldn't wait to leave.

After checking all her instruments and making sure her camera was clean and loaded, she quickly readied herself and hurried the others.

Soon they were bidding Huan Loh farewell and leaving the hut.

Beth hummed and allowed her thoughts to wander while she trekked through the forest. She remembered the first time she'd ever set eyes on a tiger. She was six years old; it was at the LA Zoo. She'd wandered away from her father and found herself at the tiger enclosure. There she sat watching a one-year-old Bengal cub frolicking in the pool, laughing and applauding the cub's antics as she fell in love with him. She cried when her father found her and it was time to go home. From that day on, she visited the zoo regularly and made her way straight to the tiger enclosure where she'd sit and watch the cub for hours.

10

The day wore on and the forest grew thicker. Beth squinted through a blur of dark foliage. Her throat contracted and her lungs were heavy while she breathed the steamy air. 'Is this taking us anywhere, Li?'

Li's eyes searched the trees ahead. 'Look!'

Beth and Yu's gaze followed Li's pointing hand. There was a break in the canopy. The distant hazy hills, which Li had pointed out earlier, were just up ahead.

'TAO!' Li exclaimed out loud, 'TAO!'

Later, Beth noticed rock through the trees on either side of them. The farther the trio walked, the higher and closer the rock became, and she realised they'd entered a pass through the hills.

The way gradually narrowed. The trees thinned and the ground sloped downwards. Eventually it opened into an enormous basin. 'Wow!' Beth said. 'It's a crater.'

'Tao!' Li repeated.

'An extinct volcano?' Beth asked, her eyes scanning the wave of rock that circled them.

'Tao!'

'Yu ... why does he keep saying that?'

Yu questioned Li in Mandarin.

Beth continued her visual exploration. Her eyes wandered to the lush forest below which filled the circular bowl. Yellow blossom covered the treetops. In the centre was a round waterhole, volcanic soil beneath its surface made it appear black. Beth closed her eyes and visualised the crater from the air as if she were an eagle drifting above it.

The Tiger Chase

'Uh hm,' Yu cleared her throat to attract Beth's attention. 'Doctor Pang says this is the heart of Blue Tiger Mountain. The place where the forces of Yin and Yang came together and gave birth to the surrounding forest.'

Beth didn't hear Yu's translation. Her eyes snapped open. 'Look!' she cried, pointing to the centre of the crater.

Yu followed Beth's gaze but didn't see anything.

Li laughed aloud. He knew exactly what Beth had seen.

'It's an eye ... a tiger's eye!' Beth exclaimed.

Yu squinted as she peered down at the crater.

Beth suddenly felt embarrassed at her outburst. 'I mean ... it looks like an eye. I didn't actually mean—' A gust of air suddenly swirled up the hillside, wrapping itself around her. She shivered and her body tingled as if she'd just received a mild electric shock. 'Whoa ... what was that?'

'The spirits are welcoming you home,' Yu said without taking her eyes from the crater.

Beth turned to face the translator. 'You said that, not Li.'

Yu didn't answer.

Li seemed to sense the situation and broke the awkward silence with the three English words he'd learnt during the trip, 'Follow. Quickly. Come,' He headed off towards the trees.

Yu lowered her head and followed Li.

Beth would speak to her later.

They made their way to the forest floor where the air was cool and the nutrient-soaked volcanic soil was black. The plants and trees were shiny and verdant.

'GRRREARGH!' A roar suddenly fractured the serenity.

Li grabbed Beth and Yu by the hands and pulled them behind the nearest tree.

'Boy, that's close,' Beth whispered, trembling with excitement.

Li put a finger to his lips, then jabbed the air with the same finger, pointing in the direction of the sound.

'GRRREARGH!'

Beth fumbled through her bag searching for her camera.

Li peeked round the tree. His eyebrows sprang to his fringe, his jaw dropped and his body quivered like an excited child.

'What do you see?' Beth had found her camera. She jostled for a look. Between the trees, she could just see the unmistakeable golden outline of a tiger lying among the undergrowth with its back to them. The two white dots on the back of its ears reminded her of the reflectors she had on her bicycle as a child. At first, she couldn't quite make out what the tiger was doing so she looked through her camera and zoomed in with its telescopic lens. 'Oh my God!' she said. 'You guys have got to see this.' She handed the camera to Li.

'Ohh ... myyy ... Gawd!' Li said, looking through the camera.

The tigress sat like an Egyptian sphinx, her front paws gripping the freshly killed carcass of a musk stag. Her head was high, her body alert. While sniffing the air, her ears rotated, her eyes darted in vigilance, and her tail twitched from side to side. She tossed back her head and roared, *'GRRREARGH!'*

'Has she picked up our scent?' Yu said.

'I don't think so, luckily we're downwind,' Beth said. 'Just being cautious I guess.'

The tigress returned to her meal. She tore a chunk of pink flesh from the glistening ribcage with her powerful jaws. Blood oozed and splashed from her mouth as she chewed nosily on the meat.

Click-click-click. Beth began to take pictures.

The tiger, unaware of her audience, continued eating.

A family of small, pied birds sat on branches just above the big cat, following her every move. Every time the tigress looked away, they would dive down and steel tiny morsels of meat.

When she caught sight of them, she roared and snapped her jaws in their direction.

The birds buzzed back to the safety of the branches.

Beth whispered to no one in particular while she took pictures. 'She's probably weak after the kill.' *Click.* 'With a one-in-twenty success rate of a kill—' *Click-click-click.* 'They burn so much energy. Built for

The Tiger Chase

power you see, not speed—' *Click-click-click.* 'They'll stalk until they get close enough to pounce. Then all their energy is channelled into the attack.' *Click.* 'If they miss, they have to recuperate without food. And if they go too long without a kill, they'll obviously grow weaker.' *Click-click-click.*

The tigress suddenly jumped to her feet. Her nose nudged the air and her face flared. *'CHUFF, CHUFF!'*

Beth knew the body language and the sound well. Wondering where the tiger was directing its call of affection, she didn't have long to wait to find out. The bushes to the left of the tigress parted and four small cubs came bounding out to their mother. 'You have got to be kidding me.' Beth zoomed back a little with the camera to take in all the action.

The cubs pounced on the carcass and fell over each other as they pulled on sinews of meat. Then, forgetting about the food, they began to wrestle. They tumbled and swiped each other before mother gave another *chuff* as if to remind them of their table manners. One cub became more interested in the pies, who were now growing impatient and taking dangerous risks. The cub began to jump at the low branches trying to hold on with its front paws, but each time it fell flat on its back.

Click-click-click went the camera. This was far better than anything Beth had hoped for. She would have been happy to see a single South China tiger in the wild, but to see a tigress and four cubs went way beyond her expectations. She felt privileged and humbled. Then she realised there was obviously a male nearby, which meant, in this perfect sanctuary, there was likely to be more tigers. *Click-click-click.*

The tigress buried the remains of the carcass under a pile of leaves.

'There's about three days' worth of food there,' Li said.

The cubs paid no attention to their mother—chasing, pouncing and wrestling was far more important.

The tigress nestled down and almost blended into the foliage, watching her cubs at play. She gave out a maternal *chuff* from time to time. The cubs would stop playing and return to her side momentarily, then be off again.

Li tapped Beth on the shoulder.

Beth jolted as if snapping out of a trance.

Li pointed to his watch even though it said midnight. She realised what he meant. It was time to return to the hut.

Beth screwed up her face like a little girl being told she had to leave the party early. But she knew Li was right. Tomorrow they would return, and tomorrow she'd have the tranquilliser gun with her.

Beth watched Huan Loh's changing expressions while Li, somewhat dramatically, retold the day's events. She guessed relief, happiness and hope was swirling through his mind, then she realised she'd misread the twinkle in his eye—it was a tear.

There were no dreams that night. In fact, Beth couldn't remember if she'd fallen asleep or not. She must have catnapped through the night, only to awaken repeatedly with the vision of the tigress and the cubs in her mind. When the first glimmers of daylight finally appeared, she rose and woke the others. 'Come on you guys, big day ahead,' she whispered, taking charge.

After a quick breakfast, they were on their way once more.

Beth set the pace and marched in front. Her eagerness made her a little impatient and cranky, especially when Li and Yu kept dropping behind. 'Come on people, keep up.' Glancing over her shoulder, she caught a glimpse of something she'd suspected. Hands snatching away from each other, reddened cheeks, eyes averted to nothing in particular. Beth realised there was more than just tigers on their minds.

Finally, they reached the spot from the day before. To fuel Beth's excitement, the tigress and her cubs were still there. They'd just eaten. The exhumed carcass was now just a mass of fleshy bones. The pies, who still darted nervously backwards and forwards, now shared the feast with a swarm of flies.

The tigress and her cubs were fast asleep. The mother lay on her back with her eyes tightly shut, her front paws under her chin. The smallest of the cubs lay across her as if it had been trying for

The Tiger Chase

a crafty suckle. The biggest of the four lay next to his mother's head, curled up with his chin resting on his front paws. The other two lay one over the other entwined as if they'd fallen asleep in the middle of a wrestling bout.

Click-click-click. Beth gave a loving smile while she took more pictures. 'Okay, folks, it's time to get to work,' she exclaimed after replacing another film. Reaching into her bag, she carefully produced the tranquilliser gun and handed it to Li.

After checking it over, Li loaded it with a dart, took a deep breath and aimed it at the tigress.

The plan, devised over breakfast that morning, was to tranquillise the mother and round up the cubs. Samples would be taken, and information collated and catalogued.

Li paused and adjusted the sight. He'd done this many times before but only from the outside of a cage and never from this distance.

Beth held the camera to her eye and realised she was holding her breath.

Li squeezed the trigger, sending the dart whistling through the air. *Phissss!*

The dart penetrated the side of the tigress's neck.

The tigress sprung up. *'GRRREARGH!'* The sleeping cub lying across her catapulted into the air. All four cubs, with their ears flat and their tails low, jumped to their feet and disappeared into the bushes.

'GRRREARGH!' The tigress roared again. Scanning the outer clearing with blazing eyes, she paced and growled, spat and snarled. Then she staggered a little. *'GERRAH!'* A half-hearted roar was followed by a whine. When her back legs gave way, she crashed to the ground.

The trio ran to the bushes and spread out—Beth to the centre, Li to the right, Yu to the left.

'Quick, over here!' Beth shouted.

Li and Yu bounded towards her.

The four cubs lay huddled together, shaking and whimpering in a small clearing. When the largest cub saw Beth, it sprang to its feet. Its face contorted and its fangs quivered as it spat like a snake.

Beth was well aware that the cub's bite could do some serious damage even at this early age.

Li had circled and got himself in position behind the cubs.

Yu crept from the left and crouched in readiness.

When Beth was sure they were ready, she gestured the count of three with her fingers, then pounced.

Li grabbed the biggest cub from behind.

Yu and Beth dived on the other three.

Perfect timing allowed them to scoop up the cubs without any casualties—to the cubs at least. Yu Quan narrowly missed being bitten by one of the males. Beth and Li sustained a few scratches and minor bites. All four of the cubs spat and fought to get free.

They quickly returned to where the tigress lay, the girls carrying one cub each, and Li struggling to hold two.

Beth handed her cub to Yu and set to work examining the tigress first. She took blood, fur and saliva specimens, and a small piece of skin for future use in DNA analysis. She estimated her age to be around seven years old. She weighed 130 kilograms and was in excellent health. Next, she cautiously examined the cubs separately. There were three male cubs and one female; they were around three months old. The largest male weighed in at 6.5 kilograms. The lightest, the female, was 5 kilograms. Specimens were taken. When the examinations were complete, the cubs were placed next to their mother.

Li led Beth and Yu back to the trees where they stood and waited for the tigress to stir.

The three male cubs ran back to their hiding place. The female climbed onto her mother and lay across her neck.

Beth had goosebumps when the cub peered in her direction. It seemed to be staring right at her.

The Tiger Chase

The tigress stirred. Her body twitched. Suddenly she bolted up. The little cub was catapulted into the air once more. *'GRRREARGH!'* The tigress roared into the air.

The female cub rubbed herself against her mother's leg and chuffed.

The tigress lowered her head and licked the cub. The three hiding cubs came bounding out of the bushes, colliding into their mother and pulling at her fur.

The tigress settled down and began to clean herself and her babies.

Beth was pleased to see them return to normal so quickly. It was time to leave. Tomorrow they would return. They'd check on the tigress again and then venture out a little farther in search of more tigers. She couldn't wait.

The trip back seemed longer this time. When they finally reached the hut, they were exhausted. After an early meal, they went straight to bed.

11

The ears of the tiger pricked up and rotated like radar dishes. Its head bobbed as it sniffed the air. Its forehead scrunched. Its ears fell forward then pulled back sharply. When it lunged forward, its claws slid and scratched on the cobblestone road. Spooked, the animal slowed and lowered its head at each alley and doorway. Frantic panting echoed while the tiger searched the empty streets of Chinatown.

Beth struggled to keep up. 'Wait!' she cried, but the police siren drowned her screams.

A cyclonic swirl of blue and red spun off the walls ahead. A cruiser turned into the street, screeching to a halt.

The tiger crouched. Its head elongated and its lips curled back from its huge fangs. Two golden eyes shone like flames in the headlight beam. *'GRRREARGH!'*

Beth slowed when she approached. He was here again. What was he doing? The tall man was kneeling by the tiger, gently stroking its head.

The tiger noticed Beth. It chuffed into the air then ran to her, circling her and pushing its body against her legs.

Beth realised it was a tigress but not the one she'd seen in the jungle. It was younger. She squinted through the headlight beam but couldn't make out the man's face. She knelt and hugged the tiger. When she looked back at the man he was gone.

***

The Tiger Chase

At breakfast, Beth purposely didn't mention her dream. She didn't understand it, and she wondered if the others had also dreamt that night.

By mid-morning they approached the spot they now knew well and hid behind the trees.

Beth peered through the camera. She increased the zoom then gasped. 'This is amazing!'

There was a large male tiger tearing at the festering remains of the carcass. The tigress was asleep with her back to them. The cubs were nowhere to be seen.

That's odd, Beth thought. She reluctantly passed the camera to Li and fidgeted impatiently while he looked.

Li's face turned white. 'Pass me the tranquilliser gun.'

'What's wrong?' Beth asked, snatching back the camera. At first, she couldn't see anything out of place. At first she focused on the male, but when she looked back at the tigress, her heart sank. A swarm of flies hovered above the motionless body. There were smears of blood on the fur around her neck. 'Oh no ... please no ...' Beth felt numb while she fumbled for the tranquilliser gun.

Li took aim and fired. The dart landed in the back of the male tiger's neck.

The animal flinched then carried on tearing at the meat. After a few minutes, he was still standing.

Beth checked the dosage. Li had used the correct amount of ketamine. 'He should be out cold by now,' she whispered. Then she remembered something she'd once read. A Bengal tiger was shot during one of the Maharaja's hunting parties in India. The giant cat had died instantly from a bullet to the temple but the tendons in its legs were so strong it remained in a standing position. Beth scrutinised the tiger, its nose was buried in the belly of the stag, but it didn't appear to be moving. 'Maybe it's out cold,' she said. 'What do you think, Li?'

'I'll shoot again but with an empty dart.' Li loaded the gun, took aim and fired.

This time the dart landed in the meaty part of the tiger's hind leg. *'GRRREARGH!'* The tiger spun round and snarled, blood dripping from its fangs. Its crazed eyes caught sight of the trio. Leaping over the tigress, it charged in their direction.

There was no time to think. No time to move. They would be torn to pieces.

Only a few metres away the mighty cat roared again. Suddenly, its front legs gave way. Its hindquarters crashed over its head. Its huge body twisted and bounced on the soft undergrowth, kicking up dust and debris. It finally rolled to a halt, unconscious against Beth's shins.

Yu turned and threw up.

Li grabbed hold of the tree to steady his legs.

Beth stood perfectly still, her eyes squeezed shut.

There they remained, momentarily silent until Beth opened her eyes. Releasing the imprisoned breath from her lungs, she sank to her knees. An expletive, which she never used, gushed from her brain and into her mouth. 'F ... F ... For goodness sake ...' She controlled the urge.

Li placed a hand on Beth's shoulder.

Beth snapped back to awareness. 'The tigress and her cubs!' She ran into the clearing. 'No!' The tigress was dead. 'Where's the cubs?' She sprinted into the bushes where they'd found them before.

Beth's throat was dry. The salt in her tears stung as she cried uncontrollably.

Three of the cubs lay stretched out. Two were huddled together. The largest one lay in front, as if he'd died trying to protect his siblings. All had puncture wounds to their necks.

Beth wiped her sleeve across her face and waved the flies away. Lifting one of the lifeless bodies, she cradled it in her arms.

Yu cried too and tried to comfort Beth.

Li began to search the bushes.

'Of course ... the female.' Beth cried. She carefully placed the small carcass back on the ground and jumped to her feet.

The Tiger Chase

Li, seeing the determination in Beth's face, took her by the arm and called to Yu to come and translate for him. 'There is a slim chance that the female cub is still alive, although it is likely the male has eaten her. He would have stumbled on the tigress and her cubs and decided to help himself to their kill. Usually, the tigress, knowing she is no match for his strength, would let him have it but on this occasion, maybe the male wanted more than just the food. He may have decided he wanted the tigress for his mate, in which case he would kill the cubs and force her to mother his. This female obviously chose to fight. Unfortunately, it was a fight she could never win. We must be quick and search the surrounding area. If the cub is still alive, it will not have wandered far.'

They split up and spread out.

'Please, God—please, God—let her be alive,' Beth repeated under her breath as she crept through the bushes. 'Chuff ... chuff!'

'Chuff ... chuff!'

That was no echo. 'Chuff!'

'Chuff!'

Beth turned in the direction of the weak calls and anxiously pushed aside the bushes. 'Chuff!'

'Chuff!'

She was getting closer. Then she heard the sound of breaking twigs when the cub bolted. 'Over here! Over here!' she cried, taking up chase.

Yu and Li ran in the direction of Beth's calls, panning out to the left and right.

Beth caught sight of the cub and found her second wind. She jumped through the bushes that tore at her bare legs and threw her bag in the cub's path, startling it.

The cub turned and inadvertently headed straight for Beth. By the time it realised its error it was too late.

Beth pounced on the cub and held it close to her body.

For a few moments they remained motionless panting heavily, the cub's tiny heart pounding against hers.

Li and Yu caught up and began to dance with delight when they saw the tiny, frightened face peering out from under Beth's chin.

The cub snarled and spat.

'Xiao Gong Zhu!' Li exclaimed. 'Xiao Gong Zhu!'

'Little Princess,' Beth whispered.

Li reminded them of the male tiger. He would awaken soon. They had to work quickly. After contemplating leaving now and hoping he wouldn't follow, they decided to give him another injection, which would knock him out for the night.

Li rushed off and administered the sedative to the sleeping tiger.

Beth slowly lifted herself up, carefully holding onto the frightened cub. The little big cat spat and swiped at her with its razor sharp claws. 'Xiao Gong Zhu … wow you're a feisty one,' Beth said, holding the cub at arm's length. 'Xiao Gong Zhu. That's a bit of a mouthful, though. Hmm, let's see, what can we call you? Little Princess …? Princess …? Too sappy. Gong Zhu …? Zhu …? Hmmm …? Zhu Zhu …? Zhu Zhu! That's not bad. Zhu Zhu. I dread to think what it means in Chinese, but it sounds pretty cool. What do you think, Zhu Zhu?'

The cub roared and lunged at her.

The opportunity of taking sperm and blood samples from a healthy purebred wild South China tiger was too good to miss.

Li held onto the cub while Beth set to work.

Like Wang, the animal was in perfect health. Its teeth were in perfect condition. Its fur shone golden and was soft to the touch. She estimated its weight at 175 kilos. It was approximately eight years old. Using the portable electro-ejaculator, she collected invaluable semen samples, and placed them in a dry ice container. When the examination was complete, they left the tiger where he lay. Apart from a headache, he would be back to normal in the morning.

It was time to leave. They would have to take the cub with them because she wouldn't last long in the wild. Beth and Li would

The Tiger Chase

take her back to the Shanghai Zoo. Her fresh bloodline would be invaluable for future breeding projects.

Beth, Li and Yu each had a tear in their eyes as they looked back over their shoulders at the dead tigress. They'd decided to leave everything as it was, keeping in line with nature's way.

Zhu Zhu constantly wiggled and fought to free herself during the journey.

Beth held her tight.

Li and Beth discussed how they should feed her and get her back to Shanghai. Li's expression changed to one of concern. 'The price of a Bengal tiger's carcass on the black market would be approximately $50,000 American. A poacher would receive around $30,000. For him this would equal ten years' pay. As for a wild South China tiger, who knows what kind of price a dealer would be prepared to pay.'

12

By the time they reached the hut, it was late afternoon. Huan Loh was waiting for them by the door. When he saw them approaching, he did a strange thing—he knelt and bowed his head to the ground, chanting.

'He is offering a prayer of thanks,' Li whispered. 'He says our journey has begun, and he is asking the forces of Yin and Yang to watch over The Little Princess.'

'How did he know about The Little Princess?' Beth asked after Yu's translation.

Li smiled and shrugged.

Huan Loh slowly rose to his feet and entered the hut. On the table, he had a dish with a small helping of raw chicken, liver and venison.

Wang was lying in the corner on a pile of straw.

After they'd all entered the hut and closed the door, Beth carefully placed the cub on the floor. It growled and spat at her, then with its ears back flat, it warily scanned its surroundings.

Beth knelt on the floor and watched while the cub scrutinized Wang.

Wang lay with his head up. His ears were alert. His eyes were focused on the intruder to his territory.

The cub edged forward.

Wang's mouth began to quiver. He snarled then suddenly swiped the cub with his giant paw.

The cub was bowled backwards. It turned, slipped on the wooden floor and bolted straight into Beth's arms.

Wang rose to his feet and puffed out his chest.

The Tiger Chase

Beth could feel the cub's tiny heart beating as it clung tightly to her.

Wang marched past them towards the door, his head high.

Li opened the door and let him out.

After a few moments, the cub sniffed the air and chuffed.

Beth gently released her when Huan Loh placed the bowl of food on the floor.

Zhu Zhu stood for a moment as if making sure Wang had gone, then she shook her fur and cautiously strolled to the bowl. After eating every morsel, she surprisingly returned to Beth's side, growled and climbed onto her lap. Moments later, she was fast asleep.

'So, what do we do now, Li?' Beth said quietly.

'Tomorrow, we start our long journey back. We must supply Xiao Gong Zhu with fresh game and keep her safe. We must avoid Lee Chong at any cost; he is a redundant poacher who would jump at the chance to make his fortune. If we enter the village at night, we can obtain fuel from the village elder. Then we will travel eighty miles north to the next village. There is a public telephone there. If we can contact the Chongqing Zoo, hopefully they will send help.'

Beth had suspected there was something strange about Lee Chong. She instinctively didn't like him. Now she knew why.

The next morning Beth was surprised to find Zhu Zhu quite calm. The cub didn't seem to want to leave her side, but Beth knew she would still have to treat her with caution, avoiding scratches and bites. She decided to give her another examination before they left. Noticing she had slight diarrhoea, she checked for pathogenic bacteria then gave her a prophylactic antibiotic to ready her immune system for the outside world.

Now, all that was left were the sad farewells.

Beth left Zhu Zhu with Li and went outside to find Wang sitting waiting for her. She knelt and hugged him, making his ear twitch when she whispered into it: 'Take care of Huan Loh and I will see you in my dreams.' She decided not to extract a semen specimen after all. Apart from respecting his dignity, it was very unlikely that an animal of his age could still produce any. She hugged him one more time.

The tears welled up in Huan Loh's eyes when he bid them farewell.

He'd given them plenty of food for the journey and assured them he would be with them in spirit.

Beth continually looked over her shoulder and waved as they walked away from the hut. The image of the old man waving with the tiger by his side would stay with her forever.

Two days later, they were safely entombed inside the blue monolith. Li had been proficient, hunting wild fowl and rabbit. Zhu Zhu had grown more attached to Beth.

After a good night's sleep in the cave, they were off again early the next morning.

'Well I'll be …' Beth said after noticing her watch was working again.

They reached the four-wheel drive by late afternoon and, as Li had predicted, they reached the village by midnight.

Li cut the engine a couple of kilometres before the village. He told the girls he would walk the rest of the way and fill the fuel cans. That way nobody, except the elder, would know they'd returned.

Beth and Yu huddled in the back seat and napped with Zhu Zhu between them.

Li returned about an hour later.

A little after dawn they reached the next village, which was basically a few farmhouses and an old Catholic church left over from the missionary days. The public phone was just inside the doorway of the building that doubled as the post office and store.

Li was only away a few minutes before he returned from making the call. 'Shanghai is arranging for a helicopter to pick us up and take us to Chongqing,' he blurted, excited and out of breath. 'They'll be here tomorrow. We have stirred great excitement among the zoo officials.'

'Okay, so where do we go until tomorrow?' Beth asked.

Li started the engine and pulled away with a purposeful expression.

13

Li drove out of the village and towards the pine-covered mountains that formed a beautiful protective backdrop.

One hour later, Beth's ears began to pop when the ascending four-wheel drive struggled to negotiate a steep narrow track. The high revving engine laboured as the wheels constantly lost traction, slipping backwards before jolting forward, and bouncing violently from side to side.

Beth struggled to hold Zhu Zhu with one hand while grasping the overhead safety handle with the other.

Yu closed her eyes tightly and held on with white knuckles.

Li pointed to a palatial building that clung to the side of the mountain above them. 'Buddha!' he shouted. 'Buddha!' Suddenly, the steering wheel spun and the vehicle veered towards the edge of the cliff. Li grabbed the wheel and jerked it back.

The early morning mist enshrouding most of the Buddhist temple was gently lifting as they approached. High sandstone walls, capped with orange pagoda tiles, clung to the edge of the rock. Tall palm trees swayed among turreted courtyards, giving the building the appearance of an exclusive resort. A bell rang across the valley as if to warn its inhabitants of approaching strangers.

The track widened and the travellers approached a set of tall iron gates.

Two young monks with shaved heads and dressed in orange gowns, struggled to open the gates. A third boy swung up and down on a rope, ringing the large bronze bell that hung from a gibbet to the left of the stone-framed gateway.

The four-wheel drive passed through the large entrance and along a winding driveway. When they approached the main building, there were two hundred monks waiting to greet them.

In unison, the monks bowed to the floor and began to chant.

When the vehicle came to a halt, one of the monks approached and peered through Li's open window. To Beth and Yu's surprise, he greeted them in perfect English.

'Welcome to our home,' he said. When his eyes caught sight of Zhu Zhu, he lowered his head and bowed graciously. With a sweeping arm, he gestured for his guests to enter the temple.

The monks scurried away in all directions.

'The bell will strike in thirty second intervals to mark the special occasion,' the head monk explained as the visitors climbed from the vehicle.

'What special occasion?' Beth asked.

A grin was the monk's only answer.

As they strolled into the building and along a stone passageway, the sound of chanting monks echoed off the walls.

Very modern, Beth thought, entering a wood-panelled office. There were twin computer monitors side by side on a curved wooden desk, a large printer and an iPhone standing upright on a charging station.

An elderly monk hobbled in and placed three chairs by the desk.

The head monk beckoned them to be seated. He took his own seat behind the desk and seemed to have difficulty taking his eyes off Zhu Zhu. 'Xiao Gong Zhu!' he suddenly said, 'The Little Princess.' He caught Beth's eye.

'How did you know that?' Beth asked.

The monk smiled. 'Although I am a Buddhist, I am of an open mind. I believe that religion is merely man's interpretation of the truth. As each millennium passes, we change the rules and lose sight of the truth. We create gods to mask our addictions and we persecute those of different beliefs, but in our dreams we see ourselves and, if we look hard enough, we can find the truth.'

Beth lowered her chin and glanced sideways at Yu. 'Here we go again,' she whispered.

The monk continued. 'Buddha taught us that with each reincarnation there are important lessons to learn. Before we reach Nirvana, we must rectify our past mistakes. In my dreams, I see the death of the last tiger. I watch helplessly as the blood is drained from its throat by the hands of a greedy fool. Then I see the first tiger, killed by a young warrior. The youth enters his village cloaked in the tiger's skin and he is crowned as chief. In his next life, he is a tiger. He is hunted and slaughtered by his descendants. His body parts are distributed around the world, consumed by kings and noblemen. His next life is devoted to the Buddha, and he is offered the chance to amend his previous mistakes.'

'Wow, the plot thickens,' Beth mumbled.

The elderly monk remained silent while he led the trio through the long passageways to their rooms.

Later, Beth sat in the sunshine in the courtyard perched on the edge of the cliff, admiring the view. Zhu Zhu napped on her lap. Beth and Li had planned to fast the cub every five days to imitate her natural feeding patterns. As the monks were strictly vegetarian, now was a good a time as any to start. On the days of the fast, they would give her only bones and water. Beth was glad Li had insisted on saving all the scrap bones from the journey.

The next morning Zhu Zhu panicked when the palm trees swayed violently, and the mountain dust was whipped up into a dry, blinding blizzard.

Beth, Li and Yu shielded their eyes with their hands as the dust scoured their faces. Zhu Zhu growled and snarled.

The head monk kissed each of them on the hand and bid them farewell

Although they were all quite short, they still ducked their heads when they ran beneath the rotating blades of the helicopter. Yu jumped in first and carefully took Zhu Zhu from Beth.

Beth followed just as Zhu Zhu was about to panic.

Li sat in the front next to the pilot.

Moments later they were circling the turrets before shooting off in the direction of Chongqing.

14

William Cloon, the American ambassador, treated Beth as if he'd known her all his life. Acting as her self-appointed spokesman, he hastily organised a press conference.

If there was such a thing as Chinese paparazzi, then they were all crammed into the Chongqing Zoo's visitor centre on this warm Friday evening. The Chinese reporters were very polite and asked questions such as: 'How old is the cub?' and 'How big is it?'

And of course, the inevitable question that Beth had discussed with Li earlier, 'Where exactly did you find it?'

Beth knew they would attract a lot of attention and not all of it good. If they revealed the exact whereabouts of the sanctuary, every poacher this side of Kathmandu would descend on it, shooting everything that moved.

Li Pang delivered a wonderful presentation on a secret and imaginary reserve somewhere on the Qinghai and Tibet border.

'Julie Rogers, ABC foreign correspondent. Are you seriously trying to tell us that you found a supposedly extinct wild tiger over two thousand kilometres northwest of its known habitat?'

Beth cleared her throat. 'Yes. Our findings show that due to habitat loss and poaching, some remaining tigers gradually moved north through corridors that are now also being lost.'

'Huh. Sounds like a smokescreen to me.'

'Well, I can assure you it isn't. My colleague, Doctor Li Pang, has studied the South China tiger for many years. It was his innovation and skill that made this find possible.'

'Well, my sources tell me that you were actually somewhere near the Guangdong and Hunan border.'

Beth shook her head impatiently. 'No.'

'Is it true you stole the cub away from its mother?'

'That's ridiculous,' Ambassador Cloon cut in. 'Why would Doctor Smith do such a thing?'

'Fame,' the correspondent quipped, staring at Beth.

An older reporter who bore an uncanny resemblance to Yoda broke the awkward silence. 'When can we see the tiger cub?'

'Well, we have many tests to conduct. You must remember she is a wild animal, and it will take time for her to adjust. But we're setting up a closed-circuit television camera system in her enclosure so we can monitor her and release the footage. Unfortunately, we will only be in Chongqing for one week, after which time we leave for Shanghai where a permanent enclosure is being prepared.'

Almost one point four billion Chinese people discussed the find that evening. The rest of the world read about it over breakfast the next morning.

LAST WILD SOUTH CHINA TIGER RESCUED BY AMERICAN CONSERVATIONIST

The world fell in love with The Little Princess when the time-lapsed images from the enclosure were beamed around the globe. *CNN* put aside a few minutes after the weather report each evening and called it *Tiger Time*. The reports included daily footage and pictures, updates and progress reports. Beth's daily blog entries rocketed her site up the search engine rankings due to the massive following. Magazines and newspapers battled each other to win an interview with the unknown American zoologist. Beth became famous overnight. When the makers of *The World Around Us* approached her to make a documentary, her employers had no choice but to apply for an extension to her stay. The Chinese government eagerly agreed and awarded Beth an open visa.

The first six months were hectic. The new enclosure at the Shanghai Zoo was given the big thumbs up by the children of the world, many of whom, in light of the new tiger awareness, had organised fundraisers through schools and clubs to help save the tigers' natural habitat.

When the documentary was finally aired around the world, Tigermania took a firm grip and attention spotlighted the poachers and the use of tiger derivatives in traditional Chinese medicines.

Beth suspected that when Julie Rogers saw her and Zhu Zhu on the cover of *Time Magazine*, she would jealously point a finger and say, 'I told you so.' She also realised the comparisons being made between herself and Joy Adamson and Dian Fossey could have a negative effect.

Zhu Zhu quickly grew from a soft, golden furball to a clumsy, mischievous adolescent. She'd steadily gained a hundred grams of weight per day and, after a cautious start, she finally settled into her new habitat.

Over the next few months, her unruly personality tended to surface whenever Beth wasn't around. She would not eat or exercise unless Beth was close by. The zoo staff playfully nicknamed Beth, Lao Hu Fuyang —Tiger Mother.

At the LA Zoo, a giant screen was erected and a thirty-minute presentation by Beth, recorded the previous day in Shanghai, was shown twice daily. The attraction became the zoo's biggest draw card. The demand for Little Princess soft toys and souvenirs was so great that zoos, toyshops and bookstores around the world sold out of the first shipment within hours. Children wore baseball caps with a picture of Zhu Zhu's eyes across the front and T-shirts with the words I LOVE TIGERS emblazoned across the chest.

Ten per cent of the sale price of each item went towards saving the South China Tiger.

Zhu Zhu's golden eyes shone with the mischief and curiosity of a child when a large first birthday cake was placed in front of her. Suddenly, her ears shot back and her face scrunched into a snarl when a member of staff crept forward to push the cake closer.

The crowd gasped but then exploded with applause and wolf whistles when Beth ran into the enclosure.

Zhu Zhu bounded over to Beth with her tail between her legs as if expecting to be chastised.

Dignitaries, movie stars and wealthy business people had flown in for the birthday celebrations. Tickets for the event had sold in minutes, two months earlier. There was a live audience of seven thousand. Two billion people watched via satellite.

Although Zhu Zhu was now 150 centimetres long and weighed 60 kilograms, to the world she would always be The Little Princess.

Beth, wearing a hands-free microphone, stood in the centre of the enclosure.

Zhu Zhu circled Beth's legs then settled down.

'Welcome to Zhu Zhu's first birthday.' The title of Little Princess was far too formal for Beth to use.

The crowd erupted once more.

Zhu Zhu looked around nonchalantly then licked herself.

Beth had to smile at the animal's regal disposition. 'As you can see, Zhu Zhu is very excited.'

The crowd laughed.

The two-hour show began with the official unveiling of the new extended enclosure that had been funded and built by donations from around the world. The Chinese President and the heads of The World Wildlife Fund and CITIES conducted the ceremony.

Beth led Zhu Zhu into the two acres of trees and bush, which included a rocky ledge complete with a cave, a waterfall and a pool.

The Tiger Chase

Zhu Zhu sprinted to the pool, dived in and swam to the other side. The audience *oohed* and *aahed*.

Beth explained that although Zhu Zhu was now captive, she was still, and always would be, wild. And she stressed the importance of keeping the enclosure as close to the natural habitat as possible. 'Okay, where'd she go?' Beth said looking round for the absent tiger.

Zhu Zhu appeared from the cave and stood on the ledge. *'GRRREARGH!'* She was the star of the show and she knew it.

'Oh, she loves to show off,' Beth said playfully.

The rest of the show saw an array of superstars performing. The comical highlight was when Danny Poe, the current US sitcom king, sat on the grass beside Zhu Zhu. The tiger, as if not allowing anyone to steal the limelight, nuzzled him then plonked herself down on top of him like a lap cat. The rehearsed lines were never delivered. There was no need for fabricated comedy. Danny, the consummate professional, with a 60 kilo tiger sprawled across him, acted as if nothing out of the ordinary was happening and ad-libbed his way through a one-way conversation. 'So, you have a guy in to clean the pool?'

Zhu Zhu looked at him and cocked her head to one side.

'Got to watch those chemicals … got to be just right, ya know … would hate to see your fur turn green … would have to call ya Ghu Ghu …'

There were many musical highlights. Sir Michael Johns performed on a white grand piano from the top of the ridge. The UK's new pop sensation, David Saxon, sang Happy Birthday to Zhu Zhu. Legendary Irish rockers Me4 penned a song especially for the event called "The Tiger's Heart".

The show was a great success.

Beth and Li had been given complete control of Zhu Zhu's upbringing. The cub would be the first founder introduced to the genetic line of South China tigers in almost forty years. After demographic and genetic computer software analysis showed her to be unrelated to any of the other captive tigers, a mean kinship value (MK) was then measured to avoid the possibility of rare and common genes being linked. In the case of all new founders, the value of zero was given, but more importantly it showed that this new genetic line would help increase genetic diversity amongst the species. The sperm Beth had collected from the male tiger that had killed the tigress also offered a new genetic line. There was much excitement among the other Chinese zoos that held South China tigers.

American zoo personnel from the Minnesota and Omaha zoos had been flown in to assist with the creation of an in vitro fertilisation program. Using what would now be termed as commonplace techniques, they were able to create a live embryo from artificial insemination. A few months later, the first cub was born to a tigress at the Guangzhou Zoo.

Although it would be another year until Zhu Zhu was entered into the captive breeding program, a mate had already been chosen from the Suzhou Zoo. His name was Chi, meaning Life Energy, named after exhibiting an amazing amount of energy shortly after birth. He was three years old. He also had an MK of zero and had yet to be mated.

When the time finally came for Zhu Zhu and Chi's introduction, the world watched with excitement.

Beth worried as any parent of a teenage daughter would. Pangs of jealousy would strike when she watched from outside the enclosure while Zhu Zhu and Chi played together. One thing was for sure though—Zhu Zhu was definitely ready.

Four months later, Zhu Zhu gave birth to four cubs. The world focused its attention on her once more. The Chinese government was delighted. Chinese and American relations were at an all-time high.

Meanwhile, Beth was summoned to Beijing to be awarded a special honour for conservation. Another first for a westerner.

15

Two years later, Beth was still in China. Her life was devoted to Zhu Zhu and the welfare of tigers. She hadn't been back to the States in all this time. Too busy. Her only friends were the zoo staff — whom she could now converse with in fluent Mandarin — and Li and Yu, who had become man and wife two years earlier.

The attention of the world had moved on. Interest in the plight of the South China tiger had become a fad from the past. Beth was growing homesick.

The South China tiger captive breeding program was gaining ground. A total of eight embryos had been created from the IVF program. Zhu Zhu's cubs had successfully bred cubs of their own. In all this time Beth hadn't asked a single request. She'd simply gone about her duties working seven days a week.

Home and her family seemed to be on her mind a great deal lately. She spoke to her parents regularly on the phone but had recently received distressing news of her father's failing health. Was he really approaching old age now? Apart from missing out on important family occasions, she began to realise she was missing the everyday contact. Worrying that she'd lost the comfort and familiarity of home, she realised she wanted to go home, but she could never leave Zhu Zhu.

Beth paced the tiger enclosure while she spoke into her cell phone. 'What do you think, Ambassador? Could it be possible?'

'Well, I think it's a splendid idea, Beth. But we'll have a problem with the Chinese. What do your superiors think?' Ambassador Cloon said.

'Sceptical at first and couldn't really see the purpose, but after I spoke to Doctor Malcolm Wilson, the Director of Conservation at the Minnesota Zoo, and won him over, they began to take notice.'

'Well, what purpose will it serve? Surely the animal is better off in this country?'

'There's good argument for and against. Sure, the South China tiger belongs in China but we're talking about captive animals that are near to extinction. How much worse would the plight of the Siberian tiger be without the captive breeding program of the Minnesota Zoo? The success rate with captive Sumatran tigers is also well on the way to reaching its target. Barbarisation can only take place if a healthy quantity of captive tigers is produced. With the expertise and facilities that could be utilised in the States, I'm sure we can work towards preservation of this species.'

'Barba … what?'

'Barbarisation, it means introducing a captive animal back into the wild.'

'Now I'm totally confused. Are you talking about setting Zhu Zhu free?'

'No … no, of course not. Forget I said that. It's not on the cards for Zhu Zhu.'

'So, what is it we're talking about, Beth?'

'I want to help increase genetic diversity by creating a new captive bloodline in the States.'

'But how are you going to achieve this with only one animal?'

'Well, Zhu Zhu's due to be mated again during the next six months. If I can take her out of the country in the early stages of pregnancy, we won't just be getting one tiger, we'll be—'

'But—' the ambassador tried to interrupt.

Beth anticipated his next question. 'I want to take her to LA. We'll create a new habitat to raise her cubs. They'll have the best veterinarian attention in the world. This will also return the world's focus onto the plight of the subspecies.'

Cloon remained silent.

Beth continued: 'Then when the cubs are fully grown, we engage them in a kind of exchange program. We'll send a male or a female to China for mating. In return, they'll do the same. In doing so, we can hopefully create a new bloodline and help increase genetic diversity.'

'Hmm ... LA. Isn't that your hometown?'

'Oh, come on, Bill, how long have you known me? And in all that time have you ever heard me ask for anything for myself?'

'No, no, I didn't mean—'

'You've offended me, Bill. I thought you of all people would understand what I'm trying to do.'

'Look ... Beth, please understand, all I am trying to do is ascertain the circumstances under which the Chinese government would allow their beloved Little Princess to be shipped off to America. We're going to have to convince them that this is for the good of the animal, and not just for your own selfish reasons. You must also understand that Uncle Sam and The Sleeping Dragon aren't exactly best of buddies at the moment.'

'So ... what are you saying?'

'What I'm saying is ... I'm one hundred and ten per cent behind you, and although I don't hold much hope for the outcome, I will do everything in my power to make it happen.'

Beth thanked him, terminated the call, and almost tripped over Zhu Zhu who was lying across the grass chewing a bone. She knew she had a difficult task ahead of her. William Cloon was right when he jokingly commented that American and Chinese relations weren't that healthy at the moment. She knelt beside Zhu Zhu. *Politicians, why do they have to make life so difficult?* she thought, running her fingers through the tiger's fur. Would people understand what she was trying to achieve? Or would they think she was doing it for her own selfish reasons?

Me4 sang, 'And the tiger's heart beats strong tonight ...'

Zhu Zhu flinched.

The ringtone stopped when Beth answered her cell phone. 'Hello.'

'Hello, I'd like sweet and sour pork, honeyed chicken wings with rice and prawn crackers for one. Oh, and if it doesn't arrive in thirty minutes, I'm not paying.'

'Hi Robert.' Beth had never met Robert Baker, the LA Zoo administrator, but she spoke with him regularly on the phone. Robert enjoyed his own humour.

'Isn't this the Chinese restaurant? Shit. Must have hit the wrong speed dial. Just kidding. How are you, gorgeous?'

'I'm very well, thank you. So how did you go with the Chinese ambassador?'

'Oh, you know me, just had to use my charm. Actually, I can't get to talk to him. But I'm bombarding his secretary, who is falling in love with me, with requests for an appointment. It looks like I'll be able to see him next Wednesday. I've also written to him with a detailed summary of what we propose to do. The best news is though, we've got the media on our side so be prepared for a few thousand calls from the newspapers and TV stations. I've also been meeting with Marsha Thompson, who is, as you know, the head of the WWF. She is arranging for me to meet with Senator Jack Daly. He's coming up for re-election in the fall and needs to boost his waning popularity. So yeah, it's all happening this end.'

'What about the new enclosure? Did you manage to get the plans through yet?'

'Oh, better than that. The city of LA wants The Little Princess. We received permission the same day as the plans were submitted. We're just waiting for the go-ahead. We'll have it built quicker than you can say, "three fried fritters".'

'Oh, that's great news, Robert. Thanks again for everything you're doing. Talk to you soon. Bye.'

Qiang Shi, meaning 'mighty', was a six-year-old male tiger also from the Suzhou Zoo. For some reason it took him and Zhu Zhu longer to accept each other, probably because the habitat at the Shanghai Zoo was vastly different from the inadequate enclosure the male was used

The Tiger Chase

to. Eventually the two came together after being separated by a chain wire fence for a couple of weeks.

The day of the meeting to decide whether Beth could take Zhu Zhu to LA had finally arrived. Although everything on the other side of the world was ready, things didn't look good in China. She'd met fierce opposition from Chinese zoo officials and members of the right-wing press. To them, America was trying to steal their Xiao Gong Zhu, and this was an abomination they would not allow.

Beth and Li stood silently in a modern glass-and-marble corridor of the Shanghai Entry-Exit Inspection and Quarantine Bureau in the Pudong New Area, Shanghai. They waited patiently outside the opaque glass door where the hearing had already started, waiting to be summoned. All they could hear and see were muffled voices and shadows through the glass. Suddenly, the door opened. Beth and Li were asked to enter.

Three Chinese officials and Doctor David Woo, whom Beth recognised from the Southeast Asia Zoo Association, sat at the head of a long rectangular, highly polished table. William Cloon, the American ambassador and two assistants sat along one side of the table. Zoo officials—Doctor Chan Jiang, formerly of the Shanghai Zoo, who had met Beth at the airport on her first day in China, and a young man wearing a blue pinstriped suit—sat along the other side. There was an area at the side of the room with a tape barrier where members of the press stood.

Beth and Li were shown to two empty seats next to William Cloon. Beth caught Julie Rogers' eye among the members of the press.

'Relax, Beth, this isn't a courtroom,' William Cloon whispered while Beth took her seat. 'This is the moment you've been waiting for.'

Beth smiled nervously.

Beth didn't hear the introductions taking place. She didn't hear the ambassador's opening statement. She was standing in front of Huan Loh's hut. The forest air was warm and sweet. Wang rubbed his body against her legs and arched his back with the pleasure of her touch.

She knelt and stroked him. It was great to see him again. She called out Huan Loh's name, but there was no answer. She entered the hut.

The old man was seated at the table. Without acknowledging Beth's presence, he began to speak slowly in broken English. 'Beware of ironies. Beware of corruption. Beware lao hu, the tiger, and do not underestimate the fool. Seek huo long, the dragon ...'

'Miss Smith ... Miss Smith ... did you hear the question, Miss Smith?'

'What ...? I'm sorry, what was—'

'The question *was*, Miss Smith, can you assure us of the safety of the tiger?' snapped the man in the blue pinstriped suit, now leaning forward in his seat and glaring at her.

'That's Doctor Smith, and yes, we have the best veterinary team in the world waiting in LA, and all the necessary security measures are in place.'

'Security? Such as?'

'Well, we've decided to keep the actual time of arrival secret. The American public is aware of our plans and has been following our progress closely but if they knew of the time and place of arrival, they could inadvertently cause unnecessary stress to the animal.'

'How so?'

'They would undoubtedly arrive in the thousands to get a glimpse. We need to keep her as calm as possible.'

'So, if she did happen to arrive safely, then what?'

'Once there, she will be quarantined under twenty-four hour guard before being moved to her new enclosure.'

The man narrowed his eyes and held her gaze for a few moments. Then he looked at William Cloon. Then at Doctor Jiang.

Beth braced herself for the next question.

The man sat back in his seat as if defeated.

Beth frowned and turned to William Cloon.

Cloon winked at her and smiled.

Suddenly, Beth and Li were being ushered out of the room. The door closed behind them.

'Surely that's not all they wanted to hear, Li?' Beth whispered in Mandarin as they stood in the hallway.

'I think there's more politics involved than the actual welfare of Zhu Zhu,' Li whispered back.

'What do you mean?'

'You must remember, like America, China is a very corrupt place. Everyone and everything has its price.'

'You mean William is trying to cut a deal in there?'

Li shrugged but Beth knew that expression—it was the same expression he'd used when leading her to Blue Tiger Mountain—the secretive I-know-something-you-don't-know look.

'God, how naive am I?' Beth said running her hands through her hair. She hadn't thought for a moment that things weren't above board. Then she remembered Huan Loh's warning. Beware the corruption. 'This is not right. We can't go through with this, Li.'

'Of course we can.'

'No ... I can't take her knowing—'

'Knowing what? Look, Beth. We need to do whatever it takes.'

Beth shook her head and fidgeted nervously.

'Relax. If someone is willing to foot the bill for getting Zhu Zhu to LA then that is good, no?'

'But who? And why?'

'Your government? Cloon?'

'You really think so?'

Li nodded and placed a reassuring hand on Beth's shoulder.

The door swung open. Doctor Jiang and his associate stormed off down the corridor without as much as a glance in Beth's direction.

William Cloon bounded out of the room grinning. 'Congratulations, Beth. You've done it.'

'What?' Beth was incredulous. 'But how?'

Ambassador Cloon threw his arms around her. 'Never mind all that. You've *won*, Beth!'

'I can't believe it. This is just unbelievable. I'm really going home?'

William ushered Beth and Li into the elevator and they travelled to the underground parking lot where his limousine awaited them. 'Lunch is on me!' he exclaimed when they'd climbed into the back of the car.

'So, how much did it cost you, Bill?' Beth asked while the waiter poured three glasses of Champagne at William's favourite restaurant.

'What? Lunch? Oh, don't worry about that, the good old expense account—'

'You know what I mean,' Beth said, cutting him off.

'Well, that's the most amazing part, it didn't cost us a cent.'

'Oh, come on, Bill, you're not trying to tell me they agreed to let their precious Xiao Gong Zhu go without a little friendly persuasion. They hardly even asked me any questions.'

'I know, I just don't get it either. I expected it to be really difficult, believe me, and I had my price set. But we never got that far. So, I naturally assumed we didn't stand a chance. Then all of a sudden, Bingo, it was all over, and we'd won.'

Beth lifted her glass. 'Yeah, right Bill, I believe you. Although I don't condone corruption, I think in this instance … I'll let you off. But seriously, thanks again for all your help. Cheers.'

'Cheers!' Li and Cloon said in unison, lifting their glasses, both with the same sheepish expression.

Part Two

Yang (The Dragon)

16

The tiger crouched and snarled. Its lips quivered over enormous fangs. *'GRRREARGH!'* it roared then pounced.

John Dean's eyes opened wide. His heart raced. A cold sweat caused him to shiver. He sat up in bed and waited for the familiar surroundings of his room to calm him. Finally, he shivered again and lay back down. At this point the dream was so clear. The girl. The tiger. The old Chinese man. The mysterious figure with the dark evil eyes. This time he would remember everything; he knew exactly what he had to do. But then, he seemed to recall thinking this before. *Perhaps this time would be different,* he thought, drifting back to sleep.

A light rain, which had showered on Los Angeles for most of the day, began to fall heavier as the evening wore on. Steam plumes, rising from the Chinatown street, swirled and flickered, almost keeping time with the faint Chinese gramophone music that drifted on the breeze.

Detective John Dean of the LAPD wiped his wet watch across his jacket and checked the time.

The offices above *The Happy Garden Restaurant* had been under surveillance for the last two weeks. John was acting on information supplied by an informant regarding the movements of Tony Spignetti, aka Tony Lee, a suspected drug dealer and well known in LA for his connections in Asia.

Elongated shadows chased by the headlights of a black limousine swung from left to right then slithered to the ground. The limo drove slowly along the deserted street.

'Hold your position, McGuire,' John whispered into the transmitter on his cuff.

Ben McGuire, John's rookie partner, acknowledged with a nod from a doorway opposite.

John shielded his eyes against the glare of the headlights. He was crouched behind trash cans, the stench of restaurant garbage making him regret his choice of cover.

The limousine stopped outside *The Happy Garden Restaurant.*

John glimpsed the licence plate when the headlights extinguished. LEE 1. 'That's our boy, McGuire,' he whispered. 'Wait until he enters the building, but make sure he has the bag, over.'

'Copy that.'

Two men emerged from the car—the first was Tony Lee.

John froze when the other man turned and looked at where he was hiding. His surroundings melted into darkness, pierced only by those demonic eyes.

The tiger crouched and snarled. Its lips quivered over enormous fangs. *'GRRREARGH!'* it roared then pounced.

'I think that's Raymond Brown, boss ... John? Can you hear me?'

John snapped back to the present. 'Yes ... I think you're right, kid.' From his informant's description he was sure the second man was Raymond Brown, an un-convicted hitman from Hong Kong, known as The Tiger. John analysed Brown's appearance. Possibly of Hispanic Asian descent, he was short and muscular. He wore a black turtleneck pullover under a tight, grey suit. His dark, deep-set eyes darted and probed as if missing nothing, and his closely-cropped hair was shaved into stripes like those of a tiger.

The two men moved towards the restaurant. Brown walked backwards, his eyes scanning the opposite buildings.

John noticed a bag under his arm. 'Okay, kid, when I give the signal, move in.'

McGuire glanced to where John crouched and nodded once more.

The red neon sign above the sleazy restaurant pulsated and

created an eerie glow on the dark street while the interior lighting struggled to filter through the grimy shopfront.

John could see the inside from his position: rows of red and white checked tables—mostly empty—plastic pot plants, Chinese lanterns hanging from the ceiling. On the left-hand wall was a small bar area, framed by a string of Christmas lights. To the right was a swinging port holed door, which obviously led to the kitchen. On the back wall, there were two mirrored French doors with brass fittings.

Tony Lee and his accomplice were in the restaurant making their way to the French doors.

John waved McGuire forward.

Lee opened one of the glass doors and climbed a flight of stairs.

Brown turned and once again scanned his wake. He nodded to the barkeeper then disappeared backwards through the doorway.

The barman didn't notice the two detectives slip into the restaurant while he prepared two drinks.

McGuire crept towards the bar.

The barman looked up, startled.

McGuire drew his revolver and put a finger to his lips.

John headed for the table in the corner where the only three diners sat. Holding up his badge, he whispered, 'LAPD. Leave quietly, please.'

The small group left in a hurry.

'So, who else is upstairs?' John asked the barman.

The barman remained quiet.

'You're gonna be in a lot of trouble, buddy,' McGuire said.

The barman shrugged and still said nothing.

'Okay, take him to the bathroom, handcuff him to something and don't be gentle.' John called for backup while he waited for McGuire to return. When the rookie reappeared, John quietly opened the French door.

Muffled voices grew clearer when the two detectives slowly climbed the stairs.

'Xiao tou!' a high-pitched voice screamed in Chinese.

'What the hell is he saying?' John recognised this voice as Tony Lee's.

The first voice grew more frantic. *'Xiao tou—Xiao tou—Xiao tou!'*

Then a third voice, which John assumed belonged to Raymond Brown, translated the Chinese dialogue into English, deep and slow. 'The price was agreed in Hong Kong. The cargo is on its way to LA, and you insult the name of the Lour family by offering a fraction of the agreed price. You are nothing more than a common thief! Thief—thief—thief!'

John was keen to move in. He'd heard the word cargo, but it meant nothing. One thing was clear though—and it worried him—the notorious Lour family from Hong Kong was operating in LA.

Tony Lee's voice rose above the rest. 'Did you really think I would be so stupid as to give you the money, *old man*? Can't you see that in Hong Kong it was you who was working for me? *You* did all the groundwork, saddled the cost … and for what? When you moved into export, *old man,* you got greedy. Unfortunately, you dealt with one who is even greedier … *me*.'

The yelling continued. John and McGuire listened as Brown translated Lee's words into Chinese.

'Here you sit, the once all-powerful, patriarch of the Lour family—Hong Kong's most feared crime lord. *Hah!* Well, this isn't Hong Kong. You're in my territory now. I have the money and the cargo, which just happens to be the purest heroin on the market today. *And* … I have you.'

That was it. John wasn't sure how many people were in the room, but he'd only heard three voices. The backup hadn't arrived yet. He had to take the chance. He motioned for McGuire to follow him.

Suddenly, shots were fired in the room.

John and McGuire rushed up the stairs.

The shooting stopped.

The door was ajar allowing John a glimpse of the smoke-filled room. There were at least six bodies slumped over tables and chairs and on the floor. Raymond Brown knelt on one knee in the middle of the room grasping a Micro UZI with both hands. Smoke rose from the tiny barrel as he twisted slowly from side to side, smiling as if daring the corpses to move.

John kicked open the door. 'LAPD, DROP YOUR WEAPON.'

Both detectives stood with their guns trained on Raymond Brown.

Brown rose calmly and turned to face them.

'Drop your weapon and put your hands in the air.'

Brown, staring into John's eyes, dropped the gun, placed his hands on his head and smirked.

McGuire edged forward.

'Hold it, kid. I don't trust this guy,' John said, grabbing his partner's arm. He motioned McGuire to cover him and, with Brown's menacing eyes locked on his, he moved towards the centre of the room and kicked away the UZI. Then he realised Tony Lee was missing.

Raymond Brown, as if reading John's thoughts, cocked his head back and laughed a deep, non-humorous laugh.

John swallowed hard, fumbled for his handcuffs with his free hand, and approached Brown. *Where the hell was that backup?*

Brown lowered his arms arrogantly.

The sound of a car speeding away distracted John, causing him to break eye contact. He was about to give chase but stopped himself. In a normal bust, he would have left McGuire to bring in the prisoner, but he couldn't leave his rookie to apprehend Brown. 'Damn!' he cussed. Lee had escaped him yet again.

Brown continued to laugh.

'Shut the hell up and turn round,' John growled.

The smirk slid from Brown's face. He didn't move.

'Okay, let's go.' John moved closer to Brown.

Brown suddenly snatched the gun from John's hand and threw it across the room.

John lifted his knee hard towards Brown's groin.

Brown easily swept John's knee to one side with his left arm, then hammered his right elbow into the side of John's head, sending him sprawling among the corpses.

Brown turned to McGuire, holding out his arms as if greeting him.

Although John was dazed, he jumped to his feet and searched for his gun.

McGuire tried to match the stare but his hand holding the gun began to shake.

John, unable to find his gun, sprung across the room and pounced on Brown's back. Having no effect, except winding himself, he wrapped his arms around Brown's throat and squeezed.

Brown, with John still on his back, marched towards McGuire until his chest touched the end of the rookie's gun.

'Shoot him,' John yelled, jostling for a better grip.

McGuire, seemingly mesmerised by Brown's hypnotic snare, dropped his gun.

John wrapped his arm around Brown's head.

The strength suddenly drained from Brown's body like a failed generator.

John had inadvertently hit the off switch by covering Brown's eyes thus preventing him from seeing the thing he thrived on most—the fear in his victim's eyes.

McGuire regained his senses and retrieved his gun.

'GRRREARGH!' Brown roared like a tiger and jerked his head back hard.

John fell to the ground, blood gushing from his nose.

McGuire aimed his gun at Brown. 'Freeze.'

'JUST SHOOT,' John shouted.

Brown, ignoring the rookie, bent and grabbed John by the lapels.

BANG! McGuire fired his gun into the ceiling.

Brown jolted upright and stood motionless in the centre of the room.

John scurried from beneath him and crawled to McGuire.

The detectives stood panting, neither sure what to do next.

'Should I shoot him?' McGuire whispered.

John shook his head and crept over to one of the tables after spotting his gun.

Raymond Brown stood tensed like a waxwork dummy.

'What do we do now, boss?'

'Shhh …' John lifted his finger to his lips. 'Do you hear that?'

McGuire cocked his head to one side and listened as a faint rumble rose like a deep gargle.

John edged forward with his gun tightly in one hand and the cuffs swinging in the other. 'Come on, kid, it's now or never—'

'GRRREARGH!'

The detectives, shoulder to shoulder, instinctively ducked their heads.

Brown dropped to a crouch then sprung into a backwards somersault, kicking out with both legs and striking each of the detectives on their chins.

Their heads slammed against the floor. Broken glass showered down on them.

Brown had dived through the window.

McGuire was the first to his feet and, closely followed by John, cautiously climbed through the broken window, lowered himself onto the kitchen roof and down into the back alley. Then he ran in one direction while John went the other.

The eerie silence made John shiver, which somehow told him he was wasting his time—the killer had gone. He reached the end of the alley. A squad car screeched to a halt in his path. Unable to stop in time, he slammed against the fender and rolled up on to the hood, cracking his head against the windshield. The backup had arrived.

The worse scenario confronted John when he returned to the restaurant. There was a room full of dead Chinese mafia, and their killer had escaped. But worst of all Tony Lee had slipped through his fingers yet again. How would he face Captain Williams in the morning? What kind of a role model was he for McGuire? For a moment back there, he hadn't known what to do. He'd relinquished his weapon to an unarmed assailant and let him get away. John wanted to punch the nearest wall. Was he losing his grip?

17

Early the next morning, McGuire was surprised when John showed up at his apartment.

'We're gonna make a slight detour this morning, kid.'
'Yeah? Where we going?'
'You'll see. I'll wait in the car.'

McGuire realised where they were going when John drove towards Beverly Hills. He knew it was useless protesting. Instead, he sat wondering about Tony Lee. He'd read Lee's file, heard all the rumours and he wondered which ones were true.

Tony Lee was a podgy Italian-American. He wore expensive suits, lots of gold jewellery, and a jet-black toupee. His passé image was a constant source of humour at the police precinct. But McGuire wondered if there was more to this man.

Lee was a somewhat disparaged student of the martial arts. At the age of thirty-three, he changed his name from Spignetti to Lee after his idol, Bruce Lee, and enrolled at the *Dong Nao Jin School of Chinese Boxing* in LA. There he trained, rather ineptly (obvious to everyone around him but himself) for six months. Then he moved to Hong Kong seeking spiritual enlightenment and more in-depth training. It was also around this time that he began dealing drugs. Soon he established a small empire, which later progressed into harder narcotics and vice.

He left Hong Kong some years later and returned to America. A question mark remained in his file as to whether he left of his own

The Tiger Chase

accord or if he was forced to flee after cheating his rival syndicates out of millions of dollars. Whatever the truth, Lee returned to LA a wealthy man and to the lifestyle of a movie star. Beautiful Asian women, whom he lavished with gold and cocaine, accompanied him wherever he went.

McGuire's mood was sombre as the car turned into Lee's driveway. He nervously ran a hand through his dark hair then rolled his eyes when he glimpsed at the house. A Chinese-styled mansion with pink stucco walls and an orange roof was partially hidden by tall palm trees. The driveway wound through botanical gardens where peacocks roamed.

When they approached the house John suddenly pressed hard on the accelerator and veered onto the lawn. With the back wheels of the unmarked police car losing traction, clumps of turf and dirt flew in all directions. The vehicle spun round leaving a circular gouge in the grass.

McGuire swallowed hard but remained quiet.

John drove back onto the driveway, sped towards the house then screeched to a halt at the front steps.

McGuire rushed to catch up when John stormed out of the car and headed towards the front door. He'd never seen his partner like this before.

The beautiful sound of classical piano music grew louder as the two detectives approached the front door.

'Für Elise,' McGuire said.

'What?' John lifted and dropped the giant doorknocker, sending a dull thud through the house.

'Beethoven.'

'Huh?'

'The music.'

John hammered the side of his fist on the door.

When the door finally opened, a small Oriental woman in traditional Chinese dress bowed. John held up his badge. She beckoned them to remove their shoes on entering, which McGuire did.

John, ignoring the request, pushed his way through and marched into the hallway.

A hotchpotch of bad taste confronted McGuire as he followed his partner into a long, Gothic-style, lime green hallway. Crystal chandeliers and European antiques complemented Oriental, Indian and African pieces like sugar would tuna. Animal heads stared down above Chinese weapons, Egyptian artefacts and Indian gods. Van Goghs, Dalis, and Picassos hung randomly among fifties, sixties and seventies memorabilia.

John marched towards a large door at the end of the hall, seemingly oblivious to his surroundings.

McGuire followed, humming to the piano music.

To the left of the end door stood a life-size sculpture of James Dean. To the right was a metre-high marble pillar with a glass case resting on top. Inside the case was a black leather boxing glove.

McGuire leaned to read the inscription beneath it: "As Worn by Bruce Lee in *Enter the Dragon*."

John flung open the door.

The music reached concert pitch.

Tony Lee didn't miss a note when John burst into the room. He continued to play the white grand piano, jerking his body and thrusting his head back, emphasising each note.

A tall Chinese girl with short, bleached hair was leaning over the piano, an empty wine glass tilting in her hand. She turned, looked at the two strangers and giggled.

John approached Tony Lee with his badge still in his hand. 'Can you tell me where you were last night around eleven o'clock?'

Tony Lee, ignoring the intrusion, carried on playing.

McGuire could see John was angry and he knew why. If they arrested Lee, he wouldn't say a word except to ask for his one phone call. Then some pompous Harvard graduate, with all the answers, would dismiss the lack of evidence, leaving the detectives with a lot of answering to do. McGuire suspected John was sick of the old routine. This case seemed to be destroying everything he believed in. Tony Lee would be laughing in his face yet again. Even though McGuire had taken pictures with his phone of Lee and Brown entering the

The Tiger Chase

restaurant in Chinatown, after inspecting them later, it was apparent that the lighting was too dark to get a clear enough shot. And because Lee was nowhere to be seen when they burst into the room, they had no proof he was even there.

John looked at McGuire then back at Lee as if he were weighing up the situation.

McGuire became edgy when his partner's facial expression changed from one of stress and anger to devil-like mischief.

John turned slowly and looked round the room as if noticing it for the first time. With wide eyes and a slight grin, he nodded as if reaching a decision.

There was an enormous flat screen TV, turned on with the volume down, at the other side of the room. John sauntered over to it, bent down and rubbed the palm of his hand across the screen.

Tony Lee glanced sideways and frowned but continued to play.

McGuire watched Tony Lee in awe. Lee's concentration hadn't wavered, he'd continued playing, impressing the rookie no end.

As a boy, McGuire was sent for piano lessons once a week to the house of an eccentric Austrian lady called Madame Bon Weisen. She would rap his knuckles with a twelve-inch ruler whenever he made a mistake. Most nights he'd go home with sore hands. 'Vren vill you learn? Vren vill you learn?' she'd yell at the top of her voice.

As much as he'd tried, he couldn't get it right. So, he'd given up. But he was left with a deep respect for anyone who could play.

Maybe he was wrong about this guy. How could a phoney like Tony Lee demonstrate such self-discipline and skill?

A loud *THUD* shattered McGuire's thoughts. He swung round to see John withdrawing his foot from a smoking hole in the middle of the TV screen.

Tony Lee rushed from the piano. 'You crazy bastard …'

The 'Für Elise' played on.

John, paying no attention, strolled over to the marble fireplace on the far wall and picked up a large blue and white vase which stood to the left of the hearth. He jostled it in his hands as if appraising its weight. He looked at Tony Lee and nodded his approval. Then he raised the vase above his head and threw it into the hearth, smashing it.

'NO!' Lee screamed, grabbing John by the arm.

John pushed him away, picked up an identical vase from the other side of the hearth and smashed it too.

'That's fourteenth-century Ming,' Lee cried. '200k a piece. Ten years' your salary, you dumb-ass.'

McGuire couldn't believe he'd been sucked in. A pianola. He should have realised. Some detective. He had to smile though while he watched the keys going up and down on the keyboard as if played by Beethoven's ghost. He gained comfort when he realised his original analysis had been correct—Tony Lee was a phoney. His smile turned to nervous laughter, however, when his attention returned to John.

'You're finished, do you hear me? FINISHED!' Lee cried, following John out of the room.

McGuire followed.

John padded into the hall, looked down at the boxing glove in the glass case and grinned.

'Don't even think about it,' Lee said, trying to push John away from his prized possession.

John stood his ground and hammered his clenched fist onto the case, smashing the glass into pieces. He grabbed the glove, placed it on his right hand and turned to face Tony Lee.

Lee's eyeballs bulged as he uttered a high-pitched cry, 'Hrahhhh!' His head rolled from side to side, his body jerked and twitched before resting into a martial arts style fighting stance.

John stepped back into an old-school boxing stance, raising the gloved fist to his chin.

Lee lunged forward and burst into a flurry of air punches and open-handed strikes. Suddenly he stopped, held his outstretched left arm in front of his face and beckoned with his fingertips for John to approach.

The Tiger Chase

McGuire laughed and stumbled, knocking over a glass gum dispenser. Hundreds of multi-coloured gumballs rolled and bounced across the tiled floor.

John and Tony Lee moved back into the main room, circling and taunting each other, ducking and bobbing.

Two Oriental guards appeared in the hallway.

McGuire reached for his gun and stepped into their path. 'Hold it right there.'

The guards backed away and raised their arms.

'Now hit the deck and lie face down with your hands behind your backs.' McGuire handcuffed them together. Then he noticed a large lion costume—the kind used for Chinese New Year—draped over a church pew below the stairs. Maybe John's mischief was rubbing off on him. He ran to fetch the costume. Unfortunately, failing to account for its size and weight, the ceramic head hit him in the face, knocked him off his feet and landed on top of him. Hearing the guards' laughter, he jumped up, dragged the costume and threw it over them.

Tony Lee was in Bruce Lee mode—his arms were revolving now in slow motion and his head twitched as if flicking his fringe from his eyes.

Suddenly, John skipped forward and let fly with a vicious right hook.

The leather glove eclipsed Lee's face and sent him sprawling backwards, smashing through a glass table and an ivory and crystal Chinese chess set. Emperors, dragons, tigers, and broken glass flew one way, Tony Lee's toupee flew the other.

John stood over his opponent, like Muhammad Ali over Sonny Liston—daring him to get up, hoping he would.

Lee lay on his back, sobbing. Blood oozed through his fingers as he cupped his nose.

The "Für Elise" played on.

John pouted and raised his arms in victory, acknowledging the applause from the imaginary crowd.

McGuire was speechless. He'd never seen his partner like this before, it was totally out of character.

Tony Lee whimpered when John tore off the glove and threw it at him.

McGuire put his hand on John's shoulder, startling him almost as if waking him.

The mischievous little boy disappeared. Detective John Dean returned. Ignoring Lee, he looked round the room and then at McGuire. 'Call it in, kid, and contact forensics.'

'Call what in? We don't have a thing on him.'

John bent and lifted Lee by his lapels. 'You have the right to remain silent. Anything you say—'

'You broke my nose—'

'—may be used against you in a—'

'My beautiful nose—'

'—court of law—'

'Do you know how much a nose like this costs? Aghhhhh!'

John flicked Lee's swollen nose with his finger. 'Shut ... the hell ... up.' He read Lee his rights then roughly spun him round, cuffed his hands behind his back and dragged him out of the room.

McGuire was about to apprehend the girl when he heard a commotion in the hall. He rushed to the doorway.

Tony Lee lay face down wincing with pain. John was wrestling a brightly coloured lion. The bodyguards kicked and punched from beneath the costume.

John punched harder.

18

If the glass in Captain Williams' office door were not the kind reinforced with a thin wire grid, it would have smashed for the tenth time this week. If the familiar sound of slamming Douglas fir was heard as far as the duty desk, it was known as the serious-kick-ass-sound. The volume of the slam was an accurate measure of the severity of the reprimand. If it was only heard in the next hallway, it was merely a clip around the ear and not worthy of an audience. The slam that had just occurred was heard in the street.

Captain Burt 'Buster' Williams was a hard, uncompromising man. He expected two hundred per cent effort from every officer in his command and always got it. In his mid-fifties, he was short and stocky, well-dressed, with grey, close-cropped hair and the kind of face you'd associate with a prize fighter. His deep gravelly voice was at one constant level—loud. John respected the fact that his boss was an authoritarian.

The captain wiped the sweat beads from his forehead and shook with anger after throwing McGuire's report in the bin. 'I have just had the mayor's office and the Department of Justice on the phone demanding your badges,' he yelled, spraying spit in McGuire's face. 'But worst of all, I've had Tony Lee's mother screaming in my ear.'

McGuire bowed his head and tried to stifle a nervous laugh.

'So, you think this is funny, boy ... huh?'

'No, sir ... I'm sorry.'

He switched his attention to John. 'So, let me get this straight, detective. You burst into this man's house—without a warrant—smash priceless antiques and furniture, assault and seriously injure him and his servants, then haul him downtown without a shred of evidence—'

'Come on, captain, you know there's more to it,' John cut in.

'Oh really? Well, how come every ass-kicker in LA is telling me this is exactly how it happened? What are you going to tell me, John? That the fourteenth-century Ming vases and priceless chess set broke by themselves? Not to mention Mr Lee's nose. How did that really happen, son?'

'Self-defence?'

'Self-defence? Three witnesses say you went crazy. John Dean, my best detective, went crazy. What the hell happened to *you*?'

John lurched forward. 'What happened to me? I'll tell you what happened to me—I lost faith in this corrupt, bullshit system we call the law. Explain to the parents why people like Tony Lee can supply their high school kids with crack. Or tell the volunteers who roam the streets in the middle of the night picking up teenage addicts from the gutter and helping them with rehabilitation, only to find them back on the street full of cheap heroin. Show these people how Lee spends his evenings, enjoying the spoils of his trade with those, ass-kicking friends of yours ... don't ask what happened to me, captain—ask yourself what happened to you.' He marched from the office and slammed the door so hard that the sheet of reinforced glass popped out of the frame and crashed down like a medieval drawbridge.

Not noticing the audience scatter when he stormed along the corridor, he headed straight for the lobby and left the building. He needed to think, get a grip on himself, so he got into his car and drove.

The captain was right, he'd blown the case. And the witnesses were right too—he *had* gone crazy. He couldn't understand what was happening to him, or what had made him lose it. Was he so sick of the job? For John, this case was different from any other he'd worked on. He wasn't getting a result. The harder he tried, the harder it was, and it was affecting him badly. He hadn't told anyone about the strange dreams. At first, he hadn't taken much notice, but now they began to bother him. Who was the girl with the red hair? Why did

The Tiger Chase

she seem so familiar? And why did he feel as if he had to help her? God, was he really losing his grip on reality?

Later that day, John found himself strolling along the promenade at Venice Beach. Girls in bikinis and healthy young guys in shorts weaved in and out of the crowd on roller blades and pushbikes. There were walkers of all ages wearing brightly coloured sports clothes and sunglasses. John hardly noticed any of them. He couldn't get the thought of Tony Lee laughing at him from his mind.

Suddenly, his ears pricked up when he heard a woman's scream. Spinning round, he saw an elderly lady falling to the ground. A guy dressed in a clown suit, clutching the woman's purse, raced in John's direction on roller blades.

People were screaming and shouting: 'Stop, thief!'

John didn't have to think; after years of policing, his automatic pilot kicked in. He continued to stroll.

The clown approached him from behind.

John walked slowly with his head down looking at the ground, waiting for the clown's shadow to come into view. When it did, he swiftly twisted his waist forward, recoiled and hammered his elbow into the oncoming clown's face.

The clown's red nose squeaked. His head stopped dead. His lower body flipped into the air, and he crashed to the ground, landing on the back of his neck.

A crowd formed, applauding and patting John on the back.

Two uniformed police officers appeared and pushed their way through the crowd trying to disperse them on their way through. 'Well, look who's here. If it isn't Detective John Dean,' said the older of the two cops. 'Rumour has it you're off the job ... lost the plot. But here you are on Venice Beach helping us with *our* jobs.'

'Jim Kowalski, still in uniform, I see. And still can't seem to be at the right place at the right time. Consistent at least.'

Kowalski curled his lip. 'Okay people, show's over, move along.' He handcuffed the clown and read him his rights while his partner took the elderly lady's details.

John knew Kowalski, mostly by reputation. The former detective had been demoted after allegedly taking bribes. To John's disgust he was never formally charged. Everyone in the force knew he was crooked. John guessed he still made money from turning a blind eye now and again, or not being where he was supposed to be at certain times.

The next day, John was suspended for three weeks with pay and advised to get away from LA. At the end of this period, he would undergo a full medical and psych evaluation. If the tests proved unsatisfactory, there would be more time off and possible therapy. Even after pleading with the captain, assuring him this was an isolated incident and that it would never happen again, Captain Williams stood firm. John knew it was a waste of time arguing.

That night, after lying awake for what seemed like hours, he finally drifted to sleep, still pondering his future.

In this lucid dream, Commander GI John waded through thick steaming jungle. He staggered into a clearing at the foot of a blue rock face. The mountain stretched to the horizon. Vertical stripes in the rock reminded John of a toppled giant candy cane. A forest of bamboo and sharp-twisting vines cosseted the base of the wall. A cloak of tempestuous cloud secreted the far-off summit.

Captain Williams appeared wearing a top hat and tails. He pointed in the direction of a moving stairway.

In an instant, John was standing on the stairway looking down on his mother who was working on her hands and knees in a rice field far below.

After stepping from the staircase at the top, he walked along the centre of a deserted highway. Soon, he passed an old Chinese man standing beneath an oak tree.

The old man's face was solemn as he watched John pass.

Yellow trees beyond a field to John's left seemed to be moving, pulsating. What sounded like a million cats meowing echoed through

The Tiger Chase

the foliage. A brass band played "The Star-Spangled Banner" somewhere in the distance.

John jumped onto the roof of a burnt-out station wagon and blew away the rain clouds, which had formed into the faces of Tony Lee and Raymond Brown. When he peered at the yellow trees, he broke into a cold sweat.

The movement in the trees was from thousands of yellow cats sitting in the branches. With black marble eyes and teeth like daggers, they spat and snarled at the GI.

John calmly lifted his automatic rifle, clenched his teeth and squeezed the trigger. The trees exploded in a mass of fur and debris as bullets ricocheted from branch to branch. The sound of the cats' demonic screams echoed among the deafening gunfire.

Still, he fired, sweeping from side to side. A cloud of dust whipped into the air and engulfed his view.

Eventually, the gun fell silent when the last round disappeared into the trees. John threw the gun to the ground and squinted, trying to focus on the settling dust. There was something there.

Sitting among the debris was a giant blue cat. Tony Lee stood to the left of it holding a large chain fastened to its neck. Raymond Brown stood to its right. Both men were laughing. John sensed there was someone behind him. He slowly turned and saw the girl. She was squatting on the road shielding her ears with her hands. Who was she? Why did he feel as if he knew her?

A bell rang.

John reached over and slammed his fist on the alarm clock. The ringing stopped. The time was 5.00 am. No work today. He rolled over and went back to sleep.

19

Regarding himself in the bathroom mirror, John Dean rubbed his bristly chin with one hand, pulled in his diaphragm, expanded his chest and stood to his full height. Moving first one way then the other like an out of shape bodybuilder, he tensed his arms and set his jaw. A sudden sporadic cough caused his chest to deflate; his shoulders dropped, and his once flat stomach flopped back to a saggy paunch. Had he really let himself get this out of shape?

John was born about thirty kilometres east of downtown LA in a small suburb called Arcadia in the San Gabriel Valley. As a kid he'd been big for his age and had looked older than he actually was. By the time he was twenty-five, he'd looked more like forty.

He joined the police academy at the age of twenty-one after deciding on a career in the LAPD at an early age. His school grades weren't exactly brilliant, but they were enough to get him in. His father had been a cop who, unbeknown to John until he was older, had pushed his police work too far, suffered from depression and fell into bouts of binge drinking. Eventually, he walked out on his family, quit his job and died a lonely man.

John grew up believing that his father had died in the line of duty. His imagination had created a superhero, whom he worshipped. His prized possession was a photograph of Joe Dean, young and in uniform, which he'd kept hidden in his bedroom as a boy.

John was devastated when his mother, for reasons known only to herself, chose his graduation day to tell him the truth about his father. He wasn't sure whom he hated most—his father for walking

The Tiger Chase

out or his mother for waiting for his special day to tell him. He lost touch with his mother for some years after that but kept the picture of his father, who he grew to understand more as he got older.

At school John was a bully. He made a mockery of the other children because he hated the thought of them being happy. He would pick fights with anyone who dared look at him twice or sometimes just for the hell of it. Yet, beneath the tough exterior was a sensitive boy who wanted to be liked. At the school dances he would be the self-appointed doorman, dishing out his own kind of justice whenever he thought necessary. He wasn't interested in playing football or hanging out with the in-crowd. He believed that being tough would make him popular. Unfortunately, the opposite proved true.

One friend he did have however, right through his school years, was a geeky, equally unpopular kid, named James Schwite.

James started school on the same day as John, in the same class. On that first day, James, or Jimmy as John called him, didn't seem to mind John's arrogant and sometimes cruel behaviour. He seemed glad to have a friend. They'd lived next door to each other since they were five year olds. John had warmed to the little four-eyed kid after receiving candy bribes and non-returnable toy loans. To this day, he can't remember his first meeting with Jimmy, although he agrees it was likely he'd beaten him up. It seemed as if he'd known him forever. One of the things he liked most about Jimmy was the great toys he'd had, like an army of GI Joes. The little figurines provided hours of play for the two GI recruits.

'Let me play, let me play,' Jimmy's little sister, two years younger, would scream.

'Go away, baby,' John would growl back.

Changes in John's home life occurred in the spring of that year. His mother seemed to be creating a new life for herself that didn't include her son. An old English lady named Mrs Smith, who lived down the street, began to babysit John while his mother went out.

At first, John hated the idea, mainly because Mrs Smith was a kind, jolly person—everything he despised. But after a few evenings he grew accustomed to her genuinely upfront and slightly eccentric manner. In fact, he warmed to her, and they became good friends.

Mrs Smith taught John how to make the perfect cup of tea, which at first, he didn't like the taste of. She also told him lots of stories. The only stories John knew were the ones he and Jimmy re-enacted from Jimmy's comics. John would picture his father as Superman or Bruce Wayne—always the hero, never the villain.

Mrs Smith, however, or Irene as John was allowed to call her, introduced him to the worlds of Robin Hood and Sherwood Forest, and of King Arthur, Excalibur and the Knights of the Round Table. These stories opened the boy's mind to new possibilities. Maybe it was better to be the good guy? Perhaps he too could be a hero like Batman, Superman, Robin Hood … his father? There was one story though, which he couldn't come to terms with—George and the Dragon. For some reason he hated Saint George for killing the dragon. He didn't know why.

That important time became a time of learning for the young John Dean, a time of self-development and change. At school, he was still the bullying, unruly kid, giving the impression of an opinionated, uncaring brat, but at home with Irene, he learned to let his sensitive side show through.

One summer break, Irene's niece, Bethany Smith, came to stay for a vacation. John had met the girl once, who was younger than he was, but he didn't like her. She called him a bully. John called her a snivelling little redhead and he ignored her for the rest of her stay.

One time he went to Mrs Smith's house for tea and had to sit and listen to the girl talking nonstop about her pet cat. John hated cats and told her so. After that he didn't go to Irene's again until Bethany had gone.

John and Jimmy moved up from elementary school to high school. John teased Jimmy for being a straight-A student but was grateful for Jimmy's help with his schoolwork. Although the pair were now in different classes, according to their academic levels, they would meet at recess and at the gates after school.

John became a pimple-faced, awkwardly-built adolescent. He'd decided on a career with the LAPD, but he would have to wait until he was twenty-one before applying.

Jimmy developed an interest in computers. This became an obsession when he began to dismantle old processors and put them together again. His mother complained bitterly about the piles of circuit boards and parts stored in his room, but she soon changed her tune when he fixed her cell phone one day.

John graduated from high school with barely the grades needed for the police academy but decided there was plenty of time to rectify this before he reached the intake age of twenty-one. So, he spent the summer of that year working part-time until he found a permanent position as a security guard at the local mall. For the next two years, he worked hard and saved his money in the hope that he could buy an apartment of his own.

Mrs Smith helped him prepare for the police academy exam. By the time he reached twenty-one, he was ready to be a cop.

Recruit John Dean graduated from the police academy six months later with the necessary qualifications. He immediately left his family home and moved into a small closet-like apartment closer to town. He couldn't wait to begin his duties as a rookie patrolman. He had no hobbies or free time—his job became his life.

After gradually moving up through the uniformed ranks, he moved into the plainclothes division and became one of the youngest ever police detectives. Something he'd always wanted.

John had lost touch with his old friend, Jimmy. Jimmy had emersed himself in the world of IT after graduating with honours from Caltech. In no time at all, he was running his own business. Soon John would be reading about Jimmy Schwite in the newspapers.

Some years later, out of the blue, John received a call from Jimmy asking him to be the best man at his wedding. It was at the ceremony that John realised how important his old pal had become. Jimmy was no longer that awkward skinny kid. He was now a distinguished handsome tycoon and the head of the multi-billion-dollar corporation, Schwite Industries. Jimmy married Alicia Rose, a beautiful Australian model. It was a wonderful wedding.

John liked Alicia. Apart from being beautiful and smart, she was down to earth and had a boyish sense of humour. She brought the best out in Jimmy, or James, as he preferred to be called nowadays. John was proud of his little pal.

John stood at the bathroom mirror smiling as he remembered those happy times. He wondered what Jimmy and Alicia were doing now. Then he remembered his current situation. He was suspended from work. He was out of shape … and he was losing his mind.

20

'Tell me about the girl.'

'What girl?'

'You mentioned there was a girl … in your dreams.'

'Did I? Are you sure this isn't therapy?'

'No, detective. This is just an evaluation. We need to prove you're fit mentally as well as physically before you can return to work.'

John was tired after being prodded and probed for the whole of the day. Now he sat on the couch of a short fat shrink called Doctor Singh. 'The dreams have stopped now. I think it was just while I was under pressure.'

'Are you sure?'

'Yes!'

'Tell me about the tiger.'

'Which one?'

'There is more than one?'

'No … of course not. You mean Raymond Brown.'

John told the doctor what he knew about Raymond Brown, but he was careful not to mention that Brown had appeared in his dreams.

Doctor Singh's expression remained stolid. 'When you think of Tony Lee … do you feel angry?'

'Yes— but not the uncontrollable kind of anger I felt before.'

'Why are you angry, John?'

'I'm angry because Lee's still on the street. I'm angry because he's a known narcotics dealer and no matter how hard we try to bust him, he manages to evade us.'

'Tell me about the girl.'

John lowered his face and massaged his forehead with his fingers. *Keep a grip. Just tell him what he wants to hear.* 'She is actually a woman about my age. She's … cute, I guess.'

'Why does she make you angry?'

'I never said *she* made me angry.'

'Then why are you raising your voice?'

Keep a grip. Keep a grip. 'I haven't got a clue. I don't know her. She just appears in my dreams sometimes and … pisses me off for some reason.'

Doctor Singh scribbled on his pad, then looked up and smiled. 'Perhaps she's your future wife.'

John smiled back. *Smart-ass!*

'There's just one more thing I'd like to know, detective. In your file you list cats as your number one hate. Would you care to tell me why?'

John had had enough but he knew if he kept his head, he'd be out of there soon. He told the doctor about an incident as a child with the neighbourhood tomcat. When he finished, the doctor stared at him as if expecting him to continue.

'But there is more,' Doctor Singh whispered after an awkward silence.

This guy's good. 'Yes. I've never told this to anyone before but yes, there is more.' John shuffled uncomfortably in his chair.

The doctor gestured with his eyes for him to continue.

Tony Lee had returned to his mansion after his lawyer had bailed him out. There he'd supposedly stayed, keeping a low profile. John knew he was up to something. Raymond Brown had vanished. On the night of the killings, a BOLO was put out, but he'd obviously gone into hiding. John suspected he may have fled the country.

The Tiger Chase

It was John's first day back on the job after his two-week suspension. Captain Williams had given him a cool reception at the morning briefing. John knew he'd have to prove himself by keeping his head. He'd made a promise to himself to put Tony Lee behind bars no matter what, but this time he'd play it by the book. He'd also decided not to tell anyone about the experience he'd had in Las Vegas during his suspension.

The first duty of the day was for John and McGuire to pay Danny Wong, their useful informant in Chinatown, a visit.

Wong had a small fruit and vegetable barrow on the Chinatown market. When he saw the two detectives approaching, his agitated expression did little to hide his displeasure at the very public visit.

'H ... Hello, Mr Dean.'

'What have you got for me, Wong?'

'I don't know anything, I'm afraid, Mr Dean. You know me. Like to keep to myself.'

John pressed a ten dollar bill into Wong's hand.

Wong lowered his gaze to the ground. 'It's something big, Mr Dean,' he whispered, glancing from side to side. 'Something that's never happened on American soil before!'

John remained quiet and allowed his penetrating stare to ask the next question.

'I honestly don't know what it is yet, but word is ... it's something involving Tony Lee and The Tiger.'

'If you're lying to me, Wong, you know what'll happen.'

'Yes, Mr Dean. Keep those notes warm. Soon as I know anything I'll—'

'You'll call me, that's right. As soon as you know.'

'Soon as I know, Mr Dean. Soon as I know.'

John and McGuire returned to the car.

'I'm sorry about what happened, John,' McGuire said on the drive back to the station.

'Don't be. It's all behind me now. Kind of like a dream, or a nightmare. All I want to do now is put this idiot behind bars. We've just got to be patient. Wait for him to slip up.'

'So, what do you think they're planning?' McGuire asked.

'Don't know, but as Wong said, it involves Lee and The Tiger, meaning Brown. It's probably drugs.'

'Yeah, with the Lour family out of action now, I'd say Lee and Brown are moving into the big time.'

'That's what they think,' John said with a determined expression.

21

Tony Lee hissed into his cell phone, 'Okay, I don't have to remind you what will happen if you guys mess this up, do I? This is it; we'll never get this chance again. Do I make myself clear …? Okay, run it by me again, I have to be sure you fully understand … uh-hm … yes … right … yes … uh-hm … okay … yes.' He sat with one leg crossed over the other in a large wide-winged wicker chair, listening while the instructions he'd drilled into his employees' heads for the last six months were translated back to him.

Raymond Brown sat silently next to the fireplace craning his neck, trying to hear both sides of the conversation.

'Right, so everyone's in place? Good. Call me in the morning.' Tony flicked his cell phone into the air with one hand and caught it with the other. Grinning at his unlikely associate, he grinned and said, 'I think this calls for a toast, my friend.'

Raymond's expression remained passive as usual.

Tony jumped up from the chair, strolled over to the wall and pulled the bell cord that hung there.

An Oriental lady servant entered the room and bowed before him.

'Bring up a bottle of Armand de Brignac and send in the girls.'

Raymond watched with narrowed eyes when Tony skipped to the jukebox across the room. *Soon,* he thought. *Soon I will consume your liver and feed your eyeballs to the—*

Dance music exploded from the jukebox and filled the house at full volume.

Tony danced round the room kicking and punching the air, his head jabbing to the beat. He picked up a candlestick for an imaginary microphone. Like Jagger, he shuffled in front of a large wall mirror, miming, spinning, strutting, and pouting to the music.

Raymond growled and clenched his fists. The thought of slowly squeezing the life from Lee gave him great comfort. He closed his eyes and for some reason his mind retreated to his first kill.

The banners and signs strung across the Kowloon street creaked when a cool evening breeze slapped and teased them. Twenty-one-year-old Raymond Brown hid in the doorway of Hou Xiang's electrical appliances store. Trembling with anger, he watched as a medley of Hong Kong's homeless entered the soup kitchen across the road. He despised weakness. He wanted to kill them all. His stomach tightened when he noticed a tall, undernourished figure staggering down the street. *Is it him? No, it can't be.* The man he was looking for was a descendant of the Mescalero Apache—American Indian—tribe. Warrior stock. It couldn't be him. Raymond squinted and caught the eye of the man. Docile, dark-ringed, uncomprehending orbs. Raymond held his breath. He knew those eyes.

Sam Brown's shoulders slouched forward while he wove along the sidewalk. He wore a crumpled trench coat and odd sneakers. Held tightly in one hand was a bottle of liquor wrapped in brown paper.

Raymond sneered and hissed when his father fell into the doorway of the soup kitchen. Stepping back into the shadows, he would wait.

An hour later, a bleary-eyed Sam was the last to leave the building.

Raymond watched him saunter to the end of the block before following. When he noticed him turn off the street, he increased his pace. Peering round the corner, his heart skipped. Sam was gone.

Ironically, it was his father's voice from Raymond's childhood that tormented him. '*Find him, you fool, don't let him get away. Find him.*'

The Tiger Chase

There was an entrance to an alleyway a short distance away. 'Perfect,' Raymond whispered with an evil grin. He checked his surroundings. When he was satisfied there wasn't anyone watching, he slipped into the alley. Once inside, he held his hand to his face to guard against the stench of rotting garbage and urine. Moving slowly forward, he kept close to the left-hand wall while his eyes adjusted to the darkness.

A trashcan fell and rolled somewhere ahead. A cat meowed and spat.

Sam stopped and took a swig of cheap wine.

Raymond marched towards his father, grabbed his shoulder and swung him round.

The two men came face to face. One was an upright figure of strength and power, the other a worthless, soon-to-be-dead, member of a once proud race.

Raymond had visualised this moment since his childhood. The charges to be laid down with each of the lethal blows were branded on his soul. This one is for the broken bones and the stolen childhood. *Smack!* This one is for a young Chinese mother abused and beaten close to death. *Smack!* And this one is for the abandonment of responsibility and pride. *Smack!* The source of his inner fears and mental instability would channel into the twitching corpse. And he would be free.

But when he looked into the bloodshot eyes of his father, he saw a man that was already dead. Dead before he was born. A warrior defeated with his ancestors defending his homeland, leaving his descendants forced to compromise with humiliation and change.

Sam's head wobbled. His lips slowly parted, revealing black, broken teeth. 'What the f—'

But his other voice chanted inside Raymond's head: '*Kill him, you weak bastard.*'

Raymond reached up with both hands and, as if about to kiss Sam on the mouth, he grabbed his cheeks and drew him closer. *Crunch.* A short, sharp twist was all it took.

Sam's corpse fell to the ground.

'Weakling!'

Raymond flinched. His father's mocking voice remained in his head. '*Pathetic!* He barged out of the alley. He should have been free know. His father was dead. '*Ya just proved what I always knew. When it came to the crunch, ya got no balls.*' A deep patronising laugh pulsated through his temples. 'You're wrong,' he cried out into the empty street. 'I am a warrior. Better than you. Greater.'

The laugh continued.

Raymond ran to the martial arts gym where he worked part-time and trained. Smashing a side window, he climbed into the old building, tore off his clothes and approached the Wing Chun wooden dummy.

After four hours of blocking, hitting, kicking, blocking, hitting, kicking, blocking, the flesh on his arms and shins was bare. His feet slipped on a warm sticky pool of blood beneath them, but he continued on, '*Oos—oos—oos—oos ...*'

The music stopped. Tony Lee flopped into his chair exhausted. 'Come on, Monkey Boy, why don't you show us what *you've* got.'

'Grrrrrrr!'

'Oh sorry, I mean Tiger Boy. Why do they call you The Tiger anyway?' Tony asked, suppressing a patronising snigger.

'*He's mocking you.*' Raymond tried to ignore his father's voice in his head, but he was right. He was always right. The fool was mocking him.

'Oh dear ... are we sulking?'

'*Tell him. Tell him how you tore your defeated opponents apart with your bare hands in Hong Kong. Tell him how the crowd would chant lao hu—tiger—at each of your fights. Tell him how the tiger was a legend in the ring.*'

Two young women, hookers, entered the room.

'Ah, the girls at last,' Tony said, grinning. He poured them each a glass of Champagne.

One of the girls smiled at Raymond.

'Grrrrrr!'

'Careful, sweetie,' Tony said, 'don't get too close.'

'Why? the girl said, squinting at Raymond. 'Looks kind of interesting.'

'Interesting? Ha. He's about as interesting as a flea. No, there's nothing there to interest a girl like you, I'm afraid. But, if you like interesting, boy have I got something to show you.' Tony led the two giggling girls from the room.

Raymond tried to ignore the internal dialogue that raged in his head. He had his reasons for sparing Tony Lee. Rising to his feet, he strode over to the jukebox and caught a glimpse of his reflection in the chrome trim. 'GRRREARGH!' His enormous fist crashed through the glass panel. A surge of electricity pulsated along his tensed arm. Aroused by the pain, he roared again 'GRRREARGH!' then he withdrew his arm from the smashed machine. 'Who's weak now?' he asked under his breath as he sauntered from the room.

'*You are ...*' his father's voice trailed behind him.

22

The hooker made the drop in broad daylight. The pimp gleefully rubbed his hands together as she handed him a small package.

'Bingo,' John said, heading swiftly towards the unsuspecting duo, followed by McGuire.

'Hey, what ya doin' man?' screamed the pimp when John grabbed him, bent him over the hood of his car and cuffed him.

The pimp's skinny, leather-like face screwed up. His over-sized baseball cap slid down over his forehead. The thick gold chains around his neck clanged and scraped the car's paint.

McGuire took the young woman by the arm and picked up the package the pimp had dropped into the gutter.

'Well, well, well … pure heroin would be my guess,' John said, holding up the package of white powder. 'What are you doing with this kind of shit, Joey? Not making enough from your girls now?'

McGuire read them their rights.

'Listen man, we're cool, right? You know Joey don't deal in this shit. We's just doing some wheeling and dealing man, ya know?'

'Wheeling and dealing?'

'Look.' Joey side glanced nervously and lowered his voice. 'This pure Chinese shit, man, going crazy cheap. This price too good to miss, ya know what I'm saying?'

'Yeah, I know exactly what you're saying. You've just told me everything I need to know to lock you up for at least ten years!'

'No—man—no! You don't wanna be wasting your precious time with small fry like Joey Kinto. You wanna know where it comin' from, yeah? You wanna know why pure grade Chinese heroin is flooding the streets at such an affordable price, right?'

John glanced at McGuire then back at Joey. 'So, you're looking for a deal ... okay, tell me what you've got, and I'll consider it.'

'Well, while you're making up your mind, consider this,' Joey said, turning and sitting on the edge of the hood.

'My big shot supplier. He's thirteen years old, man. He buys it at the school gate. His friends and him got a very lucrative business happening.'

John wrote down the name of the school in his notebook and quizzed Joey further. 'So, where's it coming from?'

'I just want you to remember that Joey is being very helpful and—'

'Just get on with it.'

'Well, word on the street is that they, whoever *they* is, are getting out of the business and moving on.'

'Moving on? What do you mean moving on?' John quipped.

'They's moving on to better, more lucrative things. There's a big deal going down and they, whoever *they* is, will be retiring. They don't care bout no drugs no more. That's why they's selling their shit so cheap.'

The two detectives glanced at each other once more with raised eyebrows.

'Okay, Joey, you the man,' John said sarcastically.

Joey gloated as John removed the handcuffs. 'Why thank you, sir. Thank you. I'm glad to be of service.'

'Don't ever thank me. You are scum and you always will be. Remember this—you belong to me now. Do you understand what I'm saying? When I come looking for you, you better be here with something to tell me, understand?' He moved in closer to the brightly dressed little man. 'I've got half a kilo of heroin here with your name on it. Do I make myself clear, man?'

'Oh yes, sir, yes. I look forward to seeing you again, sir. Goodbye!' He squirmed from underneath John, grabbed his girl by the arm and strutted off down the street cussing under his breath. 'Kick your damn LAPD ass.'

It was obvious to John that they, whoever *they* were, were in fact Tony Lee and his cronies. Danny Wong, the informant, had been right when he'd said something big was going down. Joey Kinto was small fry and would be pulled in as soon as Tony Lee's empire finally crumbled. But for now, he would be useful as another informant on the street.

23

The deep cavity finally split, and the condensed filling spewed out onto the floor. Raymond Brown checked the clock. Twenty-eight minutes. A new record. Blood pumped through his bulging biceps and shoulders, causing them to expand to almost twice their resting size. His energy levels and the power of his punches were increasing daily at an alarming rate. His unquenched thirst for the fighting arena baited his frustration into bouts of uncontrollable, chemically-enhanced fits of anger. What had been a brand new Everlast fifty-kilogram punch bag twenty-eight minutes earlier now resembled a drawn corpse swinging from a hangman's noose, its empty abdomen gaping for all to see.

Just like every day for the last month, Raymond lifted the bag down from its hook and threw it into the corner with the rest.

The basement of Tony Lee's house was a gymnasium. Jagged shards of smashed mirror hung precariously from two facing walls, while the other two were plain brick. There were chrome barbells, loose weights, and body building equipment thrown in one corner, with a speedball, punch bag and fighting equipment in the other corner. In the middle of the room was a ten-metre square, highly polished, rock-maple clad floor, which Tony had intended to use for sparring and meditation. Pictures of Bruce Lee had adorned the walls.

When Raymond Brown had entered the gym for the first time, he immediately smashed the mirrors and tore down the pictures. Bruce Lee was a fake according to this martial art master. After sorting through the mostly useless equipment, he threw to one side what he didn't need and ordered Lee's staff to purchase a dozen fifty-kilogram punch bags. When everything was to his satisfaction, he declared the room a sacred place and banned Tony Lee from entering.

Here he'd lived for the last three weeks training and meditating, only venturing upstairs when really necessary. After the first twelve days, he ordered another dozen punch bags. He'd destroyed the first bag in sixty minutes of nonstop pulverising body blows. The next one lasted fifty-five minutes, then fifty-one, and so on.

It was only a matter of time now until he attained the final item required for his immortality. Then his pent-up sexual desires would be unleashed. He would enter the world arena a complete man. The ultimate warrior. The Tiger God. And his father would be silenced forever. There was only one important task left for him to complete, and for this—unfortunately—he needed the fool.

The next day the bag didn't split when he reached twenty-eight minutes. 'GRRREARGH!' Not good enough. He'd failed to beat the time from the previous day. After yanking the bag from the ceiling, he sunk his teeth into the weakened seam. Growling loudly, he twisted his body and shook his head violently from side to side like a rabid dog. Tightly threaded nylon stitches popped as they gave way. With a massive burst of energy, and using both hands and his mouth, he ripped the bag in half down the vertical seam. It opened, sending stuffing across the floor. He threw the empty bag to the ground and stamped and spat on it before kicking it into the corner with the rest. For a few minutes he stood there shaking and staring at the pile of defeated opponents. Now he was fully psyched and ready to see the fool.

The morning rays of sun that shone in through the window highlighted each ripple and mound of Raymond's throbbing physique while he stood waiting in the drawing room. The fresh sweat glistened on his almost transparently thin skin, while large seething veins crisscrossed his giant pectorals. His trapezium muscles resembled gridiron shoulder padding, forcing his head to sit forward. His legs, flaring out from narrow hips, sat in perfect proportion with his wide shoulders. Accusations of exaggeration would be fired at any sculptor attempting to reproduce such an abstract life form.

Steven Tang, a tall Taiwanese exile and Lee's right-hand man during the Hong Kong days, sat on a luxurious white sofa between two of the temporary hookers that Tony employed from time to time to service his guests.

Tony Lee, fresh from his yacht, strutted to his chair. After theatrically sniffing the air, he gestured to one of his manservants to approach him. 'Fetch the air freshener immediately,' he whispered, just loud enough for everyone to hear.

The old Chinese gentleman left the room and returned moments later with a floral aerosol can in his hand.

Using facial expressions and hand gestures, Tony motioned for him to commence spraying the room. 'Has somebody got a problem with personal hygiene here? Is there not a shower situated off every single bedroom of this house? Is it too much to ask for a certain person to use a little deodorant?' He enjoyed nothing more than taunting and humiliating his self-important associate. 'You smell like a pussy.' The fact that he could never provoke a reaction though frustrated him.

Raymond fixed Lee with his most intimidating stare. The sight of the fool's soul cowering behind the pathetic façade relaxed him. One punch would be too easy—he wanted to savour the final moment, feel the life oozing from his veins and inhale the escaping spirit.

'*Do it now. You don't need him,*' his father's voice whispered.

'Soon,' Raymond's inner voice said. 'Soon!'

'Okay, girls, out you go ... skidaddle.' Tony slapped one of them on the butt before they left the room, then waited until the doors were closed. 'Right, everything on the other end has been taken care of, the right people have been paid, and the cargo has been released. So, what's happening on this end, Stevie baby?' Tony asked.

'Well, Mr Lee, everything's in place, just as you instructed. Our people at the airport are ready. The cargo will arrive on

Thursday at 0600 hours. The status and condition of the cargo are uncertain but—'

Raymond Brown growled and looked anxiously at Steven Tang. He needed a full report, or this could all be a waste of time for him.

Steven Tang apologised but reassured him that as soon as the cargo was delivered their professional staff would examine it and a full report would be made.

'*Kill him too ... disrespectful swine,*' Raymond's father hissed.

Tang continued. Using an overhead projector and a white board, he gave a complete rundown on the forthcoming operation. Tony quizzed him mercilessly but was satisfied when he confidently gave the right answers.

Raymond Brown hadn't listened to any of the discussion; he wasn't interested in money, that was the fool's vice. What he needed from the cargo may not even be there. If that was the case, he'd kill the fool, then go straight to China and take what he needed.

Part Three

Yin & Yang (Tiger and Dragon)

24

The plane dropped and hit a wave of turbulent air, like a small boat slamming over a ship's wake. The animal transportation crate rattled.

'Okay, baby, it's okay, I'm here,' Beth said, putting her hand through the crate's grill and stroking Zhu Zhu's ears. 'We're nearly there, baby.'

Zhu Zhu nervously whined and yawned.

The twenty-three hour flight from Shanghai to LA was drawing to a close. Beth hadn't slept the whole way; her seating area in the special cargo compartment was very cramped. Although she was only centimetres from the tiger, she was to the side of the crate, which meant they could only see each other through the small ventilation holes. So, for most of the trip she'd sat on the floor at the front of the mesh-covered end, shivering in the cool pressurised air.

The fact that Zhu Zhu hadn't eaten during the journey didn't worry Beth too much. She'd lapped up the water given to her on regular intervals. She seemed to find comfort in Beth's voice and the touch of her small hands.

Beth warily looked through the tiny porthole after the steward had informed her they were approaching the American coast. It had been a long time since she'd seen the shores of her homeland. Flying into the approaching dawn she saw the first rays of sunlight kissing the water's edge far below. Shimmering diamonds scattered in all directions while the receding shadows peeled back from the cold white sands and dispersed into a thin cleansing mist.

The drone of the aircraft's engines drowned the sound of Beth's sigh: 'Home.'

25

Ark Airlines, a subsidiary of Noah & Sons Shipping, established 4000 BC, successfully completing its latest assignment from God. Across the waters they come carrying our precious cargo to the Promised Land in aid of species' revival. Let's hear it for old Noah.' Robert Baker laughed at his own joke.

Beth's parents chuckled politely.

Jacqueline Thompson, the American head of The World Wildlife Fund; Doctor Malcolm Wilson of the Minnesota Zoo; his boss, Gerald Patterson, and the Chinese ambassador and associates stood before airport personnel at the cargo terminal. With their faces turned to the sky, they patiently watched the cargo jet approach and eventually touchdown.

The cameras of a Chinese film crew, flown in especially, were rolling and sending back live pictures to China, while Desmond Jerome from *Readers Digest* whispered into a cell phone app. No other members of the press or media were present at this secret arrival.

Robert Baker was the kind of guy who couldn't keep quiet for long. While the jet taxied towards terminal number three, he couldn't resist entertaining his captive audience. 'Two women smugglers flew into LAX from South America. Before entering customs, they ducked into the toilets. "What have you got then?" asked the first. "I've got two rare Amazonian parrots, one secured under each arm," replied the second, adjusting her bra strap. "So, what have you got?" she asked. "I've got a rare spotted South American skunk," replied the first. "Oh ... and where have you got that, pray tell?" asked the second. "I've got the skunk inside the crotch of my underwear," replied the first. "Ugh … what about the smell?" asked the second. After thinking for a moment, the first lady shrugged and replied, "If it dies, it dies!"'

The non-receptive audience was too involved watching the taxiing jet.

Robert's cell phone rang. 'Hello.' It was his boss. 'Yes, all good so far. The cat's in the bag so to speak.' There was a pause while Robert listened to the caller. 'Everything is going to plan. The plane's taxiing towards us now.'

26

The jet engines whistled when they brought the slick cylinder to a sudden halt. Motorised buggies, trucks and ear-muffed airport personnel swarmed like ants around a dying dragonfly. After thirty long minutes, the rear cargo hatch slowly lowered.

Beth rushed to reach her native soil and almost tripped on the rubber-coated ramp.

Her parents flung their arms around her.

After four years living alone in China, Beth had become accustomed to a certain lack of affection. The genuine warmth radiating from her parents felt strange, almost as if being approached and hugged by strangers. The familiar homely smell was the same, but her parents seemed somehow smaller than she remembered—her father's face was thinner and more drawn.

Robert Baker introduced himself after jokingly asking her if she'd enjoyed her trip, referring not to the flight but the stumble on the ramp. He then introduced her to the rest of the party and told her to wave to her friends back in China via the camera.

Zhu Zhu roared when the airport staff gently lifted the crate and carried it out of the plane.

The driver of the waiting forklift adjusted the height and tilt of the forks. Then he jumped from the cab and physically pushed the forks closer together to approximately match the inside width of the crate's skids.

The Tiger Chase

Beth ran to the front of the crate. 'It's okay, baby, we're home now,' she whispered.

Zhu Zhu settled when she caught sight of her.

The eager forklift driver jumped into the driver's seat and lifted the crate.

'Hold it! Wait a minute. Wait!' Beth shouted with her hands in the air. 'Let her take in some fresh air.'

The forklift driver sighed, looked at his watch and shook his head.

When they finally passed through customs, two hours had passed. Beth was tired and worried about the undue stress on Zhu Zhu. They'd planned to be out of there early enough to miss the morning traffic but by the time the crate was loaded onto the waiting truck, it was 8.45 am, the beginning of rush hour traffic.

'But why not?' Beth protested to the Chinese truck driver when he barred her from travelling in the back of the truck.

'Sorry lady, health and safety.'

Beth reluctantly agreed to ride behind in Robert's Range Rover. Just before the crate was lifted into the back of the truck, she kissed her hand and rubbed it on Zhu Zhu's forehead between the bars. 'I won't be far away, baby.'

Zhu Zhu groaned and called out when the large roller door of the truck was finally closed. *'Chuff-chuff-chuff.'*

Beth climbed into the passenger side of Robert's vehicle while her parents sat in the back. The Chinese ambassador and his staff followed in a black SUV. The rest of the party followed in their cars with the Chinese film crew behind them.

The traffic was already thick when the truck edged its way onto the freeway.

Robert honked his horn at the driver of a psychedelic Kombi van that wouldn't let him in. 'God damn hippie!' he yelled as the Aquarian gave him the finger.

The truck pulled away.

Robert forcefully pushed his way into the traffic. 'Yeah, yeah, yeah!' He waved, horns blowing and headlights flashing behind him.

Beth counted seven cars and a bread van between them and the truck. She anxiously looked at Robert, who seemed to be taking it in his stride.

The rest of the convoy was still waiting to enter the freeway. It was a typical LA morning. Brown haze hung over the city in the distance and the morning sky was like a sheet of opaque glass. Thousands of cars driven by short-fused drivers crammed the freeway in complete contrast to the smiling faces of the Chinese weaving in and out of wide streets on bicycles that Beth had become accustomed to in China.

'Come on, Robert, move it,' Beth yelled when another truck forced its way in ahead of them. She was beginning to regret the decision to keep this low key. If they'd informed the press and the appropriate authorities, as she'd suggested, they might have got a police escort. This was turning out to be ridiculous, she thought when the gap increased to ten cars.

Robert managed to make some ground. He moved over into one of the left-hand lanes, overtook six cars, then pushed his way back into the same lane as the truck.

BANG! The pickup in front wobbled when a front tyre blew. It pulled onto the hard shoulder. An orange Toyota pulled over to give him assistance, giving them another two car lengths. There was only a cab and the bread truck between them now.

Beth gave a sigh of relief. She felt even better when the taxicab darted out and overtook the truck.

Approaching the exit ramp, they had a clear view of the road below and were relieved to see it was clear.

The truck exited and increased its speed, a little too recklessly for Beth's liking. She would give the driver a piece of her mind when they reached the zoo.

Robert increased his speed and, with the comfort of his quiet, English-built V8 engine, he easily caught up with the truck.

'Jeez, is this guy in a hurry?' Beth yelled, when the truck pulled away over the speed limit.

The truck approached a large intersection and thundered through the green light with Robert close behind.

'Look out!' Beth screamed when a motorcycle raced across the intersection from the left.

Robert slammed on the brakes, but it was too late.

The motorcycle hit the front driver's side of the vehicle with such force that the front wheel of the bike disintegrated. The occupant was thrown onto the hood, smashing the windshield with his helmet. The Rover bounced into the air as a front wheel crushed the forks and handlebars of the bike. The back wheels skidded and ground to a halt.

'Shit!' cried Robert. He and Beth jumped from the car and rushed to aid the rider.

The motorcyclist was squatted at the side of the road with his head between his legs, taking in deep breaths.

'Jesus, are you alright, son?' Robert asked anxiously.

'I'm okay!' the young man said.

'He needs an ambulance,' Beth said.

'No ... I'm okay ... you can go now ... I'll be alright.'

'Don't be silly. We can't leave you here. We need to call the police and I really think you should see a doctor,' Beth insisted.

'No—no police, no doctor ... I'm okay!'

Robert reached for his cell phone and began to dial.

The youth jumped to his feet, took off down the street and disappeared into a side alley.

Beth gave chase but by the time she got to the alley, he was nowhere to be seen.

Robert was behind her, speaking into his cell phone while jogging. They ventured into the alley a few yards but turned back after agreeing he was gone.

Two minutes later, the ambassador's car arrived, followed by

Malcolm Wilson's and the Chinese film crew who immediately started filming.

'What happened?' the Chinese officials asked frantically.

Beth tried to explain how the motorcyclist had run a red light and ploughed into them at the intersection.

Robert cancelled the ambulance and called the police.

'Where is Xiao Gong Zhu?' one of the ambassador's aides demanded.

'Oh my God, the truck!' Beth said. She ran onto the centre divider and looked up the middle of the long road. The truck was nowhere to be seen.

'It's okay, Beth. He knows the way to the zoo. They've done this trip a thousand times,' Robert reassured her.

Malcolm and Desmond decided to stay with Robert and wait for the police to arrive. Beth squeezed in with the ambassador and left to find the truck. Beth's parents rode with Jacqueline and Gerald.

To everyone's relief, when they turned the next corner heading towards the zoo, the large Wittle and Sons truck stood at the side of the road.

The driver must have realised there was a problem and pulled up to wait for them. *Perhaps he's not such a bad guy after all,* thought Beth. She wanted to check on Zhu Zhu but the truck pulled away as they approached.

The rest of the journey was easy. The truck stayed below the speed limit and the rush hour traffic passed, allowing them to reach the zoo by mid-morning.

The service entrance to the LA Zoo was easily wide enough for the large truck to enter. A loud rush of expelled air gushed from its air brake cylinders and whistled when the wheels came to a halt.

The Chinese driver, climbing down from the cab with clipboard in hand, looked slightly smaller than Beth had remembered. He hastily disappeared into the office. Moments later, zoo staff eagerly surrounded the truck, joined by Beth, her parents, and Jacqueline and Gerald. The Chinese ambassador stood quietly to one side with his associates. The Chinese film crew began filming.

Beth made her way to the back end of the truck, but the door was firmly bolted with a large padlock. Putting her ear to the thin aluminium roller door, she called out, 'Chuff, chuff, chuff.'

There was silence.

'Chuff, chuff.'

Still silence.

The truck's exhaust clicked as it cooled and contracted.

'Where did the driver go?' Beth asked, throwing the question out to the crowd.

Some of the zoo staff scattered to search for him.

'Somebody see if he left the key in the cab.' She tapped the truck door with the palm of her hand. The inside echoed empty. 'Will somebody just get this thing open, please?'

A young zoo worker appeared with a crowbar.

Gerald Paterson grabbed it, ground his teeth and used the whole of his weight to break the lock. Then in one movement, he lifted and pushed the roller door to the top of its tracks.

Beth cupped her hands to her mouth. 'Oh my God, what have I done?'

The truck was empty.

The high-pitched electrical tune of *Popeye the Sailor man* broke the silence. Gerald Paterson reached into his inside breast pocket and retrieved his cell phone. 'Hello, Gerald Paterson speaking ... Hi Robert, listen we've got a major problem here. I suggest you get back to the zoo right away!'

The Chinese anchor woman jumped before the camera and frantically began reporting what had happened.

The ambassador and his staff formed a small circle and began to whisper.

Beth climbed into the back of the truck desperately and hopelessly looking in every corner. If any clues were to be found, she wouldn't have seen them through the tears.

Ten minutes later, two patrol cars arrived simultaneously. Robert Baker emerged from one and ran to the back of the truck. 'You've got to be kidding.'

'The driver. Where's the driver?' Beth yelled jumping down from the truck.

The zoo staff had searched the zoo and its offices but there was no sign of him.

'He must have made his way through the office, into the zoo and out through the front gates,' Robert said.

One of the police officers approached Robert. 'So, what exactly is the problem here, sir?'

'It's a ... a tiger ... a very rare tiger,' Robert stuttered nervously, 'stolen ... kidnapped, catnapped, whatever you'd—'

'Are we talking about The Little Princess?' the officer asked.

'Yes,' Robert replied. 'But how would you know that?'

'My six-year-old little girl's a big fan. Jeez, she's gonna be mighty upset when she hears about this.'

'Oh.'

'Yep, she's a member of The Little Princess Fan Club,' the officer said, scribbling in his notepad and shaking his head. After realising the seriousness of the theft, he radioed into the station and requested a detective to be present.

27

'Damn—damn—damn!' John Dean cussed when hot black coffee spilled into his lap. He climbed from the stationary car, threw the paper cup on the ground and desperately tried to wipe his trousers dry.

McGuire tried not to laugh while he offered him his clean white handkerchief.

A black stain spread across the front of John's pants. 'Stupid paper cup.' He hit his clenched fist on the roof of the car and grabbed the handkerchief.

The radio crackled. McGuire jumped into the driver's seat.

John continued to curse as he wiped down his trousers.

McGuire leaned across the passenger seat. 'We need to go, John.'

John climbed into the car. 'Where to?'

'The LA Zoo.'

'Oh great, just what I need. Monkey business.'

The trip to the LA Zoo took twenty minutes. John prayed it would be enough time to dry out his trousers.

When they arrived at the zoo, the large Wittle and Sons truck stood inside the rear service gate. The roller door was open and two uniformed police officers guarded the entrance. A third cop came to meet them as they drove in through the gate.

'What have we got, Gillis?' McGuire asked through the driver's window.

'Well, sir, it looks like this is a biggie. It's The Little Princess … she's been abducted!'

John and McGuire exchanged looks. It was obvious to Gillis neither detective knew what he was talking about.

McGuire said, 'The little what?'

John slowly climbed from the car, still cussing as he looked down at the stain.

The young cop continued: 'Sorry, sir, but it's been in the news for some time now. The Little Princess, or Zhu Zhu, is a South China tiger and it seems as if that Beth Smith chick finally got her way and brought it to America.'

John and McGuire still had no idea what he was talking about, frowning as they listened.

As if sensing their growing impatience, Gillis cut to the chase. 'This truck was last driven by David Wittle of Don Wittle and Sons freight. His brother, Clive, drove one identical to this—'

'So?' John butted in.

'Well, sir, David and Clive Wittle were found dead this morning in a cheap motel room not far from their depot. They'd both suspiciously overdosed on bourbon and cocaine. Most importantly though, their trucks were missing.

'One of the vehicles arrived at LAX at approximately 6.00 am, as previously arranged, picked up the tiger and proceeded in the direction of the LA Zoo. A convoy of zoo officials, Chinese dignitaries and a Chinese film crew followed closely.

'An alleged, premeditated, motor incident was then cleverly staged, and the truck was allowed to disappear out of view for a few minutes. Meanwhile, the motorcyclist who ran into the front vehicle, took off leaving the wrecked motorcycle, which has been identified as one stolen late last night from West Hollywood.

'When the convoy finally resumed, there was relief among the passengers when they realised the truck was waiting for them round the next intersection. What they didn't realise though, was that this was not the truck carrying the tiger; it was a decoy that had been switched with the original. And that brings us up to date, sir. When the truck was finally opened, it was found to be empty.'

'What about the driver?' McGuire asked.

'He disappeared soon after arrival. All we know is he was of Chinese origin, as was the first driver, and there's a possibility that the motorcyclist was also Chinese.'

The young cop closed his notebook, looked pleased with himself, then headed back to the office.

After a long, thoughtful pause, John asked, without expecting a reply, 'Who the hell would want to steal a flaming cat?'

It must have been almost thirty years since John had been to the zoo. He remembered how Jimmy had tricked him into going with him and his father after assuring him he would see a dragon. He may have only been eight years old, but he was damn sure that the monitor lizard that peered back and spat its tongue out at him was no dragon. He showed his disappointment by punching Jimmy on the arm every time his father looked away.

He didn't like the zoo much then and his feelings hadn't changed. The smell of animals and the sight of those stupid, man-made enclosures made him wonder why people would waste their time and money at such a place.

John stood in the doorway of the zoo staff lunchroom, listening. He assumed that the short redhead with her back to him was the one that Gillis had described as, 'that Beth Smith chick.'

'Why are you asking me the same questions over and over? I want to know what's being done to find Zhu Zhu?'

'We're doing everything we can, ma'am!' Gillis said shuffling from side to side.

'Yeah, like what?'

'Well, we've issued a BOLO on the missing truck, and we're scanning the vicinity by chopper. We're also questioning employees of Wittle and Sons and the Chinese Embassy. I want you to know, Doctor Smith, we're taking this very seriously.'

The doctor slammed herself down at the staff lunchroom table and held her head in her hands. After a few moments of slowly dredging her fingers through her hair, she jumped to her feet. 'What am I doing sitting here? I should be out helping with the search. Where's Robert?'

'Whoa, hold on there, Doctor Smith, I'm afraid I can't let you do that. There's a couple of detectives who need to speak to you first.'

'What, more questions? Why on earth—'

'Well, we have to ascertain who is responsible for allowing a dangerous ... wild ... animal to be transported through the busy streets of LA without notifying the LAPD first,' John said, cutting her off in mid-sentence. 'Then we have to determine how the thieves knew exactly when and how this dangerous ... wild ... animal would arrive. And until we're satisfied, we're going to ask the same questions over and over until we get the right answers. Miss?'

'That's Doctor ... Doctor Smith,' Beth growled, turning in the direction of the voice.

'Whatever,' John said, marching into the room.

'Oh great, that's all I need, Starskey and Hutch,' Beth muttered.

'Hi, Doctor Smith. This is Detective John Dean, I'm Detective Ben McGuire.'

Beth shook McGuire's hand.

'Take a seat, doctor,' John said not offering his hand and sitting down quickly so she wouldn't see the stain in his pants. 'Gillis, coffee.'

'Yes, sir.'

'Wow, Mister Personality,' Beth said.

John ignored her. 'Now, doctor I ...' he paused, distracted by the familiarity of her eyes. 'Have we met before?'

'Don't think so, *detective*.'

'Strange.'

John listened patiently for the next hour while McGuire asked the questions.

Beth grew tired and cranky. She'd told them everything from the very beginning—the plight of the South China tiger, her trip to China, and her work there. She stressed the important gap that had been bridged between the Chinese and American governments, and the significance that Zhu Zhu held for the future survival of the species. 'And ...' she added, fighting back the tears, 'she's pregnant with four cubs.'

John yawned. 'Thank you, that will be all for now,' he said, dismissing her like a schoolgirl.

John and McGuire spent the rest of the day interviewing the zoo staff. John took mental notes after speaking to Robert Baker: nervous, smart ass, hiding something perhaps?

The rest of the convoy, including the Chinese ambassador, had very little to offer. The BOLO and aerial surveillance had drawn a blank. There were no relevant prints or clues left on the truck. John and McGuire also went to the Wittle and Sons depot, where they were satisfied none of the staff were involved.

'What are your thoughts, kid?' John said while they drove back to the station. 'Why would anyone go to such great lengths to steal an oversized flea-bitten cat?'

'Well, bear in mind that this is the first wild South China tiger to be brought into captivity in almost forty years. For all we know, it may be the last purebred specimen anywhere in the world. Its worth to a private collector would be priceless ... but I don't think that's why it was stolen.'

'What other purpose could there be?'

'Traditional Chinese medicines.'

John furrowed his brow, signalling McGuire to continue.

'Since being declared illegal by the Chinese government in 1981, the trade in exotic animal parts was forced underground and flourished as the demand grew.'

'How do you know all this?'

'When I was in the twelfth grade, I participated in a worldwide high school survey, which was designed to enforce awareness of the illegal use of endangered species body parts in traditional Chinese medicines. We were invited to bombard our governments with requests and proposals.'

'And what good did that do?'

'Not a lot.'

'So, if what you are saying is true, the tiger has probably been slaughtered by now.'

'I don't think so,' McGuire said. 'I think that if this is an inside job, which it certainly looks like it could be, then the mere fact that the tiger is pregnant with four cubs will give it a temporary stay of execution.'

'Right, I see what you're saying. Why have one tiger when you could have five. Good work, kid.' John always gave credit where credit was due.

'Tell me you've found it,' Captain Williams said rising from his desk.

'Not yet, sir, but we're—'

'Just tell me what we've got,' the captain snapped, cutting McGuire off.

McGuire cleared his throat. 'Well, sir, the second truck was found abandoned in a truck stop on the outskirts of Glendale late last night. Forensics are checking it out now, but it appears to be clean.'

'And what's the word on the street?'

'We won't know until we get out there this morning, sir.'

'Have we got any leads at all?'

'Only the Chinese connection. Both truck drivers and the motorcyclist were Chinese. We're pretty sure we're dealing with an international syndicate of illegal animal traders who will sell the animal to the highest bidder.'

'So, how much are we talking about here? It seems like somebody's going to a hell of a lot of trouble for a few thousand dollars' worth of cat.'

'Imagine if you will, sir, the *Mona Lisa* being offered for sale on the black market. Collectors from all over the world would scramble to purchase it regardless of price, merely because of the symbolic importance of owning it. This purebred South China tiger is also a priceless one-off. Whether it be for a private collection or for slaughter, there'll be no shortage of buyers. Add to that the fact that the animal is pregnant … and I'd guess we'd be talking millions, sir.'

'Okay, I want all the stops pulled out for this one, boys. I've already had the mayor on the phone, who in turn has had the White House on his back. He's demanding answers, and so is the Chinese government. And now to make it worse, the media have gotten hold of it. So, it looks like we're in for a major shit fight!'

28

Doctor Chan Jiang, formerly of the Shanghai Zoo, stood on the outside of the compound with his fingers gripping the mesh. Tony Lee was to his left smoking a large Cuban cigar. Raymond Brown stood to the right and officer Jim Kowalski of the LAPD stood behind them.

Zhu Zhu's ears twitched. Her eyelids fluttered then slowly opened. The effect of the tranquilliser was wearing off. She let out an enormous groan.

'Four cubs!' Tony exclaimed through a cloud of thick grey cigar smoke.

'Do you know the sex of the cubs yet, doctor?' Raymond Brown asked in a rare moment of humility.

'No, it is impossible to tell at the moment because they're not much bigger than jelly beans. But at a guess, I would say two males and two females.'

'So, in two months' time, we go to auction with four tigers,' Tony said excitedly.

'Five, if you include the mother,' the doctor added.

'Well, I might just keep the mommy for myself … perhaps I'll present Mother with a new fur coat for Christmas,' Tony said, almost choking on his cigar.

'No matter what happens, I will take one male cub!' Raymond snapped before storming off back to the house.

Tony sniggered and shouted after him, 'Look, you're doing it again. What have I told you? Be cool, relax.' He remembered the first

The Tiger Chase

time he'd come face to face with Raymond Brown and how he'd later tried to teach him to be cool like him.

Tony Lee had been fascinated by this legendary figure, known as The Tiger, long before he got to meet him.

There was a six-month waiting list to join the Lao Hu school of Chinese boxing owned by the legendary fighter Raymond Brown. Tony had tried unsuccessfully to pay his way in but had to wait like everyone else. When the six months was over, and he received word that he could attend a training session, he turned up thirty minutes early but remained at the back of the room.

Brown was an awesome figure and an unforgiving instructor. Casualties were high among the trainees. Tony winced as he saw bones broken and egos squashed by the mighty Tiger. He managed to stay at the back of the room and avoid the instructor's attention. When the class was over, he stayed behind while the rest of the trainees limped or were carried out of the building.

Raymond remained at the front of the room, standing in meditation with his eyes closed.

At first Tony was hesitant to approach him. *What should one say when coming face to face with such an awesome presence?* he thought. *What would Bruce Lee do in this situation?* He decided to play it cool. Bruce was cool, the Fonz was cool … Tony Lee was cool.

Rolling his shoulders forward, he placed one hand on his belt and strutted towards the front of the room. 'Whasssup?' he said, using his Tony-Lee-is-cool voice.

Raymond Brown stood upright with his right fist against his left palm and his eyes still closed.

Tony moved in closer and stood toe to toe with the legend. Then something astonished him—he realised he was looking down. He was taller than Brown. With renewed confidence, he surveyed the figure from the ground up. He had stubby feet with short, manicured toenails, large smooth calf muscles, scarred shins and rippled quadriceps. *Probably got nuts the size of raisins.* Tony chuckled to himself, making him feel more at ease. His eyes continued up past the waffled abdominal sheath and to the gigantic pectorals that spread out above the tiny waist. *Maybe the legendry Tiger's a fake. Perhaps he's just a gimmick, taken out of his box every now and then to pull in the punters, like the fairground prize fighters who taunt the crowds before the start of each show.* Tony had heard of The Tiger but had never seen him before tonight. Why was that? And how come he was such a *little* guy?

He began to visualise his own physique as being far more superior. When he looked in the mirror he saw, in his mind, the body of Schwarzenegger, not Stallone or that loser, Chuck Norris. It was an image of perfection that he'd worked hard to achieve.

Maybe The Tiger wasn't a tiger after all. Maybe he was just a pussy. He could take him. Yeah. With his own natural style of self-defence, painstakingly learned and practised from analysing every single movie ever made by Bruce Lee, he could take him.

While slowly continuing his close examination, he noticed the veins in the massive—now very red—neck, bulging and contracting. Then, as if caught by a giant magnet, Tony's head shot up and, with a violent jolt, stopped at eye level.

Raymond Brown's eyes were open.

Tony's newly acquired bravado dropped to the pit of his stomach. To make matters worse, he couldn't tear his eyes away from the dark bloodshot windows which seemed to be drawing in his soul. If any normal person were in such a predicament they would have turned and ran, but not Tony Lee. He knew the importance of standing his ground and that backing down would ruin his credibility or *face*. So, in an attempt to look equally as fierce, he stood tall and tried to match the stare.

At first nothing happened and while the seconds, which seemed like hours, passed, Tony's throat became dry and his left eye began to twitch. Then he heard a noise, almost like a small burp or a tummy rumble … there it was again. This time a little louder, like the faint rumble of far-off thunder. It was coming from Raymond Brown. *Did he have gas? Maybe he hadn't had lunch. This could be the way out.*

The Tiger Chase

Tony extended his hand. 'Hi ... my name is Lee ... Tony Lee. I've followed your career from the beginning, man,' he said, trying to sound cool. 'How's about we do lun—'

Before he could finish his offer of lunch, the sound that had formed in the pit of Brown's stomach rose and rumbled in his throat like an idling motor.

Tony stood silent with his hand still outstretched. When the noise died down, he continued: '—ch? Or maybe a few drinks ... girls? Whatever you want Mr ... uhmmm, Tiger,' he said, forgetting his name. 'For you, I can—'

A hot wave of retched air belched from Brown's mouth. He lunged forward and roared, 'GRRREARGH!'

Tony's toupee dislodged and slid to the back of his head.

Raymond's giant fist hurtled towards Tony's face.

Tony closed his eyes and winced. Nothing happened. After a few seconds he opened his eyes to find a brick wall pressed against his nose. It was Raymond Brown's fist. At first, he felt relief. *Had he been spared?* Then he noticed a warm, wet sensation and a familiar smell.

Withdrawing his fist, Raymond laughed. Not a laugh of mirth, but an evil, self-satisfying laugh. Then he blew in Tony's face.

Tony later found out that Raymond Brown had had good reason for sparing him; he was planning to leave Hong Kong and needed Tony's help.

Tony's dealings with the Lour family were about to come to an abrupt end, and he didn't want to be in Hong Kong when the shit hit the fan either. And—unknown to Raymond Brown—Tony had tried to arrange a meeting for some time after realising that his credibility would increase tenfold if he returned to LA with the legendary Tiger on his payroll.

Tony made a vow to himself that evening while admiring himself in the mirror. He tensed his flabby muscles, pointed at his reflection and said, 'I don't care who the hell he thinks he is ... nobody ... I said nobody makes Tony Lee shit his pants and gets away with it.'

An odd working relationship developed between the two. Tony drew much pleasure knowing that for Raymond Brown to get ahead, he would have to do things Tony's way. He delighted in making Raymond the object of his jokes, which mostly related to his serious disposition. 'You got to learn to chill and be cool, man.'

Once he took Raymond to Venice Beach and tried to show him how to strut. 'Like this, man, bend your knees ... hold your head up ... move your arms ... no—not like that. You look like Herman fricking Munster ... relax. Watch me.' Tony strutted along the boardwalk, sliding his feet and rolling his shoulders like a pimp.

Raymond tried to copy him.

'No, stand up straight, glide ... no, no, no, my God it's like working with the hunchback of Notre Dame. Look, don't worry, monkey boy. Let's just forget it, eh? It's a waste of time.'

Raymond stormed off.

'Esmeralda, Esmeralda, I'm coming, Esmeralda.' Tony called after him.

29

Danny Wong threw a handful of grapes into a brown paper bag, held the two top corners and spun it over three times to seal it. Then, taking a ten dollar bill from the little old lady, he handed her the bag and fumbled in his leather apron pocket for change. The little old lady bowed and thanked him, but Wong's attention had been snatched away when he'd noticed Detective John Dean approaching.

'Not bad,' John said, picking up a bright red apple and tapping it with his knuckles. 'So, what have you got for me, Wong?'

'I don't really know what you expect from me, Mr Dean,' Danny whispered nervously, glancing from side to side. 'I mean you come down here, you put me at risk, and when I give you valuable information you ignore it.'

'What do you mean?'

'The tiger, Mr Dean ... the tiger.'

John moved in closer and lowered his voice. 'What about the tiger?'

'Well, I tried to tell you about the tiger last time we spoke.'

John frowned.

'If you'd acted then, perhaps there'd be a few less bowls of soup being served tonight. You know what I mean?'

'No, I don't know what you mean. What the hell are you talking about?'

Danny twitched and glanced round the market. 'Tony Lee ...' he lowered his voice, 'Tony Lee has got the tiger.'

'You're kidding. Where?'

Danny drew a loud, slow intake of breath and shuffled his fingers together.

John reached into his pocket and pulled out a twenty.

'Well, Mr Dean, let's just say they're not in LA,' Danny said with a cocky smile on his face. 'I know that for sure.'

'Okay, let's cut the crap or I'm gonna haul your ass downtown. Where's the tiger, Wong?'

'I honestly don't know at this time but if you keep a few of those crisp notes warm for me, I'm sure I can find out.'

'When?'

'I'll be in touch … soon as I hear something, I promise!'

John returned to the car where McGuire sat waiting. 'The last time I spoke to Danny Wong he spoke about Tony Lee, and he mentioned the tiger. Well, he wasn't referring to Raymond Brown as we thought; he was referring to this … this damn cat!'

'You think Tony Lee's involved, boss?' McGuire said.

'I sure hope so,' John replied, smirking.

Captain Williams finished reading John's report and spent the rest of the day on the telephone. The evening before, John had received a call from Danny Wong who had told him everything he'd learned.

'Take a seat,' the captain said, holding open the door for John and McGuire. 'Luciville, Tennessee, that's just over two thousand miles away,' he said, perching himself on the edge of his desk and looking over his reading glasses. 'I've spoken to the sheriff there, and the name Benefitto belonged to a wealthy cotton producing family. Their land was sold this year after the death of the last surviving family member and was bought by a Los Angeles businessman called Anthony Bruce Lee.'

John raised his eyebrows.

The captain, reading from a file, continued: 'The house has since been demolished and in its place now stands a pink mansion called Nirvana. What are your thoughts?'

The Tiger Chase

'Well, it's obviously Tony Lee but he's out of LA so he's out of our jurisdiction,' John said.

'Well, yes ... and no,' the captain said. 'There's much more at stake here than just Tony Lee's collar. We're under pressure to bring this tiger back to LA without the media knowing. I've had the top brass on the phone. They suggested we hand this over to the FBI. But, after convincing them not to bring in the Feds, I've been authorised to send you two guys out there to find the tiger and arrange for its transportation back.'

'Sir, although I would relish the chance of bringing Tony Lee to justice, we're cops; we don't know anything about tigers and, to be quite honest, I don't want to,' John said.

'Sure, I know you hate cats,' the captain said, the corners of his mouth turning upwards. 'But there's something else, John ... Doctor Smith will be accompanying you.'

'What? There's no way we're taking that woman with us. This is a police matter.'

'Yes, but as you've just said, you're cops, and you don't know anything about tigers. This woman is the leading authority in the country—'

'But—'

'But nothing. I want you to go down to the zoo and give that damn woman a full report because she's been phoning the station on the hour every hour demanding to know what's being done. And then you will make arrangements to fly out to Tennessee first thing in the morning.' The captain closed the file and walked around his desk. 'Oh, and detective ... be nice.'

Before heading to the zoo, John and McGuire made a slight detour and pulled up outside Tony Lee's mansion. The large gate was a piece of cake for an experienced LAPD detective to open. 'Watch and learn, kid,' John said while he pushed his credit card down between the latch. With a flick of the wrist, the gate clanged then slowly opened.

Cruising along the driveway, John and McGuire noticed there

were no gardeners tending the lawns and the house looked deserted when they pulled up at the front entrance.

John banged on the door three times but there was silence. They walked round the back of the house trying to peer in through the mirrored windows. Along the rear of the building was a row of glass bi-fold doors and a tiled terrace. In the middle of the terrace sat a heart-shaped swimming pool with a yellow twisting water slide at the pointed end. The mosaic tiles on the bottom of the pool formed the letters TL.

John approached the glass doors and peered inside the house. The furniture was covered with dustsheets.

'Looks like they've gone on vacation,' McGuire said, joining John at the doors.

'Or on a tiger hunt,' John said.

'So, do you guys actually do anything between donuts? Or is that classified information?' Beth said sarcastically.

McGuire had just given her a full report and listened patiently while she focused her frustration on him.

'What are you going to do next? Wait around until someone offers you a tiger souvenir?' she snapped.

McGuire's answers remained polite. 'Well, Doctor Smith, we're doing all we can. As I said, we've got a few leads to follow but—'

'Doing all you can? You're standing here with a cup of coffee in your hand ... is that doing all you can?'

'Now just wait a goddamn minute, lady,' yelled John, who'd been listening from the back of the room and running out of patience. He marched across the room and stood over her. 'As my partner said, we are doing everything within our power to help. Personally, I would rather be out following leads right now instead of having to justify ourselves to you. I suggest you take a good long look at yourself and your motives for bringing this animal into the country then ask yourself why you have such a guilty conscience.'

Beth looked away. Her eyes filled with tears.

John, seeing she was upset, stormed out of the room and beckoned

The Tiger Chase

McGuire to follow him. He didn't have time for a stupid woman's tears. He would do his job, find the animal and return it to the zoo. The only reason he was staying on the case was the possibility of nailing Tony Lee.

John, McGuire and Beth arrived at the station for a briefing late that afternoon.

'You will fly out to Memphis at 7.45 am tomorrow,' Captain Williams said, handing them each a plane ticket. 'Once there, you'll be met by Deputy Luke Leicester who will drive you the thirty miles south-east to Luciville. There, you'll be issued a vehicle, and reservations have been made at the Groovy Grapevine Motel. I urge you people to put your differences aside and work together as a team. If you don't, it's going to be the Feds who receive all the glory when they bring Tony Lee in and return the tiger. Do I make myself clear, detective?'

John frowned then reluctantly nodded.

Beth looked away.

What is this thing about cats? John thought as he lay in bed that night. Maybe it's some kind of penance. While his body began to surrender to the oncoming sleep, his mind drifted back to the incident he'd had as a child—the one he'd told the shrink, Dr Singh, about.

He was around eight years old and was playing with his GI Joe figurines in the garden of his mother's house. A successful raid on Jimmy's base camp, saw him take a couple of prisoners. After interrogation and torture, he decided to bury them up to their necks and leave them for a while before resuming his wartime atrocities.

The two prisoners—tied up with a pair of socks stolen from the washing line—were taken down to the end of the garden where there was a patch of loose dirt. John began to dig with his bare hands. Down a few centimetres, the earth began to feel warm and moist, which made it easier to dig. The warm, wet dirt worked its way beneath his fingernails and some of the little cuts on his hands began to sting. When the hole was as deep as a GI figurine's shoulder height, he pulled his hands from the dirt and wiped them across his forehead to remove the sweat.

Jumping to his feet, a terrible stinging stench hit his nostrils and he was forced to hold his nose with his fingers to block the smell. Then, realising the smell was on his fingers, he'd just wiped whatever it was around his nose and mouth. Spitting on the ground, he vigorously rubbed his hands up and down his clothes. Unknowingly, he'd stumbled on the local tomcat's recently used midden. The smell of fresh turds and foul-smelling urine was too much for the boy to bear—he dropped to his knees and threw up all over the prisoners of war. Seeing his lunch again didn't help the situation. The smell of steaming regurgitated meatloaf and vegetables only complemented the smell of festering cat shit. He jumped to his feet and ran towards the house, dry retching all the way.

Young John swore he could still smell the odour under his fingernails even after scrubbing them in the shower, twice a day, for the next week.

A one-boy cabinet of war was created, and a campaign of terror launched against the ginger tomcat. Yes, revenge would be his.

Unfortunately, the cat was too clever and easily outmanoeuvred any flying missiles that were clumsily thrown its way. It would casually sniff around the traps that were optimistically laid as if mocking him and laughing at his pathetic attempts at capture.

John never did get his revenge and was left with a lifelong abhorrence of all cats. 'God, I hate cats,' he muttered as he fell asleep.

Beth Smith sat on one of the low branches of a tree and slowly swung her feet backwards and forwards. The early morning sun shone through her beautiful red hair and a gentle breeze lifted it slightly, revealing her fair slender neck and petite ears.

John looked on as she watched and giggled at the golden glowing tiger that rolled and played on the ground before her. He hadn't seen her smile before; it was the kind of smile that made the hairs on the back of your neck stand up—the kind of mischievous yet caring smile that could make you feel secure, special, excited, and relaxed all at the same time.

Tony Lee strolled into view with an antique elephant gun.

Raymond Brown appeared from the opposite side.

John tried to move in, but his ankles were shackled with heavy red tape.

Beth looked up. Her beautiful smile disappeared.

Tony Lee laughed and aimed the gun at the tiger.

Raymond Brown grinned at John.

BANG! A large flash then a cloud of grey smoke mushroomed out of the trumpet-shaped gun.

'Do something!' Beth screamed at John.

The smoke cleared. The tiger lay on its back, motionless.

Beth jumped down from the low tree and ran towards the tiger, but Tony Lee grabbed her.

Raymond Brown dived onto the tiger carcass, twisted his clawed hand into its chest and wrenched out its heart.

'No!' Beth screamed.

Blood oozed from the heart and ran down Brown's arm when he held it in the air. After looking firstly at John, then at Beth, he began to eat the heart.

'No ... please no,' Beth sobbed.

John couldn't move. He was now a part of the trees. His arms mingled with the branches and his legs twisted underground with the roots. He wanted to help, he wanted to make Tony Lee and Raymond Brown pay, but he couldn't. All he could do was watch as Raymond Brown taunted him with thick, curdling blood bubbling from the sides of his mouth.

'You should have called the FBI, lady,' Tony Lee taunted. 'Didn't anyone tell you this guy's a loser? He don't wanna save no tiger. He hates The Little Princess.' Tony dragged Beth by the arm over to John. 'He's got more important things to do. Ask him about his tart from Vegas then you'll see why he don't give a shit about you or your oversized pussy. What a shame you didn't go with the FBI ... poor pussy.'

30

John met McGuire and Doctor Smith at LAX the following morning at 6.45 am. McGuire had picked the doctor up from her parents' home in Pasadena and brought her to the airport.

There was an awkward silence while the three waited at the check-in desk. John and Beth hardly spoke. John avoided eye contact. There was no way he was mentioning the dream he'd had the night before.

Deputy Luke Leicester—a large, middle-aged, tobacco-chewing country boy—met the trio outside the arrivals terminal at Memphis Airport and led them to his waiting patrol car.

'How long until we get to Luciville, deputy?' McGuire asked.

'Bout forty minutes, though there might be a fair bit of traffic on the road due to the severe storm warning an' all.'

'Storm warning? I wasn't aware there was a storm warning,' Beth said, glaring at John.

'Yes ma'am, they reckon it's gonna hit sometime tonight. A lot of folk are moving away. Roads might be a bit busy.'

'So, what do you know of the Benefitto place?' John asked.

'I know it's a damn shame what they done to the old place. My daddy used to work for the old lady, tending to the little cotton she had left. It'd been years since it was a viable business. The town folk all had a place in their hearts for the old property though. We'd all muck in and help at harvest time. It was like the hub of the community, and now … well, now it's all gone.' During the drive

The Tiger Chase

to town, the deputy went into more detail about how the tight-knit cotton community of Luciville, Tennessee, situated thirty miles south-east of Memphis, was fiercely opposed to the demolition of the architecturally and historically important home of the late Benefitto family. How they were outraged when the proposed plans of the pink monstrosity were released and passed through without a single regard to the community's objections. How the people vowed to fight on.

'How old was the place?' Beth quizzed.

'Well ma'am, the Benefitto ranch was built by an Italian missionary, Alfredo Benefitto, in 1790 and was the first property in the area. Originally, it was a Catholic mission, but it fell into the hands of Alfredo's devious brother, Mario, after Alfredo's death while out riding one day. Mighty suspicious it were too!

Within weeks Mario had sent the charitable folk of the mission packing and turned the house into a brothel servicing the traders on their way to and from the West.'

'Wow, you really know its history.'

'Yes ma'am, me and every single resident of Luciville.'

'Tell us more.'

'After only a couple of years, Mario died from syphilis and the property was passed down to the third Benefitto brother, Angelo. Angelo travelled out to America with his family from Italy but, unlike his two late brothers, he was a farmer. He set to work planting cotton. Within five years, he had him twenty thousand plants and had pioneered the way in new planting and harvesting techniques. Another five years later, and with a staggering fourteen thousand planted acres, the famous Benefitto trademark was launched. It quickly became the most successful producer in the state of Tennessee.

The property stayed in the Benefitto family until the eighty-year-old spinster, and last remaining member, Margarita Benefitto, died last year.'

'That's such a shame.'

'You're not wrong. Some of the inhabitants of Luciville cried when the house was demolished. And when the new place was built, they jeered at the building contractors, especially when they erected the eight-foot pink wall around the property.'

'Have you been to the house?' John asked.

'Yes, sir, I drove in one day and had a look just before they built the wall. It's pink with mirrored windows and orange roof tiles—kind of like Chinese style I guess.'

'Sounds familiar,' John muttered, side glancing at McGuire.

'At the time I couldn't figure out why there was a large, mesh, pyramid-shaped compound built at the back of the house. I guess it's obvious what it's for now,' the deputy added.

'What do you know about the owner?' McGuire asked.

'Nothing at all. The only people seen entering and leaving are the staff, and they're all Chinese.'

John and McGuire nodded in unison. They'd heard enough to know whose house it was.

By the time they reached the outskirts of Luciville, there was a definite change in the air. A cooling wind flowing across the wide, flat land, was whipping up dust and debris. Dark clouds raced across the horizon.

The small town sat unprotected in the centre of an enormous patchwork plane of fields with all roads leading to it. Mountains, shrouded in the approaching clouds, dominated the horizon with pine trees at their base.

Deputy Leicester pointed into the distance. 'Don't even have to point it out.'

At the back of the town there was a pink wall surrounding a house exactly the same as the one in Beverly Hills.

'Take us down so we can have a look,' John said.

The wall grew more hideous the closer they got. The ornate gate had aluminium sheets riveted to the back, making it impossible to see in.

The Tiger Chase

John and McGuire looked at each other and gave the same knowing nod.

The Groovy Grapevine Motel was in the centre of town and, although relatively new, it was of Colonial architecture, keeping it in character with the rest of the buildings. Rooms 4 and 5 had been reserved. John and McGuire would share.

In the parking lot was an early 1980s, green Chevy station wagon which had been supplied and placed there early that morning by the Luciville police department.

'Wow, a classic,' McGuire remarked.

'Piece of junk if you ask me,' John said. 'Have you got anything from this century and a bit less conspicuous, Luke? This thing's as big as a boat.'

'Sorry, we thought you might enjoy driving around town in style. That's the sheriff's pride and joy so you'd better look after it.'

'It's the sheriff's car?' McGuire asked, admiring the vehicles lines.

'Retired sheriff. Old Dan, we still call him the sheriff. He's kindly agreed to loan you his car. Truth is there was nothing else available at short notice.'

'It will do just fine,' McGuire said, running his hand across the roof.

'If you'd like to settle into your rooms and freshen up, I'll call back in about half an hour and take you to lunch,' the deputy said, handing over the keys to John.

'Oh, thank you, that'll be nice,' Beth said.

'Maybe some other time, deputy. We've got work to do. Take the doctor though,' John said.

Beth stormed off to her room.

John and McGuire went to theirs.

'So, what's the plan, John?' McGuire asked as they hastily unpacked their bags.

'All we can do for now is watch and wait.'

'And then?'

The station wagon sat across the road from the Benefitto ranch's gateway. The rain clouds were dark overhead now. A large gust of wind rocked the long Chevy from side to side.

McGuire looked at his watch. It was 1.00pm.

'Hey, you guys hungry?' the deputy called out as he pulled alongside.

Beth climbed from the patrol car and into the back seat of the station wagon carrying two take-out cartons of tacos with chilli and cheese.

31

The wind whistled and howled as the evening drew in.

'Let's call it a day. It doesn't look as if anyone's at home,' John said, starting the car engine.

'What do you mean, let's call it a day?' Beth snapped. 'Surely we haven't come all this way just to sit in the car all day staring at a brick wall. What's the plan? Are we going in there tonight?'

'Look, this isn't like one of those stupid TV shows you probably watch. We can't just go barging into the house,' John replied while trying to negotiate a three-point turn.

'Been in China for the last four years. Don't watch TV, *detective.*'

'Yeah, whatever. First, we don't know if anyone is even in there. Second, we haven't got any reason to believe there might be a tiger on the property. And third, we don't have a warrant,' John growled, righting the car and heading back towards town.

'But we have to do something. Zhu Zhu might be in there.' Beth pleaded.

'Why not get an early night, Doctor Smith and leave the policing to us, eh?' McGuire said, escorting her to her room.

Beth frowned and huffed, closing the door behind her.

Thirty minutes later, John and McGuire, dressed in dark combat gear, crept from their room out of the motel and towards Deputy Leicester's waiting Jeep Cherokee.

'They reckon this storm's gonna hit sooner than they thought,' the deputy said as the two detectives climbed into the back.

'That's okay, I'm hoping it'll act as a distraction. After sitting outside the property for half the day, we didn't see a soul enter or leave so we don't know how many are in there,' John said.

'So, what's the plan, detective?' the deputy said.

The question of the day, thought John. 'I want you to drop us at the start of the wall then head back and park out of sight. Seeing as we don't have radios, wait for thirty minutes, then follow us in. If we need you earlier, I'll call you on your cell phone, okay?'

'Right,' the deputy said. 'I know for sure you don't got a warrant, but as far as I'm concerned you did say you had authorisation for this, didn't you?'

'Of course,' John replied, tongue-in-cheek. 'I told the doctor we hadn't just to keep her out of our hair.'

John and McGuire scaled the wall and headed towards the house. They circled the building and saw the large pyramid-shaped compound at the back. The rain began to pour as the stealthy pair crept towards the facility. It was too dark to see anything inside, so John shone his torch through the mesh.

Two golden fireballs blazed in the beam.

'My God … look at the size of the thing!'

32

Raymond Brown sat on the floor in the middle of his room, meditating. His body was cut and bruised. He'd worked hard today. At first, he'd been disappointed not to have any punch bags to destroy. But after finding a large stack of concrete blocks left by the builders, he'd set a hundred of them up in a row then timed himself. Using his fists and feet, he finally smashed the last block with his head and stopped the clock. 'Three minutes, forty seconds. Tomorrow will be better.'

In his meditative state, he visualised the amazing power and sexual prowess he would possess after devouring not just one of the cubs as agreed with Tony Lee, but all of them ... *and* their mother too. Then he would kill Tony Lee and silence his father forever.

There was a knock at the door.

'Grrrr!' He didn't take kindly to being interrupted.

The knocking stopped and one of the menservants entered the room. 'Sir, your presence is requested in the drawing room.'

Raymond entered the drawing room to hear Tony ask Steven Tang, 'Is it them?'

'Yes. They've been sitting across the street all afternoon then the girl joined them. Now Detective Dean and his rookie have returned alone.'

'So, Johnny Dean and his little partner have come tiger hunting, eh? How about we supply the game.' He looked at Raymond Brown and bared his teeth. 'Grrrr, go get em, boy.'

Raymond snarled then crept from the room like a wild animal.

'You know, he's so good at what he does ... bless him!' Tony remarked to nobody in particular.

33

John and McGuire made their way to the back door of the house. The drenching rain made it hard to see. A loud crack of thunder exploded overhead then peeled off into a rolling rumble.

John peered into the dark house through the glass door. A blinding flash of lightning momentarily cast the house into daylight.

Raymond Brown peered back from the other side of the glass.

The darkness returned but small strobe-like flashes of lightning illuminated Brown like a Chinese shadow puppet.

SMASH! The glass door shattered and fell to the ground.

The silhouette solidified when Brown stepped through the broken doorframe.

Before John could aim his gun, it was sent flying across the terrace by a mighty backhand blow. Then, pausing for a fraction of a second, his attacker recoiled his hips and with all his strength he catapulted his other fist forward, hitting John squarely on the jaw, knocking him to the ground.

'Freeze!' McGuire cried, adopting a wide stance and aiming his gun.

Squinting through the pouring rain, Raymond Brown turned to face McGuire. A low growl forming in the pit of his stomach harmonised with the rolling thunder.

John painfully lifted himself from the ground just as Brown pounced at the rookie.

BANG!
BANG!
Two shots rang out.

The Tiger Chase

The first bullet hit Raymond Brown in the head. The second lodged deep in McGuire's stomach.

John scrambled towards McGuire.

'Hold it there, dickhead!'

Squinting through the pouring rain, John realised Jim Kowalski was standing in the doorway with a gun in his hand.

McGuire fell to his knees then forward onto his face. A pool of blood spread out from under his body, mixed with the rainwater and began to fill the grouted edges of the tiled ground.

John, ignoring Kowalski, rushed to McGuire's side.

'Oh, very touching,' Kowalski said. He strolled over to Raymond Brown, who lay unconscious, and kicked him. 'Freak! Some good you were.' He kicked him again. 'Shame about the kid, though ... I guess,' he said, turning.

'He needs help!' John pleaded, rolling his partner over onto his back.

'Not such a big guy now, eh?' Kowalski said, ignoring John's plea. 'I've waited a long time for this moment, detective. I hope you realise how much pleasure this gives me.' He aimed his gun at John's head.

BANG!

Kowalski jolted and dropped his weapon. Clutching at his stomach, he looked up at his killer. 'You bastard!' His body dropped to the wet tiles with a splash.

Tony Lee was standing in the doorway.

'We need an ambulance here, Lee!' John yelled, cradling McGuire's head in his arms.

Tony Lee ignored him, strutted through the rain and knelt down by Raymond Brown. 'Some tiger god, eh?'

'This is the police. Drop your weapon, we have you surrounded!'

Tony Lee rose to his feet and struggled to stand against the wind and rain. His rain-drenched toupee had expanded and sat on his head like a bird's nest, the hair dye from his eyebrows running down his face.

Another blinding flash of lightning was followed by a loud clap of thunder bursting overhead.

Tony raised his gun and fired a volley of shots in the direction of the policeman's voice. Then, dashing back to the door, he disappeared into the house.

John wanted to give chase, but he knew he couldn't leave his partner.

'Halt,' cried the deputy running onto the terrace. Seeing McGuire lying in a pool of blood he ran to his side.

'Go after Lee!' John yelled.

'But—'

'Go!'

The deputy ran into the house.

John reached into his pocket for his cell phone. The reception bar showed zero. 'Damn!'

'What happened? I heard shots—'

John swung his head round to see Beth mysteriously appear from the darkness. 'What the hell are you doing here? Hey, you're a doctor. You can help him, right?' he said, changing his tone.

Beth knelt, examined McGuire's wound then checked his pulse. 'This isn't good, detective.'

'Don't need to be a doctor to see that.'

Deputy Leicester came running back from the house. 'He's gone. Had a car out front. Listen, I tried the phones as well, but the lines must be down.'

John glanced over to Raymond Brown and realised he was also gone. 'Damn! Where's Brown?'

The deputy checked Kowalski's pulse, but he was dead.

'We have to get this man to a hospital right away,' Beth exclaimed. She checked her cell phone. There was no dial tone. 'We'll have to get him there ourselves.'

'Right, I'll fetch the Jeep,' the deputy shouted, disappearing into the darkness.

'Let's get him out of the rain,' Beth said.

The Tiger Chase

John and Beth were startled by a loud, long groan.

Beth's eyes searched the darkness. 'Zhu Zhu, where are you, baby?'

'GRRREARGH!'

'Never mind that,' John growled.

They carefully carried McGuire into the house and set him down on a sofa.

Beth checked his wound again and shook her head. She found some towels and made a crude dressing. When she had made McGuire as comfortable as she could, she told John that she'd be back soon and went out to the compound.

John knelt by the sofa.

McGuire opened his eyes. Coughing and struggling to breathe, he looked at John then closed his eyes again. 'I'm not going to die,' he whispered, trembling and licking his lips.

'That's right, buddy … you're not going to die,' John assured him.

'So dry … need water.'

John rushed outside and over to the compound.

Beth was hugging the tiger and screeching as it licked the rain from her face.

'Hey, when you've finished there. Is it safe to give McGuire water?'

'Yes, yes of course. Sorry. I'll be right there.'

John re-entered the house and found a small kitchenette. He quickly went through the cupboards, found a mug and filled it with water. When he returned to McGuire, he dropped the mug and instinctively reached for his gun. 'What the—'

'Stop, don't shoot … she can help him!' Beth said, following Zhu Zhu in through the door.

Zhu Zhu raised her snout in John's direction and sniffed the air. Her head turned towards McGuire and, as if following the scent of blood, she followed her nose. Placing her face close to his, her head rocked from side to side as she peered into his eyes. 'Chuff!' She turned and padded out into the rain.

John shot Beth a puzzled glare.

Beth knelt by McGuire and began to remove his dressing.

'What the hell are you doing?' John asked.

Zhu Zhu returned. Beth stood to one side and let her through. Zhu Zhu gently stroked McGuire's face with the side of her head then nuzzled his nose with hers.

McGuire parted his lips and drank the cool rainwater from the tiger's mouth. After a few gulps, he coughed, and water spilled over his chin.

Zhu Zhu withdrew, allowing him to breathe before letting him drink again. When he'd finished, she stepped back and sniffed the air again. *'Chuff, chuff.'* She lowered her head towards the bullet wound.

John frowned at Beth and went to move forward.

Beth put her hand on his arm and gestured for him to watch.

Zhu Zhu gently licked McGuire's wound.

McGuire winced.

'It's gonna eat him, for God's sake!' John yelled.

'Don't be silly,' Beth whispered. 'She's cleaning his wound. It must be stinging him a little, that's all. The tiger's saliva is antiseptic; they use it to clean their wounds in the wild, usually from fights or botched hunting attempts.'

'McGuire ... are you okay, man?' John said.

McGuire opened his eyes. 'Not gonna die, John ... not gonna die.'

Deputy Leicester pulled up in front of the doorway and left his headlights on. When he ran into the house, he immediately stopped and reached for his gun. 'Jesus, Joseph and Mary,' he yelled when he saw the tiger licking McGuire's stomach.

'It's okay, she's helping,' Beth said, putting her hand on his gun and lowering it.

The deputy stood staring as if in a trance.

'Where's the nearest hospital?' John asked.

'About twenty miles away,' the deputy replied, still staring.

'We have to get there, and quick!'

The Tiger Chase

'No,' Deputy Leicester said. 'I'll take him. He'll be okay with me. I think you need to concentrate on how you're gonna get the tiger back to LA.'

'He's right, John,' Beth interjected. 'Have you given it any thought?'

John, ignoring her, gently stroked McGuire's hair.

McGuire nodded in reassurance. 'I'm not going to die.'

Beth redressed McGuire's wound, and John and the deputy carefully carried him into the Jeep. Moments later, Beth and John waved when the Jeep sped off into the pouring rain.

'Okay, get the cat and let's go,' John snapped.

'Her name is Zhu Zhu and she's not a cat, she's a South China tiger,' Beth retorted.

'Whatever—did you bring the station wagon?'

'Yes, it's out front.'

'So how did you get in here?'

'Stood on the car roof and climbed over the wall.'

'Right, well let's get this thing back to the car and get the hell out of here.'

34

The torrential rain turned to drizzle then stopped. The last rumbles of thunder rolled across the sky towards the south-east. Random flashes of lightning pulsated over the distant mountains. The wind dropped and the full moon appeared through thin remnants of cloud.

Using a piece of chain from the compound, Beth made a makeshift leash for Zhu Zhu and placed it around her neck. 'Okay, baby—let's go,' she said, tugging gently on the chain.

The tiger remained seated.

'Come on, baby, we're going home.' Beth pulled a little harder. Zhu Zhu still didn't budge. Beth pulled with all her might but was no match for the tiger's strength. 'Are you just going to stand there and watch or are you going to give me a hand here?' Beth snapped, glaring at John.

John watched with his arms folded, surveying and enjoying the situation. 'So, let me get this straight,' he paused for effect. 'Little-Miss-Tiger-Expert, who is the only person qualified to transport this *wild animal* the two thousand miles back to LA, needs the assistance of this *donut-eating* detective, after travelling a mere … what shall we say … six yards?' he continued sarcastically, circling Beth and the tiger. 'The technical manoeuvre you're using there to move the animal, doctor, does that have a scientific term, or is it something they taught you in China?'

'So, you're going to be an ass instead of helping me?'

'Something like that.'

'Dick,' Beth mumbled, tugging at the chain again.

'What was that?'

The Tiger Chase

'Nothing, but if we can't get her to follow us, what do we do?'

John sighed and shook his head.

Beth grinned like a little girl and handed him the chain.

John sighed, took the chain and tugged on it slightly to see what he was up against. The tiger didn't move. He pulled harder but still she didn't move so he wrapped the chain around his right hand, grabbed it with his left, lowered his stance, took a deep breath, and pulled. Nothing.

'Come on, baby, please,' Beth urged, gently pushing the tiger from behind.

John leaned back and pulled harder.

Zhu Zhu lowered her head and resisted.

Beth pushed and tickled her while John grunted and heaved.

The tiger still didn't budge but the chain began to slip over her head and the thick fur on her neck bunched up like a lion's mane. Soon her long white whiskers were sticking out straight ahead, her ears were scrunched forward, and her face was contorted.

John pulled even harder.

Zhu Zhu snarled, shook her head from side to side and growled.

'It's okay, baby, it's okay.'

The chain suddenly slid off Zhu Zhu's head.

John fell backwards into a large puddle.

Trying desperately not to laugh, Beth cupped her hands across her mouth and turned away.

'GRRREARGH!' Zhu Zhu gave a mischievous roar then pounced on John and playfully pinned him to the ground.

'Arrrgh!' A red rash appeared on John's face from the tiger's rough licks and hot drool.

Beth pulled her away. 'No, baby, no.'

John jumped to his feet with his fists clenched.

Beth stood between him and the tiger, and while unsuccessfully trying to supress a smirk, she said, 'Should we have a plan B?'

Zhu Zhu sat and looked on while John cursed and patted his clothes down.

'Don't ask me again for any more help,' John growled.

'Look, I'm sorry I laughed and I'm sorry about the donut crack … we've got to work this out somehow. What shall we do?'

'We've got to get back to the motel. These guys could return at any moment,' John said.

Zhu Zhu groaned and yawned.

There was a few moments of silence while the pair considered their limited options, until John said, 'What do you think would happen if we just made our way towards the front gates?'

'Maybe she'll follow us.'

'Let's give it a try.'

When they'd walked only a few yards, the tiger ran up, pushed her way between their legs and walked along with them.

John shook his head and glanced sideways at Beth. 'Tiger expert, my ass!'

Beth, ignoring him, stroked Zhu Zhu's head. 'There's a good girl,' she said, blushing.

The next morning, The Groovy Grapevine Motel was deserted. The power and phone lines were down and debris from the road, including the barbershop awning from across the road, was piled against the front office wall.

John had remained awake all night. Since arriving back from Tony Lee's mansion, he'd stood at the window of his room watching and thinking, and after trying to anticipate Lee's next move, he'd formulated a plan. When dawn broke, he watched while the first rays of sun reached out across the unsullied sky and reflected off the wet road. He checked his watch then glanced at the bed. He wouldn't wake them just yet.

Zhu Zhu lay on her back the full length of the bed with her front paws crossed over her chest and her back legs in the air. Her head was to one side, her eyes screwed tightly shut, and her tongue hung from the side of her mouth and rested on the pillow. Beth lay next to her with her arm over the big cat's body and her face snuggled into the thick fur at the back of her neck. Every time she exhaled, Zhu Zhu's ears twitched, but she didn't stir.

John, paying no attention to them, pondered over the road maps he'd grabbed from the reception after realising his cell reception was still down. He'd decided to give them a couple more hours before waking them. Then he'd tell Beth his plan.

Beth was the first to awaken. At first, she peered round the room as if not knowing where she was. Then, glancing at Zhu Zhu, she smiled until she realised John was watching her with a frown. Trying to climb off the bed without waking the sleeping tiger proved impossible.

Zhu Zhu stirred and opened one eye.

'Good morning my Little Princess,' Beth said, seeing she was awake. 'Who's a beautiful girl then? Who's a—'

'Do you have to talk to it like that?' John said.

'Why?'

'It's annoying … and it reminds me of someone.'

'Reminds you of whom?'

Ignoring the question, John said, 'I've been thinking about what we should do, we need to talk. There's also a few things I need to know about … it.'

'Okay. What's the plan, Johnny?'

John closed his eyes, counted to ten and, trying unsuccessfully to sound calm, said, 'Don't call me Johnny.'

'Oh gosh, we are grumpy today … chill out, John.'

John coolly asked her to take a seat so he could tell her his plan, but Beth insisted on taking Zhu Zhu outside first so she could stretch her legs. John agreed but half-heartedly insisted on coming too.

It was six-thirty in the morning and Luciville was still deserted. Tree branches, garden furniture, broken pot plants, and other debris were strewn about the place from the storm.

Beth led Zhu Zhu out of the room and to the motel courtyard at the front of the building. When she was sure there was no one about, she clapped her hands and beckoned the big cat to chase her. 'Come on then, baby, come on.'

John strolled behind keeping a lookout. He checked his cell phone. There was still no reception.

At the left side of the courtyard stood a tall, rendered wall. Zhu Zhu rubbed herself along the length of it, rolling her shoulders and waving her tail as she went. Without warning, she suddenly reared onto her hind legs and stretched her front paws as high as she could up the wall. Then, while stomping her hind legs, she scratched at the render with her powerful front claws. Before Beth could stop her, she dropped back onto all fours and with her tail quivering in the air, squatted against the wall.

'No!' Beth cried, but it was too late.

A squirt of steaming urine splattered against the render. Zhu Zhu then turned, sniffed the air, walked farther along the wall and proceeded to do the same.

'No, baby—no … you mustn't do that!' Beth yelled, pulling her away from the wall.

'What the hell's it doing?' John said with the neck of his sweater over his nose.

'I'll have to keep a closer eye on her from now on. She's marking her territory the way she would in the wild,' Beth said.

John examined the deep gouges in the render. 'I'd like to see them explain this when they're cleaning up later. This could start one of those Big Foot conspiracies. Experts, people not unlike yourself, will fly in from all over the world and conclude that a sasquatch probably lives in them there hills.' Although his pullover was still over his nose, he lifted his head and sniffed the air. Then, frowning, he looked round to where Zhu Zhu was crouching. 'Oh, my God—no … I can't stay and watch that. Big cat, big turd. I'll be in the room,' he said, rushing away.

35

'Okay, here's the plan. The only way we can get back to LA is to drive in the station wagon,' John said.

'What? Are you crazy? How long would it take?' Beth asked.

'About thirty-five hours if we drove straight through.'

'Thirty-five hours? How far is it?'

'Almost two thousand miles. We have to be careful. I've been trying to put myself in Tony Lee's place. What would he expect us to do?'

'Well ... I suppose he'd expect the zoo to pick us up.'

'Right, but what if he has someone working in the zoo ... someone who could tip him off?'

'Hmmm.'

'I think he's still close by, which means he's probably waiting to hear if we phone in or not. If we do and give them our whereabouts, they'll be onto us straight away. But if we don't, he's gonna assume that we're going to drive back.'

'So, what do you suggest?'

'We call my captain and the zoo and give them a bit of a bum steer,' John said.

'What do you mean?'

'We'll tell them a half truth. We'll say we've got the tiger and we're on our way back. We'll say we've driven through the night and just left Oklahoma City heading for Santa Fe.'

'But if Lee sets off on the highway now, he could bump right into us.'

'True ... but if we tell them we're travelling on the smaller roads and avoiding the cities when we'll actually be sticking to the highway, that would keep them off our tail.'

'I suppose it makes sense, but there are a few problems I think you may have overlooked,' Beth said. 'First, we have with us a two-metre long, 115 kilo female tiger. There is no way she could spend thirty-five hours in the back of a station wagon. Second, have you thought for a moment the implications involved in transporting a wild animal two thousand miles across America by road?'

'So, what do you suggest? If we stay here your tiger's dead, and probably us with it, but if we phone in for assistance, the end result could be the same,' John said.

Beth thought for a moment. She looked down at Zhu Zhu who lay across her feet on the floor. 'Okay, but we can't drive straight through—the station wagon will be terribly cramped.' She paused for thought. 'I suppose if we put the back seat down, that will give her more room and she'll be closer to me, but we'll need to stop regularly. We'll have to find accommodations for the evenings, and we also need to work out what we're going to feed her. Actually, that reminds me, we don't even know when she last ate ... oh, and we must remember that she's pregnant too.'

John realised they hadn't eaten themselves since lunchtime the day before. 'I gotta eat.'

Beth was hungry too.

They packed their few belongings and were in the process of coaxing Zhu Zhu into the back of the station wagon when Deputy Luke Leicester's Jeep Cherokee trundled into the courtyard.

Beth and John left Zhu Zhu sitting on the tailgate and went to greet him.

'How's McGuire?' John asked eagerly.

'He's gonna be just fine,' the deputy said. 'Got him there in plenty of time. Luckily the storm missed Memphis, so the hospital wasn't that busy.'

'Oh, that's great news,' Beth said.

The Tiger Chase

'Thanks for all your help, Luke,' John said. 'Now there's one more thing you can do for us, if you wouldn't mind?' John told the deputy exactly what they were planning and asked him if he would phone McGuire's girlfriend and inform her of the news, which he'd already done, then to get in touch with Captain Williams at the LAPD then Robert Baker at the LA Zoo.

The deputy agreed and watched, highly amused, while John and Beth struggled to push Zhu Zhu into the back of the station wagon. 'Well, I'll be off then. You folks have a good trip back,' he said after shaking John's hand and giving Beth a hug.

John drove the station wagon through the still deserted Luciville streets. They headed west towards North Little Rock with the hope of reaching Clarksville by lunchtime and Oklahoma City by early evening. But first they decided they had to eat. 'So, what will it eat?' John said, noticing a sign at the side of the road: Burgers One Mile.

'Look, can you not address her as *it*. Her name is Xiao Gong Zhu, or Zhu Zhu for short, which means Little Princess. In the animal world she is royalty,' Beth said.

'There's no need to be so touchy. What I mean is, will it eat a burger, or do I have to go out and hunt buffalo?' John said with an uncharacteristic chuckle.

Beth loosened up. 'Well, I'm sure she would eat a burger or twenty but ideally, we need to find an abattoir so we can buy fresh horse meat and by-products, but for now a butcher shop will do. We're also going to need some bone, fishmeal, eggs, brewer's yeast, soy, bran, and some multi-vitamin and mineral supplements.'

'You're kidding? Can't we just get a couple of cans of cat food?'

'Don't be silly, she needs to eat properly. And we'll need some kind of a water container in the back of the car so she can help herself to a drink. And I think we should stop at least every two or three hours to let her stretch her legs and use the toilet.'

'Okay, but I'm going to have to stop now and get some breakfast,' John said, turning off the road and into the burger joint carpark.

'How about we use the drive-through?'

John agreed.

Beth opened the rear windows just enough to let some air into the car. The tiger gave her a lick down the side of her face.

John smirked when he noticed the red mark on Beth's cheek.

'Good morning, can I take your order please?' the spotty teenage girl said at the drive through window, while busily counting change and not looking up.

John studied the menu board to his right.

Zhu Zhu pressed her nose against the car window. The aroma of grilled burgers and French fries, sizzling in hot fat, filled her being, she pushed her snout through the gap and, with flaring moist nostrils, sniffed hard and loud.

'360, 370, 380, 390, four dollars, now what can I get—' The girl stopped in mid-sentence after finding herself looking directly into the large pink snout. Her eyebrows arched and her silver braces gleamed when her mouth dropped.

Zhu Zhu pulled her nose in and lowered her head to look at the girl. *'Grrrr.'*

'Is ... is that a tiger?'

'No, dear, of course not, it's a ... a golden ... striped Rottweiler,' Beth said, leaning over John's lap to look at the girl.

'Cool!'

On top of their order and, against Beth's better judgment, John ordered two burgers for Zhu Zhu. 'I'm not giving it any of mine,' he exclaimed.

'Okay, but this is just a snack until we get her some proper food,' Beth said.

After paying the girl, John drove towards the next window to collect their order.

Zhu Zhu, thinking they were leaving empty-handed, panicked. *GRRREARGH!'* She roared and paced causing the car to sway violently from side to side.

The Tiger Chase

John braked at the next window and leaned out to take the food, steadying himself while the car rocked.

The plump teenage boy, who broke the dress code by wearing his cap back to front and chewed gum loudly, handed John the brown paper bags and drinks.

Zhu Zhu stuck her head out of the window over John's shoulder and, licking her lips, looked the boy dead in the eye.

'Whoa, it's a man-eating tiger!' the boy yelled.

John grabbed the food, passed it to Beth then put his foot on the gas, sped out of the drive through, and back onto the highway.

Some way down the road, he noticed a deserted truck stop. He pulled into it, turned off the engine and climbed out of the car.

'What are you doing?' Beth asked, balancing the food bags on her lap.

'We're gonna eat. Come on.'

Beth climbed out of the car, handed the bags to John then checked no one was about before opening the tailgate. 'Be good now, baby.'

John headed in the direction of a picnic bench, which was almost hidden by a clump of trees.

Zhu Zhu jumped from the station wagon and bounded after John, almost tripping him.

When John reached the picnic area, he stepped onto the wooden bench seat and sat on the tabletop.

Zhu Zhu sat at his feet waiting impatiently while the first burger was unwrapped. She shuffled on her backside and drooled. *'Chuff.'* She edged forward and groaned.

John was tempted to eat the first burger but instead he threw it to the begging tiger.

Zhu Zhu caught the burger in her mouth, chewed it twice and swallowed.

Beth joined them as John was unwrapping the second burger.

'I can't believe I'm letting you do this.'

'Do what?' John said with a mouth full of burger,

'We have the rarest tiger in the world in our charge and we're feeding it burgers,' Beth said, taking one of the bags.

'I can't see the problem. It's meat, isn't it?' John said, reaching for the fries.

Zhu Zhu's attention switched to Beth.

Beth tore a burger in half. 'Now take your time with this one, you naughty girl.' She placed the half into the tiger's drooling mouth.

Zhu Zhu, as if paying attention, slowly chewed this time, throwing it round in her mouth.

Beth retrieved a burger and a small carton of fries from the bag and placed them on the table for herself.

John took a long loud sip from the carton of coke then offered it over to Beth.

'Did you only get one drink?'

'Yeah.'

'I'm not actually in the habit of eating burgers, fries and coke for breakfast. I may have preferred an orange juice or a coffee.'

'Well, excuse me, your majesty. You've got a tongue in your head, haven't you?'

Beth sighed, gave Zhu Zhu the remaining half of burger and ate her own breakfast in silence.

Zhu Zhu wolfed down her burger then shifted her attention back to John.

John threw her a few fries, 'That's it, kitty.'

Zhu Zhu caught the fries in her mouth and swallowed them without chewing.

'You'll give her indigestion,' Beth said.

Zhu Zhu began to shake her head and slap her chops. She groaned and lifted her paw to her mouth.

'What is it, baby?' Beth knelt to take a look.

'Probably a fur ball,' John said, smirking.

Zhu Zhu opened her mouth and Beth laughed. Impaled on one of her upper fangs was a slice of pickle.

The Tiger Chase

'Come here, let me get it for you,' Beth placed one hand on the side of the tiger's head and, opening its mouth wider with the other, she slid the pickle off her tooth.

Zhu Zhu swallowed it and chuffed.

'Come on, baby, let's leave Johnny here to sulk on his own,' Beth said, heading back to the car.

John frowned, sipped the last of the watery coke from the ice at the bottom of the cup then threw it, along with the wrappers, into the trash can at the end of the bench. He was regretting blowing up at her now when she'd first called him Johnny, he realised he'd left himself wide open, allowing her to piss him off whenever she pleased.

Beth coaxed Zhu Zhu back into the car. Moments later, they were on their way.

'Next stop Clarksville!' John said.

It was eight o'clock in the morning. Zhu Zhu lay on her tummy with her head resting on her front paws, her tail waving slowly from side to side across the rear window like a slow wiper blade. Soon she was fast asleep.

'We'll have to rig up a curtain or something to stop people from seeing in,' Beth said. 'How long until we reach Clarksville?'

'Depending on how often we have to stop, four-and-a-half, maybe five hours. We'll stop there for lunch then drive straight through to Oklahoma City, which is about the same distance again. Then hopefully find a motel along the highway.'

John drove back onto I-40 West and fixed his eyes on the road ahead. He almost turned the radio on but decided not to after noticing Beth had closed her eyes. Zhu Zhu was sleeping soundly in the back. The weather was fine and clear, and the traffic flow was good so, with a full tank of fuel, he moved into the middle lane and settled down into cruise control.

John's thoughts, while remaining automatically focused on the road ahead, began to wander. Vegas and what he now casually referred to as "the incident" was on his mind for some reason. Then he thought of

Jimmy, his first friend, his GI pal. Where is he now? For a moment, he contemplated getting in touch with his mother on his return to LA, but quickly dismissed it. Instead, he remembered his beloved friend, Mrs Smith, and their exclusive tea drinking rituals. He'd brought his tin of Earl Grey with him and couldn't wait to make a nice cuppa when they were settled into a motel later.

He glanced across at Beth and noticed for the first time that, although she was a pain in the ass, she was also quite attractive. She wore tight jeans and a loose-fitting blouse under a floral-lined denim jacket. Her red hair was not quite shoulder length, and she had a dozen or so small freckles across the bridge of her nose. For some reason she seemed familiar to him, not because she'd strangely appeared in his dreams, which he found totally weird and didn't fully acknowledge, but there was more. He felt as if he knew her. His natural instinct for some reason forced him into a kind of antagonist role. It felt right for him to disagree with just about everything she said. But it was going to be a long trip, so he decided to try extra hard to get along with her.

Tony Lee was also on his mind. It was obvious he'd put a lot of time, money and planning into this operation and John knew he wouldn't give up without a fight. He'd have to be vigilant and ready for trouble if or when they next came face to face. But it was Raymond Brown who worried him the most.

Highway I-40 stretched ahead and shimmered in the mid-morning heat. They'd been travelling for just over two hours and were heading through Arkansas. Beth was fast asleep on the front seat. Zhu Zhu slept soundly in the back.

John's thoughts were interrupted by a low rumbling noise coming from somewhere in the back of the car. Remembering that the car was pretty old, he hoped it would get them to LA. When he heard the noise again, he cocked his head to one side and frowned, struggling to listen over the drone of the old motor. There it was again. This time much louder. It was more of a rumbling, gurgling

The Tiger Chase

sound followed by a short burst of air like a—it happened again, but this time it sounded exactly like what it was.

Without thinking, John turned to look over his shoulder and it hit him full in the face. 'OH MY GOD!' The car swerved violently.

Beth jolted awake and almost hit her head on the roof.

John, coughing and gasping for air as the stench took hold of his taste buds, fumbled for the window switch without success. The tyres screeched and the car weaved into the next lane.

Beth, cupping one hand over her nose and mouth, held down the two front window buttons on the centre console with her other. The windows opened, letting in much-needed fresh air.

John, steering with one hand, stuck his head out of the window and gulped down the dusty highway air.

Beth also took some deep breaths.

Zhu Zhu lay with her head on her paws, looking up innocently, her ears forward.

The air inside the car was thick with the smell of tiger fart, which didn't seem to be dispersing.

John couldn't take it anymore. He pulled off the highway, stopped the car and climbed out. 'What have I done wrong? Why am I being punished like this?' he questioned the sky. The thing he hated most about cats was the smell. And after his past cat experiences, he'd vowed never to be placed in that position again. Yet now, here he was travelling across America with a two-metre long, 115 kilo, shit-stinking cat.

'You shouldn't have fed her all those burgers. It's your own fault, you can't blame her,' Beth said, who was now leaning against the car.

'My fault? How the hell … no … don't bother to answer. The tiger farts and that's my fault. Well, of course it is, how stupid of me,' John yelled, turning away in disgust.

Zhu Zhu stood up in the back of the station wagon and, as she stretched to poke her head out the front window, she farted again. This one was worse than the last.

John had to walk away from the car.

'Come on, baby, out you come,' Beth said, opening the tailgate. 'Smelly girl.' She held her nose while opening the rest of the car doors.

Zhu Zhu jumped down from the tailgate.

Beth followed the tiger closely as it swanked off into some bushes.

John noticed Beth step back and hold her hand to her mouth again. 'You've got to be kidding,' he called over to her. 'All those years of training and look at you.'

Beth pretended not to hear him.

Zhu Zhu bounded from the bushes, somewhat lighter on her feet and cantered around Beth with her tail in the air, chuffing and twitching.

'Oh, there's a good girl. Does that feel better? Yes ... I bet it does ... she's a good girl,' Beth said, unknowingly reminding John of that certain someone again and pissing him off. 'It's time we got moving,' he said, with an exaggerated glance at his watch.

Zhu Zhu, who was now becoming accustomed to the back of the station wagon, jumped straight in without being asked.

John cautiously checked the air before climbing into the driver's seat. 'We should reach Clarksville in a couple of hours. Once there we can find a gas station and somewhere for lunch,' he said when they'd resumed their journey.

'Sounds good, but we're going to need a butcher shop too. Perhaps if we keep a lookout for a small shopping mall or something, we could get everything there,' Beth said.

'But is it going to stink like that every time it eats?' John snapped.

'No ... she must have had an allergic reaction to the burgers. We need to make sure she only eats fresh food from now on. And stop calling her *it*.'

John rocked his head from side to side, silently mimicking her.

36

Becky Cecilia Johnson frowned when her child seat harness chafed her shoulder while she rocked backwards and forwards. 'When are we going to eat, Mummy?' she asked for what could easily have been the hundredth time. She didn't expect an answer; she knew she was being as annoying as only a five-year-old can. She was bored.

Her parents were taking her on their annual trip to Phoenix to visit her grandparents. Her father never spoke while driving, choosing instead to focus completely on the road ahead.

'Mummy, Zhu Zhu says she's hungry too,' Becky said, holding up her Little Princess stuffed toy.

Mummy was asleep—or pretending to be.

Becky's parents had bought the stuffed toy for their daughter's third birthday at the height of tigermania. Becky loved her Little Princess the bestest out of all her toys. Holding it tight she snuggled its face against hers while humming the tune of her favourite song, "The Tiger's Heart". A green station wagon pulled up alongside the Johnson's vehicle. Becky craned her neck to look through the window and smiled at her reflection staring back at her. Then she realised there were two reflections. She looked from one to the other and giggled. 'Look, Zhu Zhu, I can see you,' she said, holding up the stuffed toy. It took a few moments for her young mind to comprehend what she was actually seeing. Holding up the toy to the window, at first she couldn't figure out why she could see her reflection in the eyes of her toy's giant reflection which was looking back at her. Then the penny dropped. 'Mummy, Mummy, look, look—it's The Little Princess.'

Mummy stirred but didn't waken.

'Daddy, Daddy, it's The Little Princess, look!'

Daddy's eyes nervously flicked from the road to the rear-view mirror, then back to the road. He didn't speak.

'Mummy, look!' Becky yelled again.

Zhu Zhu peered back at the little girl from the station wagon and slowly waved her tail. She rubbed her head against the window and chuffed.

Becky waved when the station wagon overtook and pulled away. 'I love you, Little Princess ... I love you!'

37

When the station wagon approached the outskirts of Clarksville, a large sign at the side of the road read: "The Lone Star Shopping Village 20 Miles Ahead".

'Perfect!' Beth said. 'Hopefully we can get everything we need here without having to go near the city.'

Thirty minutes later the small cluster of log-cabin-styled buildings appeared on the horizon to the right of the highway. John took the next exit and drove slowly through the parking lot looking for an inconspicuous place to park. He turned the car 270 degrees after noticing a shaded spot at the edge of the building next to three large dumpsters.

Beth read the various shop signs. 'Cool, there's a butcher shop, a supermarket and a drugstore. Oh, and look, there's even a PetSmart' she exclaimed, while John brought the car to a halt.

Zhu Zhu lay on her tummy fast asleep with one paw over her face.

'Do you want to stay here with Zhu Zhu while I get the groceries, or do you want to go?' Beth asked.

'I'm tired as hell but there's no way I'm staying here with that thing.' John growled.

'Okay Johnny. I'll give you a list of everything we need.'

38

Becky Johnson held her Little Princess doll up so it could see the five-metre-high cowboy that greeted shoppers to the Lone Star Shopping Village.

Mrs Johnson was wakened by the sound of the car slowing.

'Hello, Mummy. You missed The Little Princess.'

'Did I, dear?' Mrs Johnson said while rummaging through her bag.

'Yes. Are we going to have lunch now?'

'We certainly are.'

'Oh goody, goody, I want a burger, I want a burger!' the little girl yelled, catching sight of the colourful playground attached to the burger joint.

A small cheeseburger and fries were a veritable feast to the five year old girl who was actually five and three quarters so was technically six—In her mind. Cramming half the burger in her mouth, she raced outside to the playground with the carton of fries in her hand.

'Play carefully, Becks,' her mother called after her.

The little girl struggled to push open the large glass door then nearly slipped on the vinyl turf that surrounded the yellow spiral slide. The enclosed multi-coloured structure had a platform at the top with a ship's steering wheel and a large abacus on the side.

Becky crammed another handful of fries into her mouth, then puffed and panted and stamped her feet while she climbed the concealed stairway of the slide. When she reached the top, she gazed

The Tiger Chase

over the parking lot trying to hum, chew and breathe all at the same time. Her bulging cheeks rose into a smile when she noticed the green station wagon parked along the fence underneath a large tree. She peered down to where her parents were sitting. Her father was reading one of the complimentary newspapers while her mother sat across the table from him filling out a competition coupon. Becky swallowed with a gulp, threw in another handful of fries then slid down the slide.

An elderly gentleman caught sight of her struggling with the glass door, so he held it open while she passed through. A teenage boy ambling into the building, didn't notice the young girl slip out through the entrance before the door closed behind him.

Once outside, Becky checked on her parents through the window then skipped off in the direction of the station wagon.

On her tiptoes she could just see into the car and made out the orange and black stripes on the tiger's back. Not noticing Beth asleep in the front seat, she tapped on the window, but nothing happened. She tapped again.

Zhu Zhu opened one eye.

'Wake up, Little Princess, wake up,' Becky called out.

Zhu Zhu leapt to her feet. *'GRRREARGH!'* She roared and lunged at the glass.

***

Beth was jolted from a light sleep. She swung round to find Zhu Zhu snarling and growling at something through the window. There was a little girl trembling outside. Beth gently ran her hand through the tiger's fur. 'Calm down, baby, calm down.'

Zhu Zhu continued to snarl and quiver at the little girl.

'It's okay, it's just a little girl.' Beth climbed from the car. 'Hello,' she said to the little girl who was crying. 'Don't cry.'

The little girl looked up at her and sobbed. 'Doesn't Zhu Zhu like me?'

'It's not that she doesn't like you, it's just that she doesn't know you.'

'But I only want to be her friend.' Her little lips trembled.

'I know but you have to remember Zhu Zhu is a very dangerous animal. It takes a long time for her to get used to someone … what's that you've got there under your arm?'

The little girl held up the stuffed Little Princess toy for Beth to see. 'It's Zhu Zhu. My Mummy and Daddy gave it to me for my birthday.'

'Where are your Mummy and Daddy?'

'Over there, eating lunch.'

'And what's your name?'

'Rebecca Cecilia Johnson, but you can call me Becky,' the little girl said, cheering up.

'Well, it's nice to meet you Becky. My name is—'

'You're Doctor Elizabeth Smith although my Mummy says you're not a real doctor, she says you're a vegetarian.'

'A veterinarian,' Beth corrected her gently.

Becky didn't appear to hear her. 'I know everything about you and Zhu Zhu—I'm an official member of The Little Princess Fan Club.'

'That's great.'

'Why is Zhu Zhu cross with me?'

'She's not cross, sweetheart.'

'But in the cartoons and books she is everyone's friend.'

'I know, but they're just stories. I think your parents might be wondering where you are.'

'Yes, I better go.'

'Okay, nice to meet you, Becky.'

'Goodbye, Doctor Smith, it was nice to meet you too. Goodbye Zhu Zhu,' she called over her shoulder, skipping back to her parents.

Beth watched the little girl return to the burger joint. Those blessed cartoons, she thought. It wasn't that she was against them being made, they certainly had brought in valuable revenue to help fund the species' revival program for which she was grateful. No, it

The Tiger Chase

was the content she disagreed with. Zhu Zhu, the cute, humanised cub, a friend to everyone. Zhu Zhu at the beach. Zhu Zhu the pop star. Zhu Zhu saving the world. It really was sending children the wrong messages. She'd fought against the concept. She'd pleaded for more of the documentaries and true-life stories but who was she against the mass-media-marketing-machine. There was nothing she could do about it. The TV shows were syndicated around the world. The DVDs, video games and books had sold by the millions. She couldn't help wondering where all the money was really going.

'Are you sure we need all this stuff?' John said, when he returned, struggling to control the heavily laden shopping cart.

Beth returned from her thoughts as the little girl disappeared into the burger joint. 'Would you rather we feed her burgers?' she replied, holding her nose and waving her hand in front of her face.

John shook his head and drew a sharp intake of breath.

He'd managed to get almost everything on Beth's list: joints of beef, lamb, pork, two chickens, fresh liver, and three sheep's brains. And the butcher happily threw in a couple of large marrowbones for John's big dog, free of charge.

'And what about—'

'Patience. I'm getting to that.' At the supermarket he'd purchased eggs, dried brewer's yeast, two boxes of natural bran, and a large cooler box to store the meat in. From the drugstore he'd bought a family-sized bottle of multi-vitamin and minerals, some soy meal and oats.

'Well done. Did you get us anything?' Beth asked.

'Chinese.'

'Cool. I just need to feed Zhu Zhu first,' Beth said.

John pointed to an area at the side of the building. 'There.'

Beth pushed the shopping trolly while John reversed the station wagon into a deserted loading bay.

Beth cautiously opened the back of the car and let Zhu Zhu sit on the tailgate. 'There you go, baby, some real food,' she said, handing Zhu Zhu some of the meat.

Zhu Zhu wolfed down two large joints of meat and some of the fresh liver.

Beth mixed a half dozen eggs with soy, bran, brewer's yeast, one of the sheep's brains, and some crushed vitamin tablets. She tut-tutted when Zhu Zhu gulped it all down. 'Naughty girl.'

John and Beth ate their Chinese food, and within a few minutes they were back on the highway.

39

The early evening traffic was dense as they reached the outskirts of Oklahoma City. It had been a long hot day. John was tired. Zhu Zhu had slept all afternoon. Beth had catnapped most of the way, which John was glad for. He hadn't felt much like talking. They'd travelled almost five hundred miles.

John suggested they leave the highway before the traffic got any worse, find a motel close by and hopefully sneak the thing in without anyone noticing. Fifteen minutes later, they spotted a Holiday Inn sign and took the next exit. 'Damn!' John cursed. The traffic on the smaller road was even thicker than on the highway. It took another fifteen minutes to reach the motel.

When they finally pulled into the driveway, Beth jumped out of the car and, feeling refreshed, headed for the reception.

John climbed wearily from the driver's side, stretched his shoulder blades together, and took a long deep breath through his nose.

Five minutes later, Beth came skipping out of the building twirling a key ring on one of her fingers. 'There's good news ... and there's bad news,' she said.

'What's the bad news?'

'No ... you're supposed to say, "Great, what's the good news?" To which I'd reply, "We've got a room for the night. Yay" And then you'd say, "Cool! What's the bad news?" And I'd say, "They only had one room, so we'll have to share,"' Beth said, sounding like a kindergarten teacher.

John looked horrified. 'So, I've got to sleep in the same room as the cat?'

Beth winced and nodded.

'Great, just great!'

The motel was small, but it had good amenities: a restaurant, a pool, self-contained apartments, a laundry, and undercover parking. They were able to park the car directly outside their room, which made it easy to smuggle Zhu Zhu in through the front door.

'Bummer!' John said, entering the room.

Beth searched his face for an explanation.

'Well ... there's good news, and there's bad news.' He adopted the same patronising tone Beth had used earlier. 'The bad news for you is that there's only one bed, so you're sleeping on the floor. And the good news for me is because I've been driving all day, I'm sleeping in the bed.'

'Okay, Johnny.'

John sauntered across the room and went for a shower.

Although he was forced to bend beneath the small chrome showerhead, which gave out more of a trickle than a jet of hot water, and the cold vinyl curtain kept sticking to his legs, John felt reasonably refreshed after his shower and decided to have a shave. He peeked round the bathroom door to see Beth giggling at Zhu Zhu. The tiger was on the bed lying on her back with her hind legs in the air. 'That's Johnnie's bed, you'll be in trouble.'

'Uh hm,' John cleared his throat pretending not to hear when he bounded from the bathroom with a towel around his waist. 'Left my bag in the car.'

On a coffee table by the TV set was a neatly arranged fan of brochures and booklets. Beth picked up the house menu and read it aloud when John returned.

'Sounds good,' John said.

'Which bit?'

'All of it.'

'Listen, thanks for driving today. How about I shout you a nice juicy steak.'

'Yeah, why not.'

After John had finished in the bathroom, Beth took a shower.

Zhu Zhu lay in the same position fast asleep.

'Make the most of it, pussy, cause you're not sleeping there tonight,' John mumbled sitting on the edge of the bed and pulling on his socks.

No reservations were required at the restaurant. They agreed that Zhu Zhu would be okay in the room as she was already asleep.

John, although tired, enjoyed a large char-grilled T-bone swilled down with a cold beer.

Beth chose a healthier meal of roast chicken with boiled vegetables and gravy, with freshly squeezed orange juice to drink. 'So where are you from, John?' she asked, breaking an uncomfortable silence.

'I'm from Arcadia, which is—'

'I know where Arcadia is.'

'Right ... well that's where I'm from, but now I live in downtown LA.'

'And are you married?'

'No ... yes ... well ...'

'You are or you aren't?' Beth said, loading her fork with salad.

'It's kind of embarrassing but it all happened a couple of months ago.'

Beth gestured with raised eyebrows for John to continue while flicking her fingers to grab the waiter's attention.

The beer was making John relax. 'Thanks to our friend, Tony Lee, I got suspended from work. I guess you could say I lost it for a while.'

Beth, gaining the waiter's attention, pointed to John's almost empty beer.

'Anyway, I was ordered to take three weeks off. I didn't have a clue what I was going to do with myself. I was desperately out of shape and emotionally at an all-time low. Before I knew it, I was in a bar trying to drown my sorrows. Then for some reason I got this crazy notion that I should go to Las Vegas. I saw a billboard across the street from the bar that said: 'Luck at Las Vegas.' I liked the clever word play.

'This started me thinking about *my* luck and my life. Spontaneity isn't one of my stronger points but, "What the hell," I said and found myself on a flight to Vegas the next day. I booked into the Bellagio.'

'Wow, that's spontaneous.'

'Yeah, I'd never been to Vegas before and I can tell you when I arrived in that town and checked into my suite, I felt like a million dollars. For the first time in my life, I felt free, you know ... free to do whatever I wanted.

That night I hit the town—dinner and show at Caesars Palace, a couple of bars. Inevitably I ended up in a casino, tried my hand at Blackjack, then settled down in the piano bar. By this time, I'd had a lot to drink. Feeling kind of spacey, I noticed a young woman giving me the eye. She was a dead ringer for Scarlett Johansson, or at least in my slightly inebriated perception she was. We got chatting and, for some reason, I took on the role of the happy-comical-drunk. She spent most of the evening giggling.

'We seemed to be getting on really well, you know ... laughing a lot. Her name was Nancy Rawlings. She told me how she was a dancer and that she'd performed all over the world. God, I must have been wasted. It was obviously all bull. I couldn't see through it, though. Guess I was smitten.

'We talked all night. We rode an open-top, double-decker bus and we held hands and kissed. Then before I knew it, we were standing at the altar of The Joining Hearts Wedding Chapel.'

'You're kidding?'

'No.'

'Don't tell me ... Elvis was there, right?'

John blushed. His beer arrived. He downed it in one.

Beth ordered him another.

'We got married and stayed in my hotel room for a week. For the second week we did pretty much the same, apart for some sightseeing.

The Tiger Chase

We flew over the Hoover Dam and the Grand Canyon in a helicopter. You know, touristy things like that.

'When it was finally time to return to LA, we realised we had done the wrong thing and decided to end it there and then.'

'As simple as that?'

'As simple as that!'

'Why?'

'We just weren't right for each other, that's all.'

'Come on, there must be more to it.'

'Nope.'

Beth probed him further after applying more beer. 'So, tell me, John, why do you hate cats so much?'

'Well, there was an incident when I was a kid, but I don't like to talk about it.' He was beginning to slur now.

'Tell me.'

'No.'

'Tell me.'

John gave in and told her about the incident in his garden with the ginger tomcat.

Beth laughed. 'But that's no reason to hate cats ... are you sure there isn't more?'

'Jeez, you doctors are all the same.' He paused and looked down at his drink.

Beth remained silent sensing there were more revelations to come.

'No, it's nothing, really.'

'Oh, come on, you can tell me.'

'Well, it's to do with Nancy.'

'There's more? She had a cat?'

John chuckled and shook his head. 'We didn't actually split in Vegas. When our honeymoon was drawing to a close, we had to talk about our future. Nancy seemed to get edgy whenever I brought up the topic. I suspected she was hiding something. We finally decided that I would go back to LA first and find a bigger apartment while Nancy tied up all her loose ends in Vegas.

It was difficult to find a place, especially when Nancy insisted on it being on the ground floor. Eventually I got one though.

On the Thursday of that week I was scheduled for an early meeting with my captain. Then Nancy informed me that she would be arriving on Thursday morning from Vegas. I couldn't cancel my meeting, so we arranged to leave the key with the elderly couple who lived next door. I gave Nancy the address. She would be settled in by the time I got home.'

'All sounds great so far. What happened?'

'Well, there were a few things about her life that she'd forgotten to tell me. I didn't get back until later than expected. I'd been told that I'd have to undergo a full medical on the Monday before I could start back at work.

When I got home, Nancy was waiting for me at the door. We kissed and cuddled for ages there outside and I got the feeling she didn't want me to go into the apartment. Then she says, "There's something I've been meaning to tell you about myself, Johnny." She always called me Johnny.

'*Oh my god*, I thought, *she must have kids and been too embarrassed to tell me*. This sent me into a bit of a spin, I can tell you. I'd never even considered children in the equation. But after a few moments, I calmed down and we went into the apartment. Before we went through the front door, however, she insisted that I close my eyes. She even clasped her hands around my head so I couldn't peek.' John took a long drink from his beer and grimaced as the memories returned.

'How many kids did she have?' Beth asked eagerly.

'Not kids.'

'Huh?'

'Not kids ... cats!'

'Cats?'

'Cats ... twelve of the damn things.'

Beth cupped her hand to her mouth trying not to laugh.

'They were all over the apartment, swinging on the plants, shitting on the floor, making a hell of a noise and one hell of a stink.'

'What did you do?'

'I stormed out of the apartment to get some air. Nancy followed me. She tried to assure me that I'd grow to love them, but I can tell you there was no way. I told her there and then, the cats had to go! She started to cry. She said how sorry she was and that she would try to find them new homes in the morning. That wasn't good enough for me, so I stayed at McGuire's for the night.'

'Did she get rid of them?'

'No. When I returned to the apartment the next day she was gone. A few days later I got divorce papers from her lawyer in Vegas.'

'Wow, she must have really loved her cats.'

'I realised afterwards that I didn't know anything about Nancy Rawlings.'

'Do you miss her?'

'No!'

'So that's why you hate cats.'

'That's why I hate cats.'

'I still get the feeling there's more.'

'That's enough about me. Tell me about you. How come you never got married?'

'Never found Mr Right.'

John gulped his beer and nodded for her to continue.

'Oh, there's nothing to tell really. I'm from LA. I studied to be a vet, worked in different zoos then went to China.'

'Pretty boring.'

'Yes, I suppose I am.' Her expression cooled.

'Tell me more about China,' John said, changing the subject.

Beth told him about Blue Tiger Mountain and Huan Loh. John listened, fascinated, while she described her adventures.

The evening turned out to be surprisingly pleasant for them both and, as the waiter patiently hovered round trying to look busy, they decided it was time to check on Zhu Zhu. They strolled back towards their room. The air was warm and the full moon hung directly overhead reflecting off the calm surface of the swimming pool.

'I know somebody who would really enjoy a swim right now,' Beth said, mischievously.

'Cats don't swim. Everyone knows that,' John slurred.

'Tigers do. They love the water.'

'Yeah? Well, I wouldn't mind a swim myself.' He looked round to see if there was anyone about.

Beth watched in surprise while John weaved towards the pool, stripping as he went. By the time he reached the edge of the water, he was down to his jocks, and after one last glance round, he dived in.

The water was cool, exhilarating and cleansing. The white moonlight illuminated the tiny bubbles that rushed from his outstretched fingertips as he drifted along the bottom of the pool. He resurfaced, wiped his fringe from his eyes and swam back to the edge. 'Are you coming in?' he shouted. But there was no reply. Lifting himself up, he rested his elbows on the side of the pool. Beth was nowhere to be seen. Allowing himself to slip back under, he pushed off the side with his feet and dived to the bottom. The cool water seemed to flush away the alcohol in his system. He drifted back to the surface and floated face down with his arms and legs stretched out to the sides. The water suddenly dispersed, and a wave came crashing over him. Something heavy had landed in the middle of the pool. John sucked in a mouthful of water and struggled to lift his head for air.

Zhu Zhu swam towards the side of the pool with her head high and her front paws slapping the water.

There was a scream and then another splash. Beth—attempting a dive—had tripped and belly flopped, slapping the pool surface.

John laughed when she resurfaced and, just as she was about to chastise him, he splashed her with his open palms.

Beth splashed him back.

John splashed back harder.

Zhu Zhu turned and headed towards them, panting and whining while she swam. When she reached Beth, she playfully placed her paws on her shoulders and licked the side of her face.

The Tiger Chase

John climbed from the pool, took a run and jumped as far as he could, tucking his arms and legs in close to his body, landing like a bomb in front of them.

Beth squealed and tried to turn away, but Zhu Zhu held her firmly.

John bobbed up and pushed both their heads down with his hands.

Beth took a deep breath and, being freed from the tiger's grip, dived down to the bottom of the pool, turned back to where John was treading water, grabbed hold of his feet and pulled him under.

John played dead and slowly drifted back to the surface.

Beth swam to the other side of the pool.

Meanwhile, Zhu Zhu decided she'd had enough and tried unsuccessfully to negotiate the high pool wall. She kicked with her hind legs and lunged out of the water, clawing at the wet tiles with her front paws, only to slip back down.

Beth, hearing her whines, swam over and tried to push her from behind. 'Give us a hand, you big lug,' she called over to John.

John climbed from the pool and sauntered round to where Zhu Zhu was now panicking.

Zhu Zhu lunged her body upwards.

John grabbed hold of the thick fur around her neck and pulled.

Beth pushed from behind.

John strained and grunted. He leaned back and pulled harder. Suddenly, all 115 kilos of wet tiger came bursting out of the water and bowled him over. His head hit the tiles hard. Zhu Zhu landed on top of him.

Beth rushed from the pool.

Zhu Zhu planted a rough lick on John's cheek.

'Arrrgh, get off me, you overgrown rug,' John yelled. His mood had completely changed by the time Beth tugged on Zhu Zhu's fur and pulled her off him. He struggled to his feet, grabbed his clothing and stormed back to the room.

Beth patted Zhu Zhu on the head and giggled like a nervous schoolgirl. 'Come on, baby, it's time for bed.'

40

Anticipating the kind of reaction he would receive when he told his boss of the news, Steven Tang hesitated before pressing the last digit on his cell phone—and he was right. Tony Lee screamed down the phone at him.

'What the hell am I paying you for? All you had to do was locate them, then call us. Is that too much to ask?'

'No, sir, but you must understand there are two thousand miles of highway and—'

'Who the hell do you think you're talking to? I don't need to hear excuses. Stay where you are; we're coming out!' Tony yelled, before hanging up.

Steven poured himself a large brandy. *Surely, they realised they'd given him an impossible task,* he thought, finishing his drink. He'd driven straight through from Tennessee to Arizona and now stood exhausted in his executive motel room, trembling at the thought of his boss's wrath.

Forty-five minutes later, an R44 Raven helicopter landed on the motel helipad. Tony Lee, Raymond Brown and Doctor Jiang climbed down and hurried across the tarmac. They headed for room 133 where Steven Tang nervously waited.

Tony entered the room first, followed by Doctor Jiang, then Raymond Brown, who now wore a black patch over his right eye. 'I'm very disappointed in you, Tang … you've let me down,' Tony said, lighting one of his large Cuban cigars.

The Tiger Chase

'But Mr Lee, I've driven straight through from Tennessee as you instructed. I can assure you I didn't see them, so they must still be on their way.'

'Tell me something I don't know, fool. And tell me why you've driven all this way on the highway when you were specifically told to look for them on the small roads.'

'Mr Lee, surely it is obvious that they would use the highway. It would take them weeks otherwise.'

'Obvious? What are you implying, Tang, that I'm stupid?'

'No, Mr Lee, no, I didn't mean that at all. It's just an impossible task that you have given me.'

'You know what, Steven? You've gotten lazy. You sat in your car and drove all this way with your head up your ass. No wonder you didn't see them.'

'No, sir, I looked. Honestly, I did.'

'You were good in Hong Kong, but I bring you to America and this is how you repay me.' Exasperated, he glanced at Raymond Brown and nodded.

41

Raymond Brown stepped forward. Enjoying the fear in his victims' eyes, he moved towards the larger man, tensing his upper body muscles one by one, clenching his fists and cracking his knuckles.

Steven Tang dropped his glass and backed off towards the wall. 'Please, I'll go back out ... I'll find them ... just give me one more chance.'

Raymond stood directly in front of him. A deep, slow, growl began to roll up from his diaphragm. '*Kill him!*' his father demanded.

Steven Tang must have figured he had nothing to lose. He threw a half-hearted punch.

Raymond didn't even bother to block it. The punch landed on his chin with no effect. However, in the split second that Tang was left outstretched, unbalanced and wide open, Brown twisted at the waist and pounced with a thunderous left uppercut to the big man's heart. A loud *CRACK!* rang out when Tang's sternum split in two.

Raymond smiled, staring into Tang's desperate bulging eyes. He paused for a moment, twisted back in the opposite direction then followed through with a right uppercut. This time his fist smashed through Tang's left rib cage. Tang doubled over and spluttered.

Instead of retracting his fist, Raymond pushed it deeper into the man's rupturing internal organs. '*Yes!*' his father hissed. '*Yes, yes, yes!*' Grabbing Tang's hair with his left hand, Raymond lifted his head so he could once again look into his eyes. Blood poured from Tang's mouth.

The veins in Raymond's neck contracted and throbbed and his good eye narrowed. Suddenly, his open right hand shot forward, and the hard heel of his palm smashed up through Tang's nose, driving cartilage and bone into his brain.

Tang's neck snapped backwards, and his lifeless body fell to the floor.

'Bravo ... bravo!' Tony Lee cheered, clapping.

Doctor Jiang looked away with a worried expression.

'Okay, let's get out of here,' Tony said, marching towards the door.

'But what about Mister Tang?' Doctor Jiang said.

'Don't worry, doctor, my people will take care of the mess. Perhaps you would do better concentrating on the task ahead and thinking about what happens to people who fail me.'

'Yes, of course, forgive me. What do we do now?'

'We let the tiger chase begin!'

42

John lay on his back somewhere in that twilight place between sleep and awake. Although his eyes were shut, he sensed it was early. His wife, Nancy, was laying next to him still asleep, her arm resting over his chest, her breath warming his cheek. He didn't understand why she was there. It didn't matter. Her body was warm against his. He ran his fingers through her soft hair. She responded and gave him a wet kiss on his cheek. He kissed her back. She squeezed him tighter and gave him a rough lick on his cheek. Her hot breath smelt kind of meaty. John opened his eyes. Two golden orbs stared back at him. 'NO!' he yelled, flinging the tiger's paw from his chest and jumping out of bed. 'Get the hell off me!'

Beth, sitting upright with a blanket up to her neck on the uncomfortable lounge chair, giggled.

John realised she'd been awake, watching. 'What the hell are you laughing at?' he yelled, struggling to pull on his pants. 'Why are you doing this to me? You know I hate cats.'

'Doing what? I was just sitting here snoozing when you two started getting it on,' Beth said, trying to control her laughter.

John looked at his watch. 'Let's get out of here.'

It was 4.45 am. The weather was crisp and clear, and the dawn chorus held centre stage. Beth peered cautiously out of the front door to make sure there was no one around then beckoned Zhu Zhu and John to follow her. She led the tiger to a small, shaded, garden area that was situated on the far side of the swimming pool.

The Tiger Chase

John reluctantly brought the meat and eggs from the fridge and the rest of the supplies from the car.

Beth expertly mixed the ingredients for the tiger's breakfast then sat back and watched while it was devoured in a matter of moments.

When they finally crept back to the room, they quickly packed their bags and got ready to leave.

'Wait,' Beth said. 'We need a curtain or something to hide her with.'

On the wall behind the bed was a wide, half height window close to the ceiling with a lace curtain across it. There were narrower versions in the bathroom and kitchenette.

'We'll send them back when we get to LA,' John said, reaching for the curtains over the bed.

Beth removed the ones from the bathroom and kitchenette and within fifteen minutes John had fixed them on the inside of the station wagon's rear windows.

'Perfect. You can see out, but you can only see in if you get up really close,' John said, admiring his handiwork.

Breakfast would be another quick stop. They decided to look for a highway gas station cum diner. Driving out of the motel and back towards highway 1-40, the first sign they saw read: Gas Station and Diner.

John took charge. 'I'll get the gas and food, you stay in the car with the thing.'

'Okay, Johnny,' Beth said, using a Marilyn Monroe voice for the extra comeback value.

43

Beth opened the window to let in some fresh air while John disappeared through the sliding glass doors of the gas station. Not having slept much last night, she closed her eyes.

'Okay, lady, get out of the car!'

Startled, Beth opened her eyes to find herself looking up into the face of a scruffy teenage boy holding a knife.

'I said get out of the car!' the youth bawled.

Beth could see from his shaking hand that he was nervous. She noticed his clothing, scrunched up and dirty but good quality. His hair was stylishly long. His face was pimply and pale. In an instance she'd analysed him: Just a kid. Been to an out-of-town party. Spent or lost his money. Slept rough. Desperate to get home.

'If you don't get out of the car, lady, I'm gonna cut you. Don't try me.'

'Ah, you're not going do that, and believe me, you really don't want me to get out of the car,' Beth said calmly.

The boy scowled and began to twitch. 'Look, lady, I don't want any trouble. I just need your car … get out.' He reached through the window with his other arm and grabbed Beth's shoulder.

'Okay … okay, I'm coming, but don't say I didn't warn you,' Beth said, opening the door and stepping out.

The boy ran around the car and climbed into the driver's side. He cussed when he realised the keys weren't in the ignition and was about to yell at Beth when the back of his neck felt strangely hot. There was somebody in the back. With the knife held tightly in his hand, he spun around.

The Tiger Chase

'*GRRREARGH!*' Zhu Zhu lurched forward. Her open jaws almost enclosed the boy's head, and a burst of foul-smelling breath swept his hair back like streamers on an electric fan.

'Arrrgh!' He stared in terror at the gaping mouth and the giant, bone-crunching teeth that dripped and quivered millimetres from his face. Squealing like a girl, he sprang backwards out of the car, bumped his head, dropped the knife, and pissed his pants.

Beth couldn't help but laugh at the way he looked at her in disbelief from across the roof of the car. His face was deathly white, his eyes were glazed, and his bottom lip quivered. He reminded her of one of the fairground clown heads that oscillated with their mouths open, waiting for a ball to be thrown in. He bolted blindly, ran head-on into the gas pump ... *Dong!* ... and landed flat on his back. Disorientated, he lay on the ground for a moment. Then he jumped to his feet and took off towards the street.

Zhu Zhu gave out another loud roar.

The boy whimpered and almost fell again, scrambling to get away.

John returned carrying bagels, flavoured milk and chips. 'What are you looking so coy about?' he asked Beth as he climbed back into the car.

'Oh, nothing, I see we have yet *another* healthy breakfast,' Beth said, eyeing the chips.

John slammed the car door behind him. 'Okay, from now on you can choose breakfast, lunch and dinner. How's that?'

'Fine!'

'Fine!'

When they were back on the highway, Beth checked the GPS map on her cell phone. The next stretch of their journey would take them to Amarillo. After that they'd continue on and hopefully reach Santa Fe by late evening. It would be another long day.

Oklahoma City became a part of the early morning haze when Beth glanced over her shoulder.

John set the car in cruise control and turned on the radio.

'Did you love Nancy?' Beth asked after a speechless hour.

John seemed to snap out of a trance. 'What?'

'Nancy ... did you love her?'

Oh God, he suddenly remembered he'd told her about Nancy and the cats the night before. 'I thought I did but in retrospect I guess it was just lust. What about you, have you ever been in love?'

'No, never,' Beth said blushing. 'Except for my job and the animals I care for. There's been no time for a social life.' Beth began to reminisce. She spoke of her time at high school and of college, her likes and dislikes and her hopes for the future. 'I know it's hard for someone like you to understand but the plight of the South China tiger has to remain at the front of people's minds before it's too late. If only we could get the idea across that tiger parts are useless as medicines and that it's our foolish acts that have driven this subspecies far closer to extinction than most of the other endangered species.

When we think of whales and dolphins being slaughtered for our selfish needs, we become angry and appalled, and when we hear of people buying ivory goods, we ask ourselves why is this still being allowed to take place? When we see tigers on TV or in articles, they're usually Bengal or Siberian. Yes, they are also endangered and need our help and, thanks to the efforts of many dedicated people, their plights are being recognised, but when it comes to the South China tiger, which just happens to be the ancestor of all tigers, most people have never even heard of them.'

'So, what's the answer?'

'We need to bring to people's attention the fact that in places such as Vietnam, tigers are still publicly baited and slaughtered. If the people who buy tiger products could be re-educated and convinced of the many cheaper and more effective alternatives—'

'Viagra?'

'Sure ... scientifically proven to work, why not? Ninety-nine per cent of the products made from tiger derivatives and other endangered species are fake; this is a fact. If we don't do something soon for the South China tiger, it's going to be too late.'

'You really feel strongly about this, don't you?' John said.

'I'd be willing to dedicate my life to their cause.' Beth turned and stroked Zhu Zhu's fur.

John hunched up and looked down at the sleeping hulk through his rear-view mirror.

'You've got to admit it, she is cute,' Beth said.

'Cute, my ass!'

***

The journey continued. Beth closed her eyes but couldn't sleep. She could hear John getting annoyed with the radio when it began to lose its signal. He was pressing the buttons impatiently until he found a station. She was surprised when he settled for a classical music station. The Baroques? She peeked at him through half-open eyes to see him almost in a trance, obviously enjoying the music.

They ate lunch sitting on the hood of the car, hidden by trees at the side of a small river, near Amarillo. This time Beth had insisted on healthy salad sandwiches and fruit. She giggled at Zhu Zhu, who was lying on her back, stretching and wiggling in the long grass. 'She can do tricks you know.'

'Yeah, right.'

'Yes, she can ... do you wanna see her dance?'

'Not really.'

Beth slid off the hood and beckoned to the tiger, wiggling her hips. 'Come on, baby, dance with me ... come on.'

Zhu Zhu's ears shot up. Her eyes darted and her body twitched while she watched Beth moving from side to side. She sprang to her feet, reared up onto her hind legs and, as if walking on stilts, moved precariously forward and backwards, keeping her balance with her tail waving and her tongue hanging out.

'Yeah, baby!' Beth took Zhu Zhu's front paws and placed them on her shoulders. Then, with the tiger towering over her, she hummed the Vienna Waltz as they danced. 'Okay, now watch this,' Beth said after the dance. 'Zhu Zhu, sit … Zhu Zhu, lie down … Zhu Zhu, roll over … good girl! Zhu Zhu, play dead.'

Zhu Zhu rolled onto her back, closed her eyes and lay with her legs in the air and her mouth open.

'Good girl. Zhu Zhu, dying fly.'

Zhu Zhu moved her legs back and forth.

'Good girl … all right, Zhu Zhu, sit … now, Zhu Zhu, puppy dog.'

Zhu Zhu sat up and the end of her tail wagged while she shuffled on her backside and chuffed; only this time she chuffed in short sharp bursts like dog barks.

'You gotta be kidding.'

'Good girl … she's a good girl. So, what do you think?' Beth asked, patting and stroking Zhu Zhu.

'Not exactly Lassie, is it?'

Beth carried on fussing over Zhu Zhu. 'Take no notice of Johnny; he's just a grumpy old sour puss.'

'I thought tigers were supposed to be ferocious,' John said.

'They are. A wild tiger is one of the fiercest animals on Earth. Even a captive, tame, tiger can turn on its keeper without warning. I grow concerned and angry when I hear of tigers being kept as pets. I look forward to the day when the law is changed, not only in this country but around the world, to prevent people from buying exotic animals. You can't extract an instinctive killer from a natural environment and then expect to train it to act like a pussycat. It just doesn't work that way. I get so pissed off when I read that a big cat, caged in a back yard, has attacked someone, and then the animal is to blame because someone has lost an arm or worse, their life. At the end of the day, it's the ego of the person who owns the animal that should be to blame, but until the law is changed this kind of thing will continue.'

'But aren't you being just a little bit hypocritical here? You just had it doing tricks for God's sake.'

The Tiger Chase

'I guess it could look that way, but Zhu Zhu is special. Did you know that of all the tiger subspecies, the South China tiger is impossible to train? Chinese circuses gave up trying to use them years ago because they were too ferocious.'

'So how did *you* train *it?*'

'I didn't. And stop calling her *it*. We just seem to have this amazing bond. Zhu Zhu isn't an ordinary tiger ... but to answer your question, yes, all tigers are ferocious. When you see a tiger interacting with a handler at a zoo, you have to remember that the handler is a highly trained professional, and even they know that their lives are at risk every time they come into contact with the animal.' Beth sat back on the hood of the car next to John and bit into a big shiny red apple.

Zhu Zhu strolled to the back of the vehicle, jumped onto the roof then lay on her tummy like a sphinx.

'If they could see me now,' John said, shaking his head.

'John, you were telling me about Nancy's cats last night and why you hated them.'

'I was?'

'Yeah, but you cut it short.'

'How do you know I cut it short?'

Beth shrugged and grinned.

'You should be a goddamn shrink.'

'Perhaps I am.'

'When I said I stayed the night at McGuire's, that wasn't true. I actually stayed the night in the apartment.'

'With all the cats?'

'Yep ... it's strange, but until that night, I hadn't noticed how annoying Nancy's voice was. "What's the matter, Johnny, don't you like my pussies?"'

Beth laughed at John's impression of his ex-wife.

'And she had stupid names for all the cats—Tigger and Monty and JZ and God knows what else. And she used to say: "It's all right, babies, mommy's here." It just about drove me up the wall.'

'So, what happened next?'

'There were incidents that night. I'd moved into the apartment a few days earlier; it was all new, you know? It had that fresh new smell. I really liked it. The first thing I did when I unpacked was to frame the photo of my father, my prized possession, and place it on a shelf over the TV. Then I unpacked my third prized possession, my teapot, and made a nice cup of tea. I was totally relaxed at that time. I didn't have a care in the world.'

'What's your second prized possession?'

John frowned. 'Do you wanna hear about the cats or not?'

'Sorry.' Beth took another loud crunchy bite from her apple.

'When I came back to the apartment from my meeting with the captain and saw all the cats for the first time, I just about freaked. I mean, there were twelve of them with twelve kitty litter boxes set up against one wall and all the windows and doors were closed.'

'Poohey.'

'Yeah, that's right, and the damn cats were everywhere—sprawled across the bed, on the furniture, in the kitchen. You can imagine the noise. But then I noticed she'd set up photos of them all round the place and to my horror, she'd replaced the picture of my father with a picture of a big fat—'

'Cat,' Beth said finishing his sentence.

'Where's the picture of my father? I yelled. "Oh, that old thing. I threw it out, Johnny." As you can imagine, I was pissed. I rushed down to the basement, climbed into the dumpster beneath the garbage shoots and began to sift through the garbage.'

'Did you find it?'

'No, I recognised the brand of bin bags that I'd bought a few days earlier and started to tear them open. One was heavy and jammed, so I pulled it hard. The bag split open, and I realised it was full of used kitty litter.'

'You don't mean?'

'I do ... I was covered from head to toe in cat shit.'

Beth tried not to laugh while John continued.

'I go through about half a dozen bags, when I hear a voice from above, "Is this what you're looking for, Johnny?" I look up to see

Nancy peering through the garbage shoot hatch above me. She had the photo in her hand. I remember yelling at the top of my lungs then jumping out of the dumpster and falling flat on my face. See that scar there?' He pointed to a small gash just below the hairline of his forehead. 'Jeez, did it bleed!'

'So, she hadn't thrown the photo away?'

'It was screwed up in the wastepaper bin.'

'What happened then?'

'I stormed back to the apartment. I didn't say a word to her; just headed straight for the shower.

'When I got to the bathroom and started peeling off my slimy clothes, I look up to see a big grey and white cat lying across the top of the shower rail, kind of like a lion on a branch. The damn thing spits and lashes out with its claw.'

'Did it scratch you?'

'No, but at this point, I was naked. I jumped back and slipped on the floor, thanks to Nancy for leaving wet towels all over the place, and I cracked the back of my head hard on the toilet.' He took hold of Beth's hand, lifted it to his head and stroked her finger across a small ridge on his crown. 'Yet another cat scar!'

'But didn't you say you slept the night?'

'Yeah, in the spare room. And to top it off, I had another one of those damn strange dreams that night.'

'Strange dreams?' Beth asked, her expression becoming serious.

'I think it's time to go.'

'Tell me about your dreams.'

Blushing, John ignored her and slid off the hood. 'Let's get the thing back in the car and get the hell out of here.'

The rest of the day was like the previous day—long, hot and boring. Beth catnapped again while Zhu Zhu slept all the way.

By the time they reached Santa Fe, it was already dark, and John was exhausted. When he drove off the highway, he complained of having a numb backside and told Beth to look out for a motel.

Zhu Zhu was now wide awake and rested her head between the two front seats. Luckily, John didn't notice a large bead of drool drip from her panting tongue and land on his sleeve.

Beth tried to draw Zhu Zhu's attention to her side, but as she did so, the tiger shook its head and dislodged a splodge of hot slaver, which hit John in the face.

The car swerved.

'Ohhh—myyyy—Godddd!' John tried to wipe his eyes with one hand and spat when he tasted the thick snot on his lip.

Once again Beth struggled to suppress her laughter but, realising John was tired, she pushed Zhu Zhu's head into the back of the car and handed John a tissue. 'You're a naughty girl, Zhu Zhu,' she said, turning back to the tiger.

John wiped his face then glared at the road ahead without saying a word.

The Motel on the Park was exactly what its name implied: a large, country-style motel on the edge of a forty-acre park with a lake and botanical gardens. The apartments were spacious, air conditioned and had two double bedrooms.

After Beth had checked them in, she directed John to drive slowly through the wooded driveway while she looked for the apartment called Poinsettia—the apartments had names of plants rather than numbers. When they finally found it and let themselves in, John headed straight for the nearest bedroom and flopped on the king-sized bed. Moments later, he was fast asleep.

Beth opened the curtains, which almost covered the whole wall in the dining area, then unlocked and opened the large sliding door that led out onto the park. She slid through the doorway and closed the door behind her. Crickets, keeping time with the skipping, and automatic sprinklers were the only sounds. The rest of the apartments seemed to be empty. She checked to see if there was anyone in the park. When she was sure there wasn't, she opened the door and allowed Zhu Zhu to step out. 'Come on, baby, let's go for a walk,' she whispered.

The Tiger Chase

Zhu Zhu padded beside her like an obedient dog and the two strolled into the dark. After a quick run through the park and dodging the sprinklers, they returned to the apartment.

Beth gave Zhu Zhu a hug and made a bed for her on the floor with a pile of spare blankets from the linen cupboard. After another hug, she whispered goodnight and retired to her room.

As soon as Beth climbed into bed, she heard the tiger saunter off towards John's bedroom and push her way through the half-open bedroom door. She had to smile when she heard the bedsprings creak under Zhu Zhu climbing onto the bed. But then her expression changed when she thought she heard John say: 'Goodnight, Beth.'

44

Tony Lee stayed up late into the night pondering over the route from Tennessee to LA on an iPad.

Doctor Jiang sat by his side but was unable to offer any suggestions, so he merely nodded and agreed with everything Tony said.

'Let's just say they've been cunning and told us they were in Oklahoma when they were actually still in Luciville. And let's say they're not driving straight through but stopping off as they go. What do you think, doc? Does that sound more feasible to you?'

'Yes, we have to remember they've got a full-grown tiger with them. There's no way they could drive two thousand miles without stopping.'

'Okay, so let's say they drove to Oklahoma on the first day then stayed overnight. Then on the second day, which is today, they've driven all the way through to Santa Fe.'

'That's still a big drive.'

'Yes, but this is John Dean we're talking about. He'll want to get back as soon as possible. So, my guess is …' He followed the road map on the screen with his finger then brought it to rest at Santa Fe. '… they're here.' He threw the iPad down onto his desk with a decisive look on his face.

The doctor nodded then winced when he heard Raymond Brown outside smashing wooden planks with his head.

45

The next morning, John awoke startled. He knew at once without looking that the large bulk lying beside him was Zhu Zhu. Turning his head, he squinted to find himself looking directly into her eyes. Before he could curse, she released a mighty lick that caught him the length of his face and flicked into his mouth.

'Hey, no tonguies, get out of here.' John jumped out of bed and quickly rinsed his face with cold water.

Zhu Zhu stayed on the bed and watched him dress.

John crept from the bedroom and looked in on Beth. She was still asleep. It was 5.00 am.

Zhu Zhu had followed him out of his room and sat by the patio doors. She shuffled and whined as if asking to be let out.

'Okay, I'll take you out, but you better behave yourself.' He let her out of the doorway after first going out himself and making sure there was no one around. Zhu Zhu bounced onto the grass and trotted into the park.

'Come on ... thing,' John called over his shoulder, jogging past her.

Zhu Zhu came bounding after him and playfully jumped up against his back. Her front paws hit his shoulder blades with such force that he went sprawling forwards flat on his face. The tiger skipped and jumped around him in a circle, then pounced on him and began to lick his head all over.

'Get the hell off me!' John yelled. He struggled to push the animal from him and scrambled to his feet.

Zhu Zhu cowered close to the ground as if ready to pounce again, but instead she sprang to her feet, turned and took off into the park.

'Hey, wait … come back … oh shit!' John gave chase.

Zhu Zhu ran into the wide-open space with long flowing strides.

John couldn't keep up. Wheezing, he ran as fast as he could but had to watch helplessly while she disappeared into a large clump of conifers.

46

Beth stirred, stretched and yawned. Although it was still early morning, she felt refreshed after a good night's sleep. She got out of bed and put on one of the flannelette motel dressing gowns from the closet. She called Zhu Zhu's name then peered round John's bedroom door. 'John ... Zhu Zhu?' *He must have taken her out for a walk*, she thought. Looking out of the window, she smiled when she saw them both running back through the park. She couldn't help but giggle; it's not every day you see a man jogging in the park with a tiger by his side.

Then her giggles turned to laughter when Zhu Zhu caught sight of her through the window and became excited. She bounded and skipped in front of John, tripping him. John fell but to Beth's amazement, he didn't curse as he usually did. Instead, he jumped up, playfully grabbed Zhu Zhu around the neck and wrestled her to the ground. They rolled around on the grass for a few moments until John had to give in and let her lick his face.

Beth waited for them at the door. John's disposition changed dramatically when he noticed her watching. 'That's the last time I take that stupid animal out,' he growled, as they entered the apartment.

'Why, what happened?'

'What happened? It took off for a start. Then I think it may have eaten a peacock.'

'What?' Beth knelt and inspected the tiger's mouth. There were traces of blood on her gums. 'She's eaten something. What happened?'

'I followed her over to the lake, but she was too fast and way out in front. When I got there, I noticed there was a little old lady feeding the ducks. Luckily, she was short sighted and said she'd thought she'd seen a big dog across the lake.

'I looked over the water and saw a jogger with a small terrier dog running just behind him. Then I noticed a large peacock go tearing off into the trees.'

'Was Zhu Zhu there?'

'I didn't see her, so I ran around the lake but by the time I got there, the jogger and the peacock were gone. I've covered the whole park looking for that damn thing!'

'So where was she?'

'I decided to double back and take another look where I'd seen the peacock. I shouted its name and it appeared from the bushes with its tail between its legs. Then I noticed a trickle of blood in the corner of its mouth.'

'How did you get it—*her* back?'

'After surveying the area, I just started to jog. Thankfully it ran beside me.'

'Will you stop calling her *it*?'

'Listen, lady, I've just ran about ten miles looking for that thing. Don't tell me what I can and can't call it!'

Beth put her hand on his shoulder. 'Okay, Johnny, be cool.'

John pulled away and headed for the bathroom.

Beth called after him, 'We better get ready and go. Maybe someone saw her.'

They showered, dressed and after deciding on yet another drive-through breakfast, they left Zhu Zhu in the apartment while they packed the car.

'Excuse me, you haven't seen a little Jack Russell terrier, have you?'

John looked up from the back of the car. The jogger stood before him dripping with sweat. 'No, I'm sorry, I haven't.'

The Tiger Chase

'That's strange. He comes out with me every morning, always a few paces behind. One minute he was there, the next he was gone.' The middle-aged man jogged off in the direction of the park.

John looked at Beth who was standing with her mouth open. 'You don't think?'

'Let's get out of here,' Beth said.

Ten minutes later, they were on their way once more.

'I want to try and make it to Winslow Arizona by lunchtime, then California, possibly Los Angeles, by nightfall,' John said. 'But it means it'll be the biggest day's driving yet. What do you think?'

'Let's just play it by ear and see how we go.' Beth had decided to fast Zhu Zhu for the next couple of days and just give her bones to chew on. 'Do you think we should phone the zoo or the LAPD to let them know we're okay?' she asked, watching Zhu Zhu gnawing on a large femur.

'I've been thinking about that but I'm worried. If there is someone on the inside, the last thing we want to do is tell them where we are. By now Tony Lee will have realised that we're still on the road so it's very likely we might bump into him between here and LA.'

Beth sighed and furrowed her brow. 'What about your captain … do you trust him?'

'With my life.'

'Then why don't you call him?'

'Well, I know I should, but something's telling me not to.'

'Yes, I know what you mean. I've got the same feeling.'

They sat in silence and stared at the road ahead of them.

John turned on the radio.

Beth checked on Zhu Zhu, who was still enjoying her bone.

47

Five and a half hours later, John needed to pee. It was time to stop. They hadn't quite made it to Winslow, but he knew he had to find somewhere that wasn't too populated to stop at. He also knew that the helicopter, which had been tailing them for the last two hundred miles, was Tony Lee's, and that he would be waiting for them to stop so he could make his move. He hadn't said anything to Beth because he hadn't wanted to alarm her.

The Hungry Trucker was a gas station and diner with a small cluster of shops behind the main building. John pulled into the parking lot and turned to Beth. 'There's something you need to know.'

'What, that there's been a helicopter following us since Santa Fe?'

'You don't miss much, do you?'

'No … what do we do now?' Beth asked seriously.

'We'll think of something.' He parked the station wagon. Then he saw it—that something. His mind raced with the possibilities. His expression changed. The mischievous boy was back.

48

The helicopter pilot skilfully brought the chopper to rest in a field behind The Hungry Trucker. Tony Lee, Raymond Brown and Doctor Jiang, carrying a rifle, stepped from the craft and walked briskly across the grass. When they reached the shops, they hid behind a wall.

Tony peered round the corner at the station wagon. 'Okay chaps, this is it, let's go.' He produced a handgun from his inside pocket and beckoned the others to follow him.

When they approached the station wagon, there didn't appear to be anyone inside.

Tony pointed at the covered windows that were open a couple of inches. 'The tiger must be in the back, probably asleep. This is going to be too easy,' he whispered.

Doctor Jiang released the safety catch on the rifle.

Raymond Brown, not really interested in their plan, stood back, folded his arms and watched while Tony gave the doctor his instructions.

'Okay, you go around the other side, place the nozzle through the top of the window, then wait for my signal.'

Doctor Jiang tiptoed around the car and did exactly as he'd been told.

Tony cocked his gun and moved to the near side of the car. He peered into the window but couldn't see through the thick-netted curtain. When he tried the handle, it was unlocked. Carefully, with uncharacteristic bravado, he opened the door and leaned in. 'Damn!' he yelled when he realised the car was empty.

Doctor Jiang, thinking he'd been given the signal, blindly fired the rifle into the car.

'Arrrgh!' Tony staggered from the passenger side with an enormous red tranquilliser dart sticking out of his neck. Bewildered, he looked from the doctor to Raymond Brown.

Raymond's devilish laugh slithered across the car lot.

Tony blinked heavily and fell against the car. His eyeballs rolled and his head wobbled. Dropping to his knees, he began to gurgle and drool.

Doctor Jiang stood with his hands clasped to his mouth, nervously looking down at his unforgiving boss.

Tony jabbered like a baby then fell on his face.

Still laughing, Raymond lifted Tony, threw him over his shoulder, carried him to the helicopter and threw him into the back.

Doctor Jiang followed, his face a sickly shade of white.

Raymond straightened up his jacket and marched towards the diner.

A large, tattooed trucker kicked a chair across the room and shook with anger. 'Doggone LAPD, stealing a guy's truck, who'd they think they are?' A young waitress stood filing her nails, taking very little notice.

Raymond Brown moved in closer. 'What are they driving?' he asked the trucker calmly.

'Who the hell are you, freak boy?' the trucker growled, turning to face him.

'What are they driving?' Raymond said again patiently.

'What's it to you?' The trucker squared up to him.

'I need to know what they are driving—the licence number and in which direction they went.'

'Oh, you do, do you? Well, see if you need this.' The big man lurched forward and swung a wide punch towards Raymond's head.

Raymond stepped back, caught the giant fist with his right hand and jerked it backwards.

The trucker roared when his wrist snapped.

Raymond wrenched the arm round, forcing it to bend the wrong way, breaking it at the elbow.

The trucker, holding the limp arm with his other hand, fell to his knees and groaned.

'Now, let's start again ... I need to know what they are driving, the licence number, and in which direction they are headed.' Raymond grabbed the trembling trucker by the hair and yanked his head back.

'Okay, okay.'

Raymond released his grip, strolled over to the counter, grabbed a pen and ripped a page from the waitress's order book.

'Candy-apple-red Mack truck. Licence plate BJ 111. Cab only with Big John's Haulage painted on the side. Heading west.'

Raymond scribbled down the trucker's words, bowed his head politely then left.

49

It didn't take John long to get used to driving such a big truck. In fact, he was amazed at how easy it was. He hadn't liked to use force, but his badge wasn't enough for the trucker who was twice his size, and who wasn't prepared to let his truck go without a fight. John had been forced to produce his gun and, to his relief, the big guy had backed down.

In a matter of minutes, they'd transferred Zhu Zhu and all their stuff into the spacious cab, while the trucker unhooked the trailer and his valuable cargo of, ironically ... Yum Yum Cat Biscuits.

There was more room in the cab than in the station wagon. Behind the two large seats was a sleeping compartment complete with mattress, portable fridge and a television.

Zhu Zhu immediately made herself at home and sprawled out on the mattress.

Beth leaned back and cocked her nose up when she noticed a pile of girlie magazines stacked behind her seat. 'Gross!' she said, grabbing them and throwing them out window.

John enjoyed the sheer power of the big red truck. He was a GI Joe special agent. He looked through the rear vision mirror. The enormous nuclear missile on the back of the truck, with a giant red cone at the sharp end, rocked and bounced when the vehicle increased speed. He had to get it to the secret military installation by sundown, but instead he might just keep it for himself and hold the world to ransom. He sat up straight, gripped the large wheel and honked the horn.

'Uhm ... you all right there?' Beth said, smiling.

John snapped out of his fantasy. 'What's that?'

'You're just a big kid, aren't you?'

'Huh?'

'Nothing. How about we put the radio on ... Big John?' she said, turning on the radio without waiting for a reply.

They settled down and headed west on highway I-40 once more.

'I'm going to call the zoo,' Beth announced later.

John glanced sideways while she fumbled in her jeans pocket for her cell phone. 'Do you think that's a good idea?'

'I'll speak to Robert Baker—I'll be discreet.' She retrieved the number.

'Okay, then I'll phone Captain Williams,' John said.

'Beth, where are you?' There was a sense of urgency in Robert Baker's voice.

'We're nearly home. Make sure the enclosure is ready and prepare the lab for a full examination.'

'That's not a good idea, Beth. There are Feds and Chinese officials all over the place. They want your head, I'm afraid. Tell me exactly where you are and I'll arrange to have you picked up safely ... Beth ... Beth, are you—'

Beth hung up.

'Maybe our Mister Baker is the man on the inside,' John said. 'It would make sense. How else would they know exactly when the tiger was arriving from China?'

Beth nodded thoughtfully.

'I'd say they have someone in the Chinese zoo as well,' John added.

'I have to admit, John, when we first thought of bringing Zhu Zhu to America, I didn't think for a moment we'd be allowed to. But we were, and it was easy ... too easy.'

'Money talks, baby.'

The phone rang three times, then Captain Williams' secretary answered. Moments later, the captain was on the line. 'Where are you, detective?'

'We're approaching the California border, sir.' John went on to explain how Tony Lee and his gang had caught up with them, and of his suspicions regarding Robert Baker.

The captain listened then confirmed that the Feds were now involved. 'Is there anywhere you can hole up for a few days while I try to put them off your scent?'

'With all due respect, sir, there aren't that many places you can hide a tiger.'

'Just two days, John, that's all I need. I'll check out this Baker guy and organise a safe passage to the zoo—'

'But sir—'

'You'll be glad to hear McGuire is doing fine, they flew him back to LA yesterday. The only harm, other than the blood loss, was an unexpected appendectomy, so he should be up and about in the next few days.'

'That's great news, sir, thank you. But about this—'

'Just two days, detective. Call me when you find somewhere.' The captain hung up.

'So where do we go now?' Beth asked.

'I haven't got a clue.'

'What about your apartment?'

'Too dangerous—they'd be watching it.' John struggled with the gearshift and slowed down for roadworks.

They sat in silence, deep in thought.

'I've got it!' Beth exclaimed, rising from a slouch. 'My brother's place, we can go there.'

'But that'll be easy for them to find. They'll probably be watching your brother too.'

'No ... no, trust me, they won't be. I've just got to make a call.'

John concentrated on the road ahead.

Keeping her voice low so John could hardly hear over the drone of the mighty truck engine, Beth made a phone call then, looking pleased with herself, said, 'It's all sorted. When we get closer to LA, I'll give you the directions.'

'Well, that was all a bit cloak and dagger.'

'You'll see why.'

Soon, Beth was asleep again. John couldn't help side glancing her while she slept. He felt like he'd known her all his life.

The night was drawing in and the cab was growing dark. Beth began to mumble in her sleep. 'No, leave her alone, no …'

John was amused when he watched her body twitching.

She began breathing heavily. 'No! Get away, damn you. Leave us alone … help us, Johnny, help us!' she bawled.

Steering with one hand, John leaned over and rested his hand on her shoulder. 'It's okay!'

Beth screamed and jumped up. 'Get away from us!' She punched out.

John tried to duck but she caught him on the cheek. 'Hey what are you—'

She swung again with her other fist; this time catching him on the nose.

The truck swerved into the left-hand lane. John was momentarily blinded. 'What the hell are you doing?' he yelled while drivers behind them honked their horns.

Beth sat upright, her wide eyes searching the cab as if, once again, not knowing where she was. Her breathing was coming in short, sharp bursts. 'What happened?'

'Well, I was hoping you could tell me.'

Beth slumped back into her seat. She looked at John who was rubbing his cheek. 'Did I just hit you?'

'You could say that.'

'Gosh, I'm sorry … I was having a terrible dream.'

'Do you want to tell me about it?'

Beth peered over her shoulder at Zhu Zhu.

Zhu Zhu, startled from her slumber, moved between them.

She chuffed until Beth stroked her. Then she rested her head on the centre console.

'I've been having a lot of strange dreams,' Beth said, gazing through the window into the dark sky. 'They took her away again.'

'They?'

'The two strange men … they took her away and there was nothing we could do.'

'Is that all you can remember?'

'They want to kill her. They'll kill us too if they get the chance.'

'It was just a dream. Nobody's going to get killed,' John said.

'There's a man with cropped hair like tiger stripes … he's the Boogeyman, John … and he's coming for us.'

John leaned over and put his hand on her shoulder again. 'It's going to be all right.'

When the night wore on, John became more inquisitive. 'So, these dreams you've been having, tell me about them.'

'Now who's the shrink?'

'Have I been in any of them?'

Beth mumbled something inaudible.

'What's that?' John asked.

'Nothing.'

50

Beth had programmed the address into the truck's built-in GPS. She checked the map again. 'Okay, it's only about two blocks now.'

Suddenly, the truck spluttered and gurgled.

'Damn!' John said.

'What is it?'

'We're out of gas!'

The engine coughed, rattled then cut out. The truck cruised to the side of the road until it slowly came to a halt.

'What now?' Beth asked.

John checked his watch; it was half past midnight. He looked out of the cab window. Expensive apartment buildings above boutiques and fancy shops lined both sides of the street. Between some of the shops were apartment lobbies, mostly deserted except for the odd security guard reading a magazine or going about their business. The street was empty.

'Well, if we're only two blocks away, we can walk,' John said.

'Are you serious?'

'There's no other option, come on.' John climbed down from the cab, went round to Beth's side and opened her door. 'We'll need to rig up a leash this time; the last thing we need is for it to take off again.'

Beth climbed down.

On the underside of the cab was a big chrome toolbox. John opened it and found some rope and a knife. He cut a piece of rope about two metres long. Remembering the difficulty they'd had in Luciville, he handed it to Beth. 'There you go, doctor.'

Beth helped Zhu Zhu out of the cab and tied the rope around her neck. 'Yet another situation I can't believe we're in. We're going to walk the rarest tiger in the world through the streets of LA,' she mumbled, securing the rope. 'Okay, baby, let's go.' She gently pulled the rope. Zhu Zhu didn't move. 'Oh, please, baby, come on.' She pulled again. Zhu Zhu chuffed and fidgeted on her backside. But still didn't move.

John, quickly growing impatient, grabbed the rope from Beth's hands. Then he knelt and whispered something in the tiger's ear. Zhu Zhu licked him on the nose and rose to her feet.

Beth stood, bewildered, while John strolled down the street with the tiger by his side.

'Are you coming or what?' John called over his shoulder.

Beth skipped to catch up.

They turned the corner at the end of the block and were immediately aware of loud muffled music coming from one of the buildings. When they crossed the road, they realised they were approaching the entrance to a nightclub.

'Ere mate, what ya got there then?'

John looked up to see a large doorman watching them.

'Is that a bleedin' tiger?' he asked with a British accent.

'Yes, we're just taking her for a walk,' Beth said.

The doors of the club burst open, and the music spewed out into the street, making Zhu Zhu flinch. Two girls and two guys staggered out of the club and stopped on the sidewalk.

'Shit, what the hell's that?' slurred one of the guys.

'Oh, wow, I don't believe it,' yelled one of the girls, lifting her hands to her mouth. 'It's The Little Princess.'

'It don't look very little to me,' the doorman said.

Before John could stop him, one of the young guys went to touch Zhu Zhu.

'*GRRREARGH!*' Zhu Zhu roared and snapped at his hand.

The boy quickly pulled away.

'It's not a very friendly Little Princess, is it?' the doorman said.

John tugged on the rope and tried to continue walking.

The Tiger Chase

The girl who had recognised Zhu Zhu asked Beth, 'What are you doing here?'

'Whatever happens, you haven't seen us,' John growled.

'It's okay, we're on our way to the zoo,' Beth said.

'You're a bloody long way from the zoo, darlin',' the doorman said.

John continued on.

Zhu Zhu followed.

Beth politely bade them goodnight and also followed.

As Zhu Zhu passed the doorman, she cocked her tail in the air and squirted hot urine on his pants.

'Hey, bleedin' hell!' he shouted, making his way towards her.

Zhu Zhu turned and snarled.

'Whoa.' The doorman backed off. 'All right, all right ... nice pussy,' he said and returned to the door, shaking his leg and cussing under his breath.

'How much farther is this place?' John asked when they turned another corner.

'It's just down here.'

'Wow! What does your brother do?' John asked when they approached the plush apartment building.

'I'm not quite sure.'

'You can't bring that thing in here,' the short, balding man seated behind the reception desk said when they entered the building.

'Oh, no, well just watch,' Beth said sarcastically, snatching the apartment card key from his hand.

'LAPD, pal, nothing to worry about. This is official police business,' John said, holding up his badge in front of the man's face. 'Oh, and this is top secret. Don't say a word to anyone,' he added over his shoulder, heading towards the lift.

They entered the elevator. Beth placed the key into the top button—the one with a golden P on it.

'Penthouse? You sure your brother's not mafia?' John said, joking.

The lift opened into an enormous marble-clad foyer with gold embossed floor tiles and beautiful stone-carved incidental furniture. In the centre of the circular room stood a two-metre-high reproduction of Michelangelo's *David*. Orbs on the walls, like giant pearls, glowed brighter as the guests entered the room.

Zhu Zhu's claws clicked loudly on the highly polished floor when she followed John and Beth through the foyer and into the main living area.

'Wow!' John's wide eyes followed the floor to ceiling windows and the illuminated city below. 'Has to be drug money!' he mumbled, exploring the rest of the apartment.

Beth busied herself tending to Zhu Zhu. Then she realised the butcher's meat and supplies were still in the truck.

'Some pad!' John said returning from his exploration.

'Sure is. We have a problem.'

'What?'

'We've left the meat and supplies in the truck.'

'Not a problem. I'll go fetch it.'

'Great. While you do that, I'll fix us something for supper. Hungry?'

'Always!'

Beth was busy in the kitchen when John returned with the bags and cooler. 'Fish and veggies.' John plonked the supplies down on one of the counters. 'Fantastic, I'm starving!'

Beth gave Zhu Zhu some of the meat then carried on with the cooking.

John took another look around the apartment. He entered the main bedroom. 'Damn cat,' he grumbled, spotting a large indent on the king-sized bed where Zhu Zhu must have laid.

After a few reluctant moments drumming up the courage to taste the thick cheesy sauce that covered his dinner, John finally ate every scrap and sincerely complimented the chef. They shared a bottle of wine, which they continued to sip while they loaded the dishwasher. Before Beth could stop him, John gave Zhu Zhu the rest of the creamy sauce that was left in the pan.

'You'll be sorry!' Beth said.

The Tiger Chase

When the kitchen was tidy, John instructed Beth to sit on one of the high stools at the island counter declaring he had something special for her. Moments later he produced a small silver tin and a porcelain teapot from his bag. He smiled at Beth's quizzical expression as he filled the electric jug from the filtered tap. 'This is my second most prized possession,' he said, handing her the small silver tin.

'Wow,' Beth seemed strangely choked.

'It's a tea caddy and it was given to me by a very special person.'

'Wh ... who?' Beth asked, clearing her throat.

'An old English lady called Mrs Smith. She was my babysitter when I was a kid.'

A soothing smile appeared on Beth's face as if she were reliving a fond memory in her mind. She asked him to tell her more.

'She showed me how to make a proper cup of tea. "You must never wash the pot, dear," she would say, "heaven forbid."'

The ritual unfolded before Beth's eyes.

John explained every step and told her of the important dos and don'ts, just as Mrs Smith had taught him all those years before. 'You should always heat the pot first and use the finest tea, preferably Indian.' The tin was full to the brim with tea leaves. Underneath the lid there was a small silver spoon. 'One for each cup and one for the pot.' He scooped three spoonfuls into the pot. 'You must always make sure the water is boiling, and after pouring it in the pot, you must leave it to stand, or brew, for a couple of minutes.' He poured the water from the jug. A cloud of steam rose to the ceiling.

'This is so not like you, John Dean.'

'Wrong, this is me.'

While the tea was brewing, John placed two cups and saucers on the counter. Then he placed the lid back on the silver tin, flipped it upside down and opened the other end. 'This is the strainer,' he said, taking out a small silver sieve and holding it up. He placed the strainer on one of the cups. 'Sugar?'

No, thank you.' Beth was sitting on her hands like an excited child. 'This is amazing, I love tea!'

John poured the tea, added a little measure of milk to each cup, then carefully handed her one.

'Thank you!' She gently blew into the cup and took a sip. 'Mmm ... this is wonderful.'

John continued to tell her more about Mrs Smith.

Beth shuffled uncomfortably on the stool. 'And she gave you this?' she asked, holding up the silver tin.

'No, her sister did after Irene's funeral a couple of years ago.'

For a moment Beth seemed taken back. 'Oh ... I'm sorry. Did she give you the pot as well?'

'No, that's mine, I actually bought that myself. That was another thing about Nancy. She actually washed it out, can you believe it?'

'Oh, heaven forbid. No wonder you divorced her,' Beth said sounding strangely like Mrs Smith.

They retired to the lounge, taking their cups with them.

John looked out of the window at the sleeping city below and gave a deep relaxing sigh. 'So, where's your brother? And how come there are no family photos anywhere, or clothes in the closets? This place looks as if it's never been lived in,' John said.

'That's because it hasn't. A wealthy Asian businessman apparently bought it when the building was built but it sat empty for quite a while. According to my mother, my brother bought it for a very good price. Settlement was only a few days ago so he hasn't even seen it yet because he's away on business. In fact, he doesn't even know we're here. I arranged all this with my mother. Lucky for us, she'd just stocked the kitchen for his return. Although she's not sure when he'll be back, she knows it'll be soon.'

John sipped his tea. *Hmm, dealings with an Asian businessman. Extravagant lifestyle. Nobody knows where he is or when he'll be back. Maybe my first hunch was correct. This guy would know all about what Beth was doing in China and would also have the clout to throw money in the direction of the Chinese officials. But why? Surely with all this wealth, he'd have no need to deal in the animal trade ... or maybe that's how he makes his money. Shit!* John almost cussed out loud when he realised something for the first time. What if Tony Lee was her brother? Or Raymond Brown? He couldn't believe he hadn't thought of this before. Suddenly it all made sense. Her brother is away on business—Luciville perhaps? He scrutinised Beth while she peered through the window. *She obviously doesn't know her brother has set her up. Or does she? Oh crap! What if she's led him here and Tony Lee was on his way?* No… he was being irrational. He was tired and not thinking straight. *Her name was Smith not Lee or Brown. Could have changed it? That's just dumb.* He decided not to say anything just yet. It would be better to wait and see what happened next. He hoped he was wrong.

When they finally bid each other good night, John retired to one of the bedrooms, while Beth settled in the one next to it.

Zhu Zhu had lain in the corner of the kitchen chewing on a bone all this time.

John had also been throwing her scraps of food all night. He'd begun to see her more as a big dog now rather than a giant cat.

He climbed into bed and was almost asleep when he rolled to the centre of the mattress. Zhu Zhu had climbed beside him and began kneading the covers with her front paws. 'Get out of here! Go choose one of the other beds,' he yelled, straining to push her onto the floor.

Zhu Zhu curled up on the floor by the door. When she was sure he was asleep, she climbed back on the bed, flopped her herself down beside him and gave a long, deep sigh.

51

Tony Lee opened his eyes. His throat was dry, and his body ached. He was lying in a four-poster bed with the curtains drawn. He sat up but flopped back to the pillow wishing he hadn't.

Raymond Brown and Doctor Jiang were standing at the side of the hotel bed.

'Water ... I need water,' Tony croaked.

Doctor Jiang, as if anticipating his needs, handed him a full glass.

'What happened? All I can remember is approaching the station wagon then, *BAM!* Everything went blank.'

'You hit your head on the car as you tried to look in through the window,' Doctor Jiang said.

Raymond Brown grinned at the doctor.

'Is that right? Is that what happened?' Tony asked, sitting up painfully and peering through squinted eyes at Raymond Brown.

Raymond Brown chuckled.

Tony Lee surfaced by mid-morning after a handful of painkillers and a cold shower. He made a call to the LA Zoo. When he'd finished speaking on the phone, he grinned and placed the butt of a Cuban cigar into his mouth but threw it straight into the bin when the taste almost made him throw up.

'We need to regroup ... *be more professional,*' Tony yelled across to his associates. 'I've spoken to our man at the zoo, and he informs me they are still on the road, but they've gone into hiding. So, we must find them, and we must be ready. I've put more people out there and there'll be professional animal handlers at our disposal. This time I'm going to finish Detective John Dean myself ... once and for all.' He slammed his fist down hard on a table and immediately regretted it. Wincing with pain, he steadied himself before slumping into a chair, massaging his temples.

His mobile phone *dinged*.

Tony's face lit up with surprise as he read the text from his FBI mole. He held up the phone to his associates so they could read the screen. To his surprise, neither understood the significance of the message. 'Of course, forgive me, I constantly keep forgetting you're both morons. Don't you see? This vital piece of information will lead us *straight* to them. My worker ants are scurrying and searching as we speak. I guarantee we'll have an address anytime now.' He looked at his watch.

His mobile rang.

Tony's head bobbed like a nodding dog from the weight of his cocky smile.

52

He didn't have to open his eyes—he knew the tickling under his nose was the end of a long stripy tail slowly flicking from side to side. He was getting used to being awoken this way. Opening one eye, he lifted his head. Yep. There it was. He blew it away when it brushed across his mouth. Then he opened the other eye and turned his head. To his dismay, the tiger was lying with her head at his feet; her tail was coiled over his chest and her backside was way too close to his face. He tried to move, but he was pinned beneath the stiff new sheets. 'Get off!' he yelled, 'Get off me.' But as he struggled to free himself the bed started to bounce.

Zhu Zhu, thinking it was a game, sprung to her feet, turned and slammed her front paws onto John's chest.

'Umphh—get off—get off!' John cried with 115 kilos of tiger expelling the air from his lungs.

Zhu Zhu reared up slightly and playfully tapped either side of his head with her paws like a kitten playing with a ball of string.

Beth, hearing the commotion, came running into the room. 'Come on, baby, off you get … you are such a naughty girl.' She giggled, coaxing the tiger off the bed.

John bounded into the bathroom, once again without saying a word.

Beth led Zhu Zhu from the bedroom and into the kitchen.

A few minutes later, John appeared from the bedroom. He looked at the tiger and growled.

The Tiger Chase

'Come and sit down, I know what you need,' Beth said pointing to the stools.

When John took a seat, Beth handed him a cup of steaming hot tea. He looked at the cup suspiciously. The colour was about right. He took a cautious sip. 'Hey, that's not bad ... for a first attempt.'

'Why, thank you, but I already knew how to make tea.'

'Yeah right, who taught you?'

'Oh, I don't remember, must have been a long time ago.'

'Is there anything else I should know about you?'

'There's a lot you don't know about me, John Dean,' Beth said, smirking.

John took charge and cooked bacon and eggs for breakfast. When they'd finished eating, he watched closely while Beth made another pot of tea.

With steaming mugs in hands, they retired to the terrace and relaxed on the comfortable outdoor furniture.

The terrace was a large rectangle shape with terracotta tiles and a waist-high tinted glass barrier around the outer edge. There was an arrangement of potted palms and trees, a BBQ, an entertainment area, and a kidney-shaped swimming pool in the middle with a beach style shallow end.

'We have some new problems we need to overcome,' Beth said, leaning against the glass barrier.

John furrowed his brow inviting her to continue.

'Well, take a look around us. How are we going to exercise Zhu Zhu, and where is she going to do her toiletries?'

'Toiletries? You mean where's it gonna crap?'

Beth, ignoring John's vulgarity, paced the terrace for a few moments thinking. 'Do you remember how you told me that Nancy used kitty litter?'

'*No* way, don't even think about it,' John said, the next scene of his recurring nightmare flashing through his mind.

'It's the only way, Johnny.'

It was John who now paced the terrace. He wasn't just reliving his nightmare; he was being forced to relive it tenfold. If this was some kind of sick cosmic joke, then somebody up there had a rotten sense of humour.

Ten five-kilo bags of kitty litter were far too much for Beth to carry, so she was grateful when the lady at the local PetSmart arranged immediate delivery to the apartment.

John watched in amazement while a young delivery boy wheeled a trolley, heavily laden with the ten bags, out of the lift, and stacked them in the foyer. Then he watched, without offering any assistance, as Beth struggled to carry one bag at a time to the main bathroom, where she poured the litter into the large Jacuzzi tub.

'Perfect!' she said, after filling the tub just over halfway.

Zhu Zhu, as if knowing exactly what was happening, sat on the cool tiled floor waiting patiently.

Beth stepped to one side.

Zhu Zhu jumped straight into the bathtub, squatted down and did a long steaming wee.

Beth looked over at John, nodded smugly and flicked on the exhaust fan.

Zhu Zhu jumped out of the tub, slipped across the bathroom floor and almost knocked John over.

Beth, trying not to laugh, said: 'We just have to make sure we leave this door open at all times and use this when the need arises.' She produced a small stainless steel shovel and leaned it against the bath.

'No, no, no, no, no ... not *we—you* ... you're the vet, I'm the cop ... I clean up the crooks—you clean up the cat crap.'

Beth breezed past him with deaf ears.

They returned to the terrace and relaxed in the warm midday sun, read the newspapers and indulged themselves in some much-needed R & R. Beth sat at the aluminium table on one of the trendy outdoor chairs, typing a social media post on the dos and don'ts of travelling with a large animal. John lay on one of the sun lounges contemplating their next move between naps. Zhu Zhu sat in the shallow end of the pool with the water up to her neck and her eyes closed as if in meditation.

'What would you like for lunch, Madame?' John suddenly said, rising from the lounger.

'Surprise me,' Beth said looking up from her iPad.

John strolled into the apartment humming. He entered the kitchen, flung open the large stainless steel freezer door and rummaged through the icy packaged food. 'Burgers? I don't think so. Fish? Nope. Chicken …?' He went back out to the terrace. 'Hey, you fancy barbequed chicken?'

'Mmm, yummy.'

John approached the shiny new barbeque cautiously.

'How about I prepare some salad?' Beth called over to him.

'That'll be great.' John lifted the lid of the barbeque and randomly turned the nobs.

Beth closed her iPad and went into the apartment.

Zhu Zhu's ears pricked up. She jumped out of the pool close to John and shook her fur, wetting him through.

'Hey!' John shouted after her when she padded into the apartment leaving a wet trail behind her.

John fired up the gas barbeque, after discovering how it worked, then went into the kitchen. Moments later, he returned with two chicken fillets and a bottle of olive oil. He placed the food on the timber slats at the side of the grill then turned to look out over the city. *This is almost too good*, he thought when a warm breeze gently swished through the palm trees. After checking the heat of the grill and deciding to leave it a little longer before putting the food on, he headed back into the apartment. 'Would Madame care for a glass of wine?' he asked, peering round the kitchen door.

'*Oui oui monsieur,*' Beth said.

John hummed merrily while he poured two glasses of Australian chardonnay from the fully stocked bar, then strolled back onto the terrace. Something caught his eye. His body jolted; his muscles tensed involuntary. He dropped the glasses of wine and without thought, launched into an almost automated single movement of whipping off his right shoe with one hand and throwing it with all his might. 'Get the hell out of here!' He hadn't felt anger like this since his last meeting with Tony Lee. For it to come on so suddenly, after being mellow for the last few days, would have been totally unthinkable to him only moments earlier.

His shoe whistled across the terrace but missed the cat and went sailing over the side of the rail.

The ugly cat arched its back, turned to look at him and spat.

John ran at it.

The cat quickly picked up a piece of chicken in its mouth, jumped onto the rail then up onto the roof.

'You bastard!' John shouted after it, but by the time he got to the barbeque, the cat and the chicken had gone.

Beth came running out. 'What happened? What is it?'

John stood looking up at the roof with his fists clenched by his sides. He was red faced and breathing heavily.

'John, what is it?' Beth said again, putting her hand on his shoulder.

John took some deep slow breaths and began to blow, trying to calm down.

'Are they here? Is it the Boogeyman?'

'No, worse ... I think it was the devil himself.'

Beth noticed he was wearing only one shoe. 'What happened to your shoe?'

'I threw it ... at the cat.'

'The cat?'

'Not just *a* cat. God, this thing was ugly. Pure evil!'

'A cat?'

John turned to meet Beth's patronising gaze. 'It stole your piece of chicken!'

The Tiger Chase

'My piece?' Beth said, crossing her arms and looking at the remaining fillet. 'So, you almost have a coronary over a little cat?'

'It wasn't just a little cat, I tell you. It was weird.' John peered over the rail.

'Did your shoe go over there?' Beth laughed.

'Yeah ... damn!' John cussed when he couldn't see it. 'Good job, I've got an extra pair.'

'How about I thaw out another piece of chicken in the microwave, you fix us two more drinks and we'll cook lunch together?' Beth said.

'Okay, but if I see that cat again, I'll ring its neck.'

After eating lunch out on the terrace, they spent the afternoon watching television while Zhu Zhu napped in the shade taking advantage of the cooling breeze that blew up from the city.

John shook his head but had to smile when he flicked through the TV channels and came across Thomas O'Malley and his alley cat friends singing, 'Everybody wants to be a cat.'

'So, what do you think we should do next, John?' Beth asked later.

'We'll stay here for another day, but I'll phone the captain in the morning and see if anything's happening.'

'I feel like staying here forever.' Beth snuggled down into the large Easy Chair. 'So, tell me more about your childhood, John.'

'What? That's a bit random, isn't it? Tell me about yours.'

'Oh, there's nothing to tell. Would you like more tea?' Beth jumped up and headed for the kitchen.

She's definitely hiding something, John thought. *It's gotta be something to do with her brother. I'll get the captain to check him out in the morning.*

53

The lights in the apartment were controlled by movement sensors but John, becoming tired with Zhu Zhu activating them in the night while pacing from room to room, had set them all to manual. Everyone was asleep. The apartment was dark and quiet. Suddenly, the button at the side of the elevator door illuminated.

Zhu Zhu was lying on the large, silk-covered sofa in the living room. She jolted from her sleep.

The elevator was on its way up.

There was a high-pitched *DING* and the elevator door slid open.

Zhu Zhu stole down from the sofa and crouched with a clear view of the foyer.

An intruder stepped from the elevator and walked casually across the marble floor towards the living room.

The stealthy killing machine followed as the stranger headed towards the kitchen. With her eye on her prey at all times, every sinew of her body was taut, alert and ready. *GRRREARGH!*' She roared and pounced.

The intruder cried out, turned and leaped onto the counter like a desperate gazelle.

***

John jumped out of bed and bumped into Beth when they both ran from their rooms towards the kitchen and the sounds of flying saucepans, terrified screams and Zhu Zhu's constant, deafening roar.

The Tiger Chase

Entering the kitchen, John peered through the dim light at the figure standing on the counter wielding a large frying pan.

Zhu Zhu was circling the counter.

John fumbled for the light and, when he finally turned it on, he blinked heavily and shook his head in disbelief. 'This has to be another of those damn dreams,' he said, standing in his underwear.

Beth pushed past him.

Zhu Zhu backed off.

The intruder turned to face Beth in readiness for another attack.

John stood with his mouth wide open but managed to muster only one word…

54

'Jimmy?'

Each of them stood with their mouths agape until Jimmy warily climbed down from the counter.

John bounded across to his old friend and flung his arms around him. 'Why ... what ... how? What the hell are you doing here, man?'

Jimmy stood shaking in disbelief. 'Well, I could ask you the same thing. What the hell is John Dean doing in my kitchen, in his underwear, with my little sister and a ... a bloody tiger? This must be a dream. Pinch me, please?' He grabbed Beth and gave her a big hug.

John turned to Beth. 'Little sister...? Hey! Wait a minute ... this means you were that freckle-faced, annoying little brat with pigtails and braces. Why didn't you tell me? And where do you get the name Smith? Surely it's Schwite?'

'Hold it, hold it. Before we get into twenty questions, I think you guys have some answering to do for me, don't you?' Jimmy said, undoing his top button and loosening his tie.

John made tea. For the next hour they sat at the dining room table and told Jimmy everything that had happened, and how they came to be staying in his new apartment with a tiger.

Jimmy was amazed when Beth explained why the crooks wanted the tiger and to what lengths they were prepared to go to get it.

When they'd finally told Jimmy everything, John turned to Beth and raised his eyebrows.

'Okay ... okay, I know what you're going to say,' she said, blushing and staring into her empty cup.

'Before you get into all that, I'll take a look around my new apartment and leave you two lovebirds to talk,' Jimmy said, rising from the table.

'What? Don't be so ...' John and Beth said in unison.

Zhu Zhu growled as Jimmy left the room.

'All right, I officially changed my name from Schwite to Smith just before I went to college. He was already making a name for himself, and I didn't want to be bogged down with people asking me about him all the time, or assuming that I was rich just because I was his sister. I had to go out and find my own identity. As for telling you who I was ... maybe I should have, but as a kid you were so mean and aggressive. I hated you. You'd either pinch or punch me on the arm, or totally ignore me.'

'Yeah, I *was* a shit. But that was twenty-five years ago. I used to treat all the girls like that—ask Jimmy.' John smiled mischievously.

'I knew Mrs Smith as well. That's where I got the idea for the name. On the odd occasion, she would babysit for us too, and she taught me how to make tea. But you know what? All the time I was with her, all she did was talk about you. Whenever I told her some of the nasty things you did, she'd say, "He's not a bad boy really, dear."'

'Hey guys, sorry to interrupt, but is there a reason why there's a pebbly beach in the guest hot tub?' Jimmy said, poking his head round the door.

Beth and John laughed.

'Uhm, it's not actually a hot tub anymore,' Beth said.

'It's not?'

'No ... it's Zhu Zhu's toilet—but only temporarily, of course.'

'Oh, of course.'

'Anyway, sit down, mister. I think it's your turn to answer some questions now. Like where's Alicia—the sister-in-law I haven't met yet?'

'She's flying in from Sydney tomorrow morning. She should be here quite early. After both of us working extremely hard and travelling the globe in opposite directions, we decided to spend two weeks relaxing in our new apartment.'

'Hey, listen man, we'll be out of here tomorrow. If we knew you were coming back, we wouldn't have imposed,' John said.

'Are you crazy? I've been followed round for the last three months by sycophants and fools—"yes, sir; no, sir; whatever you say, sir." I can't think of anything better than spending time with my most favourite people in the world. Besides, you're going to need my help. It'll be like old times, John. The GIs against the world.'

'But what about Alicia?' Beth asked.

'As Alicia would say, "No worries, mate!" You know, in the newspapers, it might look like we're having fun at all those gala events or royal weddings, or whatever, but the truth is, our lives are very boring. It's all work and no play. Believe me, she's gonna love all this adventure. Although, she may want to keep the tiger.' He looked over at Zhu Zhu.

Zhu Zhu bared her teeth and snarled.

Jimmy was grateful that they hadn't used the master suite and they all retired for the night.

John found it hard to get back to sleep. He couldn't believe his old friend, Jimmy, was here and that Beth was his little sister. *Strange how fate works,* he thought.

55

The next morning, John awoke to the glorious smell of fried food wafting in from the kitchen. He was amazed when he looked at the clock—it was 10.30 am. After climbing out of bed, he dressed and made his way to the kitchen. 'Alicia!' He was surprised to see one of the highest paid models in the world, cooking breakfast, wearing a pair of tatty knee-length board shorts and an INXS T-shirt. Her long sun-bleached hair was held in a ponytail with an elastic band. Her feet were bare, and she had a deep tan, which made her beautiful blue eyes even more piercing. He hadn't seen her since the wedding, and she looked very different from the photographs John usually saw on the front of the women's magazines in the supermarket. But what John liked the most about Alicia Rose was her down-to-earth, boyish and mischievous manner.

Zhu Zhu sat by her side begging.

'G'day, John, it's great to see you, mate!' Alicia said, skipping across the kitchen with her arms wide open.

Beth entered the kitchen moments later with Jimmy.

'Alicia, I would like you to meet my baby sister, Beth.'

The two girls hugged.

'I've heard heaps about you, Beth,' Alicia said. 'I've followed your career and I think it's just great what you're doing for the South China tiger—oh, it's so great to finally meet you,' she added excitedly.

'And Zhu Zhu, The Little Princess, what an honour, I just love her to bits. I'll never be able to let her out of my sight now, though.'

'Well, I'm sorry. I'm afraid she's already spoken for. She's fallen in love with John. In fact, they've slept together ever since they first met,' Beth said, smiling.

John frowned and blushed, and everyone laughed when he mumbled something about hating cats.

They all sat down to an unfamiliar breakfast of steak and eggs. 'Good old Aussie tucker,' Alicia exclaimed.

After breakfast, John made tea while Jimmy turned the radio on and loaded the dishwasher. Everyone fell silent when the news came on.

'Reports last night of the abduction of The Little Princess have been confirmed by the FBI …'

'Damn, that's all we need,' John said, handing each of the girls a mug of tea.

The bulletin continued: 'Media attention was captured yesterday by a leaked FBI document that outlined the secret arrival into America and the attempted abduction of a South China tiger known as The Little Princess.'

Jimmy turned on the TV and scanned the main news channels. The story was headline news. Creating their own series of events and scenarios, it seemed over-zealous reporters were collecting stories of sightings and contacts that had been flooding in by the thousands. Tiger awareness was sweeping America once more.

'We've got no dirt on Robert Baker except for a few parking fines, although he has got a lousy credit record. It seems he likes to live beyond his means,' Captain Williams said on the phone. 'My hunch is he's our man though.'

John nodded in agreement but remained silent while the captain continued.

'I'm gonna haul him in, see if we can put some pressure on him. I've been talking to Doctor Malcolm Wilson from the Minnesota Zoo. He's flying down this morning with a team of specialists. They're going to be taking over at the zoo then we'll pick you up from the apartment.

'Top security and specialised transport for the animal will be the priority. As for Doctor Smith, I checked her brother out as you asked and you're not going to believe it, he's actually James Schwite, the tech billionaire.'

John smiled and thanked the captain for his help.

56

Beth was pleased to hear Malcolm Wilson would be taking over at the zoo. She'd worked with him in the past and had enjoyed showing him around Shanghai when he'd visited China two years earlier. It also meant that transportation to the zoo would be organised on a more professional scale as opposed to Robert Baker's botched attempt.

Alicia couldn't leave Zhu Zhu alone; she wanted to watch and pat her all the time.

Beth suggested it was time Zhu Zhu was bathed and groomed. 'Would you like to help me?' she asked Alicia.

'Bloody oath, mate!' Alicia replied.

They led Zhu Zhu out onto the terrace. Beth unravelled the hose and while trying to figure out which way to turn the nozzle, and not noticing where it was pointing, she turned it on.

Alicia shrieked when a powerful jet of freezing cold water hit her in the centre of her back, knocking her off her feet.

'I'm sorry!' Beth yelled, struggling to bring the hose under control.

Alicia lay on the ground laughing then fell into hysterics when Beth directed the water at Zhu Zhu.

Zhu Zhu flinched and hopped like a giant rabbit. Turning her back to the strong jet, she lifted her tail, allowing it to spray her behind. She turned face on and snapped at the plume with her jaws as if trying to eat it. Then she rolled on the ground allowing Beth to hose her belly.

'Give us a go!' Alicia cried, almost slipping on the wet floor.

The Tiger Chase

Beth reluctantly handed over the hose and disappeared into the apartment.

Alicia giggled, hosing down the tiger.

Beth reappeared carrying a bottle of flea shampoo.

Alicia, with her tongue wedged in her cheek, directed the hose in the opposite direction and watched patiently while Beth rubbed the shampoo into Zhu Zhu's wet fur.

'Oh, you like that don't you, baby?' Beth said, covering the tiger from head to toe in thick soapsuds. Now it was Beth's turn to scream when Alicia set the hose on her and Zhu Zhu.

John appeared from behind Alicia, grabbed the hose, and pushed her to where Beth was cowering. 'Yeehaaaa!'

The girls tried to hide behind the tiger. Zhu Zhu was enjoying every minute.

After ten minutes of vigorously drying the sopping wet tiger with towels, the girls retired to the apartment, showered, changed, and relaxed, leaving Zhu Zhu to lie in the sun.

57

Zhu Zhu sat alone on the terrace looking more like a fluffed-up poodle than a deadly carnivore. Her eyes suddenly flickered. Her ears shot forward and her brow furrowed. Lifting her nose, she sniffed the air.

The hairless Sphynx sauntered along the guttering above the terrace.

For a while, Zhu Zhu watched and stared into the odd eyes of the cat—one blue and one brown. Then she began to pace the terrace. She chuffed and gave out a low roar.

The cat turned away, cocked its tail into the air and disappeared over the roof.

Zhu Zhu bolted to the end of the terrace, jumped onto the barbeque then onto the roof.

Above the penthouse was a meadow of contemporary turrets, apexes, and geometrical shapes and domes in a variety of sizes—a cat's paradise.

The wind ruffled Zhu Zhu's fur when she peered over the edge at the concrete jungle forty floors below.

'Meow!'

She turned to see the cat calling to her from the highest part of the roof. Zhu Zhu chuffed into the air then began to scale the steep angle. When she reached the top, she stood with her front paws on the apex. *'GRRREARGH!'* She was on the top of the world.

'Meow!'

The opposite side of the roof sloped down to a flat section with a large glass pyramid in the middle.

The Tiger Chase

The cat was sitting at the base of the pyramid with a fresh pigeon carcass by its side.

Zhu Zhu crept down the steep roof with the ease and elegance of a street cat.

'Meow!'

'Chuff—Chuff!'

When she reached the bottom, she sat facing the cat for a few moments staring into its odd eyes.

The cat ignored the tiger.

Zhu Zhu cheekily reached out with a paw and tried to nudge the pigeon towards her.

'Meowww!' The cat arched its back, lurched forward and swiped her on the nose.

Zhu Zhu cowered when the cat snarled and spat. She backed away, lay on her stomach and rested her head on her front paws.

The cat picked up the pigeon, turned with its tail in the air and, as if giving her the cat version of the finger, sauntered away and jumped into one of the lower turrets.

There was no wind between the apexes. The sun was warm on Zhu Zhu's fur. She circumnavigated the roof, squirting urine and leaving deep scratch marks on all four turrets. Then she returned to the largest of the turrets on the far side with her prey between her teeth. She jumped up into the open tower, released her grip on the small carcass and roared into the smoggy Californian air. *'GRRREARGH!'* The territory was officially hers now.

58

Beyond the dining room was a fully stocked bar complete with tall bar stools, a jukebox and a pool table.

'You always were useless at ball games,' John said when Jimmy sent the white ball flying off the pool table and bouncing across the tiled floor.

'I was good at pocket billiards.'

Alicia and Beth sat at the bar sipping lemonade, talking and giggling, while The Beatles' *White Album* played in the background.

'So, tell me about James and John. What were they like when they were kids?' Alicia said.

'Smelly, nasty, horrible! John was a bully. James was his disciple and followed him everywhere. I think John used to stick up for him. But God, they were annoying. They had this private little club—GIs only.'

They laughed as they reminisced some more.

On a more serious note, Alicia asked, 'So what's going to happen to the South China tigers now? Is Zhu Zhu really the last wild one?'

'I don't believe she is; I think there are still some left in the reserves, albeit only a handful, perhaps twenty or so. These are the ones that we have to concentrate on!'

'Did you say twenty?'

'Yep, someone needs to make a decision pretty soon.'

'What kind of a decision?'

'Well, if there is a small population left and the current trend of deforestation and poaching is allowed to continue, they'll be forced to move farther north through small corridors to areas that can't sustain them. The bottom line is if somebody doesn't do something soon, we're going to lose this very important subspecies forever.'

'What can people do?'

'Ideally, what we really need is a celebrity or high-profile businessperson to help bring the plight of the tiger to the attention of the world. Look at what Live Aid achieved. With the right organisation, a special benefit could be set up to help fund the fight against poaching and a change in government policies. I believe we need to find and study the tigers in the wild and protect them. If we're not too late, that is.'

'So, if you found some tigers in the wild, what then?'

'First, we could learn a lot just by capturing and examining them. We would take semen, DNA and cell samples for future introduction into the captive animal bloodline. This would give us an important insight into how environmental changes are affecting them. Then, if all the wild animals were categorised, we could release them back into the reserves, which the Chinese government have gone to great lengths to reclaim. There we could protect them.'

'Okay, we'll do it!' Alicia exclaimed.

'What?'

'We'll do it ... me and James. First thing Monday morning, we'll start the ball rolling. We'll go to the media, we'll call a meeting with our people and lawyers, and we'll get you your fund. I will do everything in my power to help save the South China tiger ... and so will James.'

'Oh, Alicia, I didn't mean—'

'No, I've decided—'

'Alicia, when I said somebody famous, please don't think—I mean—I wasn't—I didn't mean you and James. In fact, it never even crossed my mind. Surely, you're much too busy.' Beth blushed.

'Being here now with you and Zhu Zhu has opened my eyes, so much so that if I have to give up the fashion industry to champion the cause, then so be it.'

'Oh Alicia ... I couldn't expect you to ...' She noticed the determination in Alicia's eyes. 'Okay ... we'll do it together.'

'You've got yourself a deal, mate.' Alicia held out her hand for Beth to shake.

They shook hands, finished their drinks and decided to check on Zhu Zhu, leaving the boys to their game of pool.

Wandering out onto the terrace, the girls were surprised not to see Zhu Zhu fast asleep in the sun.

'Zhu Zhu, where are you?' Alicia called out.

'She's most likely on John's bed,' Beth said.

'Isn't she still a bit wet?'

'Probably.' They laughed. 'Don't worry, it's part of his penance for hating cats and being a dick as a kid.'

They checked John's room. She wasn't there. They looked in the rest of the rooms then checked the terrace again. Beth began to panic. 'Zhu Zhu, where are you baby? Come on, girl.'

There was no sign of the tiger.

Alicia ran to fetch John and Jimmy.

59

After another search of the apartment, the group returned to the terrace. 'How the hell can you lose it?' John growled.

Beth, ignoring him, was staring at the roof.

'What?'

'Up there ...'

'Surely you don't think?' John strode to the end of the terrace where the barbeque was. 'Be pretty difficult to get up there.'

'Not for a tiger,' Beth said.

'I mean for us.'

'There must be another way up,' Jimmy said. 'The janitor would know.'

'Right, you guys go and find him,' John said to Jimmy and Alicia. 'I'll wait here with the tiger expert in case it comes back.'

Jimmy and Alicia rushed from the apartment.

Beth waited on the terrace with John. 'Stop calling her an *it*, and don't be so sarcastic. Tiger expert. It's not my fault,' she said with a hint of a sulk. She was growing impatient. 'What if she's not up there? What if Tony Lee has somehow managed to steal her from under our noses?'

John leaned against the glass railing again and looked up. 'It would've had to have jumped onto the barbeque then up onto the guttering. It wouldn't have been easy ... shit, what if it fell over the side?' He looked over the side of the building.

Beth also looked over. She couldn't wait any longer. She surveyed the distance between the top of the large stainless steel barbeque and the gutter. If John stood on the barbeque, he'd be a little under head height with the roof. 'We'd need to go up there!'

'What, are you crazy?' John said.

'We're wasting time. She might not even be up there.'

'Okay, but I'll go. You stay here. You'll only slow me down.'

'I'm coming too.'

'No, you're not.'

'Try and stop me, Johnny.'

John sighed inwardly; his temples were beginning to throb. 'I'll go first, then if you think you're still up for it, I'll pull you up.' He carefully climbed onto the barbeque then reached up for the guttering. After checking the strength of the guttering, he jumped up and lifted himself onto the roof. 'Okay, your turn. Just be careful.'

Beth followed John's lead but when she reached for the gutter, she was way too short.

'*Phhh* ... girls!' John grabbed her wrists and lifted her up.

Beth frowned and stuck her tongue out after scrambling onto the roof.

'I don't believe I'm doing this,' John mumbled as they trekked upwards toward the pinnacle of the roof. At the exact moment they reached the top, Jimmy and Alicia stepped out of a small doorway beneath one of the turrets.

John crouched down then, seated on the back foot with the other foot stretched out in front, he slid down the side of the roof and landed just before the glass pyramid.

Beth's expression showed great concentration while she tried to emulate John's manoeuvre. She squealed when she started to slide. Then she stopped about halfway.

'Unbelievable. 'Come on!' John yelled, shaking his head.

Beth slid down a little farther, then stopped. She slid some more and continued to slide in increments until she finally reached the

The Tiger Chase

bottom. By the time she'd stood up and called John an impatient jerk, Jimmy and Alicia had joined them.

'How'd you go with the janitor?' John asked.

'Good. He said his cat's probably up here. It's a hairless Sphynx named Bowie,' Jimmy said.

'Bowie?'

'After the singer. One blue eye, one brown. A dead ringer for The Thin White Duke, apparently.'

'So perhaps Zhu Zhu followed it up here,' Beth said.

'Yeah, or eaten it!' John quipped. His expression suddenly changed, and he pointed to the largest turret. 'There!'

Zhu Zhu lay on her tummy with her head resting on her front paws, staring down at them.

'Zhu Zhu, you naughty girl. Where have you been?' Beth rushed over to the far side of the roof. 'Come on, baby, let's go.'

The others caught up.

John smirked while he listened to Beth's pleas. 'Here we go again. You see ... what we're witnessing here guys is years of animal training. So, tell me, what delicate and sophisticated moves are we going to see today, Doctor Smith?'

'Shadap, Johnny!'

Zhu Zhu lifted her head, yawned, then lowered it onto her paws again.

'Give us a bunk up, Jimbo,' Alicia said.

'What?'

'Bend down. I'll climb on ya shoulders.'

'No, no, no! Step aside, girls. This is a job for the GIs!' Jimmy said, grinning at John.

Jimmy bent down and groaned when John climbed onto his back.

Beth put her hand on Alicia's shoulder. 'Let the little boys have their fun. Meanwhile we'll work on plan B.'

John reached up, grabbed the edge of the turret where Zhu Zhu lay, pushed off Jimmy's shoulders with his feet, and scrambled up onto his elbows.

'Go, Johnny!' the girls shouted then burst out laughing when Zhu Zhu smothered him with rough licks and wet kisses.

'Get—stop—no—' He tried to push her away but in doing so, lost his grip, fell and landed on Jimmy.

'Thank God for the GIs.' Alicia gave a sarcastic salute.

Zhu Zhu jumped to her feet and chuffed.

'Even Zhu Zhu's laughing at ya', Johnny,' Beth said, enjoying John's embarrassment.

John grunted and looked the other way.

Zhu Zhu suddenly sprang from the turret and sailed over their heads. She landed silently, scurried across the roof then scrambled up the glass pyramid, slipping on the glass.

'Baby, no!' Beth called after her.

Zhu Zhu reached the apex of the pyramid, stood with all four paws gripping the glass pinnacle and, looking like a cartoon character, she roared over her territory, *'GRRREARGH!'* Then she nestled onto the glass point, lifted a front paw and licked it nonchalantly.

'Struth! What now?' Alicia asked.

'We can't climb up there, that's for sure. It's too dangerous. That glass could give way at any minute,' John said.

'Come on, baby … come to Mommy,' Beth called up.

'Come on, baby … come to Mommy,' John said, mimicking Beth.

Alicia playfully punched him on the arm.

'I've got it,' Beth said. 'James, fetch some of that ribeye from the fridge. She'd sell her soul for that.'

'Yes, Mother.' Jimmy ran back to the turret and disappeared into the small doorway. Five minutes later, he was back with a large piece of fresh steak.

Zhu Zhu rose precariously and sniffed the air.

'That's it, baby. Come on.' Beth took the steak from Jimmy and held it up so Zhu Zhu could see it. 'Here you go, baby.'

The Tiger Chase

Zhu Zhu chuffed and whined, sat down and began to shuffle forward. Suddenly, she slid down on her backside with her head and tail in the air.

'Wahoo ...!' Beth squealed.

Even John couldn't help but smile at the surreal sight of a fully grown tiger sliding down a glass pyramid on its butt.

'Crikey, look out,' Alicia yelled when Zhu Zhu picked up momentum and came flying down towards them.

Everyone managed to get out of the way just in time except, of course, John. The tiger bowled him over then trampled on him as she scampered towards Beth and the steak.

'She's a good girl,' Beth said, feeding her the meat.

Thankfully, Zhu Zhu followed when they made their way back to the stairwell.

John looked at his watch. Time was getting on, and he was expecting a call from the captain. He hurried them down the stairs, checked the corridor, then ushered them back into the elevator.

One minute later, they were standing in the foyer of the penthouse, looking up at the glass pyramid above *David's* head.

60

John, Jimmy, Beth, and Alicia sat in the living room, waiting patiently while Zhu Zhu lay on the tiled kitchen floor.

John was growing anxious.

'We're like The Famous Five,' Beth said, breaking the awkward silence.

'The Famous what?' John said impatiently.

'The Famous Five ... you know? Enid Blyton? Oh ... sorry, that's right, all you guys ever read were Superman and Robin or—'

'That's Batman and Robin ... stupid ... soppy Famous Five.'

'Jeez, you're bloody good at winding him up, eh?' Alicia said, offering Beth her hand for a high five.

Beth high fived with pride. 'It's just getting too easy.' She turned back to John. 'They weren't soppy. They were very good.'

'Whatever. I think it's time we got ready,' John said, deciding he'd heard enough. He headed for his room.

'Struth, you two are just like a married couple,' Alicia said, feigning seriousness.

'Worse, even we don't argue this bad,' Jimmy added.

It didn't take long for them to pack. Jimmy and Alicia insisted they would come along for the ride. John didn't like it, but they wouldn't take no for an answer. He suspected they secretly revelled in the idea that there might be some action. Placing his gun in its holster, his anxiety returned.

61

The doorman fell to the ground when the butt of the Beretta 92FS 9mm came down hard on the back of his neck. Four henchmen stood to one side allowing Tony Lee, Raymond Brown and Doctor Jiang to enter.

While one of the thugs dragged the doorman into the deserted foyer, another ducked behind the counter and began to search the drawers. Moments later, he returned carrying a card key.

They filed into the elevator.

Doctor Jiang swiped the card and pressed the button for the penthouse.

As the elevator rose, Raymond Brown watched Tony Lee with a slight grin. The thought of grabbing him by the throat and dislodging his fifth vertebrae with his index finger and thumb flashed through his mind.

'Do it! Do it now!' his father yelled.

No! His patience would pay off. He'd kill John Dean first then everyone else in sight, saving the fool until last. This he would enjoy almost as much as devouring the tiger. If it weren't for his sexual impotence, he'd be aroused right now.

62

John was pacing the apartment uneasily when the green light by the elevator illuminated catching his attention. 'Strange.' He checked his watch. The captain would have contacted him to tell him they were on their way. Needing to think quickly, he rushed through to the living room and ordered the others into the farthest bedroom. When he returned, the elevator stopped and *dinged*. He just had enough time to hide inside a closet to the side of the foyer before the metallic doors slid open.

For a few moments, nothing moved. Then two henchmen stepped out and stood each side of the elevator. Tony Lee appeared next, followed by Raymond Brown, then the doctor.

They moved slowly through the foyer and cautiously around the statue of *David*. The two henchmen moved up behind them.

'Police!' John yelled, stepping from the closet with his gun aimed at Raymond Brown.

The intruders turned at once and raised their arms.

John moved between them and the exit.

'Oh dear, how embarrassing,' Tony Lee said. 'After all this time and preparation to be so easily beaten yet again by my nemesis, *Detective John Dean*.'

John felt cold steel against his temples.

'You must be slipping, my old friend,' Tony quipped. 'You see, four henchmen are so much better than two, don't you think?' He grabbed the gun from John's hand and slapped his face.

John hardly flinched. 'You're too late, the tiger's already gone.'

The Tiger Chase

'Oh please. We know it's still here. We also know that one of the richest men, or should I say *nerds*, in the country is here with his wife—who just happens to be the hottest supermodel of the moment. I'm sure Mr Schwite wouldn't mind parting with a few hundred million dollars in return for the life of himself and his loved ones.

Sadly though, you're just a worthless, dispensable cop. Nobody's gonna pay a ransom for you, are they?' He lifted the gun to John's forehead. *'Bang!* Oh, I wish I could, but unfortunately, I promised my associate here the pleasure. He, whose interests include fine dining, French wine, shopping, and tearing people limb from limb. A delightful chap really—once you get to know him.'

John could tell Tony was enjoying every minute. He also realised Raymond Brown was growing impatient.

'Okay, split up and find them,' Tony said, waving his hand toward the different doorways.

Raymond Brown stood before the statue of *David* and began to shadow box, pulling his punches only millimetres from the white marble.

Tony Lee yawned then looked over at the doctor, who stood nervously holding the tranquilliser gun. 'Be ready with that gun, doctor. We wouldn't want any nasty accidents now, would we?'

After a few minutes, Tony glanced at his watch. 'What's taking them so long?'

Suddenly, 'Freeze ... slime balls!' Jimmy appeared in one of the doorways pointing a gun from Tony to Raymond to the doctor, and back.

John was amazed to see his old friend with Alicia and Beth on either side of him, each with a gun in hand.

'Oh my God, it's Charlie's Angels. Which one are you, Schwite?' Tony said, manoeuvring behind John and pushing the gun closer to his head.

'Drop your weapon, Lee. It's over,' Jimmy said.

Doctor Jiang dropped the tranquilliser gun and raised his arms.

'Doctor Jiang ... why?' Beth asked.

The doctor looked away and said nothing.

Raymond Brown took a deep breath then flicked his wrists. Two wooden darts flew out. One pinned Beth's shirt cuff to the wall and forced her to drop her gun. The other one embedded itself in Jimmy's neck, causing him to also drop his gun and yell out in pain. Raymond lurched forward and slapped the gun out of Alicia's hand.

Alicia involuntarily kicked out and connected with Raymond's crotch.

John expected him to double up in pain, but he didn't.

Raymond merely stood and smiled. He didn't even flinch when Alicia followed up with a solid punch to his jaw.

Jimmy yanked the dart from his neck, pounced forward, and tried to stab Raymond in the chest with it. But as the dart made contact with the rock-hard pectorals, it snapped in two, splintering his hand. He tried to throw a punch, but Raymond ducked, causing him to fall against Alicia.

Beth was struggling to free her wrist from the wall when she realised Raymond's demonic stare was now focused on her.

John launched his elbow into Tony Lee's fat gut then repeated the movement into his face when he bent forward. He spun round and punched him in the mouth, sending him flying back into the elevator.

Raymond Brown turned and redirected his stare at John. He dropped into a wide stance with one hand clenched into a fist and the other rigid like a knife. A low, deep growl emulated from his gut and rose in volume.

John slowly circled him, bobbing up and down like a boxer. Remembering their last encounter, and realising his opponent specialised in the art of defensive counterattacks, he decided to hold back and try to provoke him into making the first move.

Raymond Brown soon grew bored and, as if deciding to end it, stood up straight and marched towards John with his arms by his side and his chest puffed up like a British bulldog.

John punched low with a left to the abdomen and followed up with a right. Both blows sent his arms ricocheting back with little effect. He jabbed twice to the jaw with his left, then threw a right with all his strength. *CRACK!* His fist smashed into Raymond's jaw.

The Tiger Chase

Raymond stood firm, clicked his neck, grinned, and kept coming.

John skipped backwards leading his attacker around the foyer.

The grin suddenly fell from Raymond Brown's face like melting snow from a roof. He lurched forward and drove his elbow up under John's chin like a piston.

John's head whiplashed.

Raymond dropped to one knee and, with the open heel of his right hand, hit John hard in the groin.

John doubled over in agony.

Raymond remained in the same position for a few moments then looked up at Beth. He cracked his knuckles then bent and grabbed John by the hair.

Beth yanked her cuff free and flung herself at Raymond.

Raymond threw John's head to the floor and grabbed Beth by the throat. He stared into her eyes, slowly twisting his shoulder back, lifting and clenching his other fist.

A growl reverberated around the room once more.

This time, however, it wasn't from Raymond Brown.

Only John noticed when Doctor Jiang slid into the elevator, but he was more concerned with Beth than trying to stop him. The elevator door closed, and the lift went down.

'GRRREARGH!' Zhu Zhu pounced through the doorway and swiped at Raymond Brown's arm, digging her fully extended claws deep into his shoulder.

Beth broke free and ran to Alicia and Jimmy.

Zhu Zhu, snarling and growling, swiped with her other paw and slashed Raymond's neck. 'GRRREARGH!'

'Stop—please stop!' Raymond Brown scurried to the wall and cowered behind one of the stone chairs with his hands over his head. 'Please, get it away from me, please?' he yelled, his body trembling.

Zhu Zhu stood over him and roared once more.

John sat up and watched in disbelief at the hulk crying like a baby and clawing at the wall as if trying to scale it.

'Please, help me ... I'll give you anything you want. Just get it away from me, pleeeeeze?'

Beth and Alicia began to giggle while Zhu Zhu moved in closer, tormenting the once great Raymond Brown, forcing him to curl up into a ball.

'You all right, John?' Jimmy asked, helping his friend to his feet.

John's attention was drawn to the light on the elevator wall panel. The lift was on its way back up.

Beth ran to Zhu Zhu's side and gave her a big hug. 'Well done, baby, well done.'

Raymond Brown peered out from behind the chair. 'Please ... help me,' he sobbed.

'Get up, or I'll tell her to rip you to bits—NOW!' Beth yelled.

Raymond crawled warily from behind the chair and into the living room, where he cowered into the corner and sat with one fist pushed up against his mouth. 'Two tigers!' he mumbled. 'Two tigers ... one golden ... one blue!'

John instructed Jimmy and Alicia, each with a gun in hand, to take cover. 'When the doors open, fire.'

Moments later, the familiar *DING* rang out through the foyer and the elevator door began to open. John dropped to one knee and took aim.

'Hold your fire!' Captain Buster Williams yelled, stepping through the entrance, wearing a bulletproof vest. John dropped his aim and gave a sigh of relief.

Beth stepped back.

Jimmy and Alicia were still aiming their guns. 'One move, and you're a goner, mate!' Alicia growled.

'It's okay, you two ... it's my boss,' John said.

The captain explained to John how Tony Lee had been caught with his hands around Doctor Jiang's throat. Unfortunately for the doctor, being a frail man, his neck was broken by the time they reached the ground floor. The captain stepped back into the elevator then

The Tiger Chase

returned holding Tony Lee forcefully by the arm. 'There you go, detective, do what you've wanted to do for a long time.'

John smiled, read Tony Lee his rights and slapped the cuffs on his wrists.

Raymond Brown remained on his knees and whimpered when the captain yanked him to his feet.

John felt strangely lightheaded when Tony Lee and Raymond Brown were taken away.

'Shut the hell up you damn freak!' Tony screamed at Raymond, who was still sobbing uncontrollably. 'Tiger God, my ass!' he yelled when they were shoved into the elevator.

'Blue tiger,' Raymond muttered. 'Blue tiger.'

The captain told John to relax for a moment while he took care of the details. John led Jimmy, Alicia, Beth, and Zhu Zhu out onto the terrace so they could all get a much-needed breath of fresh air.

'So, what happened to the four heavies?' John asked.

'Oh, you would've been proud of us,' Jimmy said.

They all tried to talk at once.

'Hold it, hold it,' John held up his hands, trying not to curb their excitement. 'One at a time.'

Jimmy jumped in. 'We were hiding in the small bedroom at the back of the apartment when I realised that there was no way I could leave my old GI Joe partner on his own, so I told the girls to stay where they were, and I crept out.

I saw one of the thugs going out onto the terrace. I quietly followed him. Then I spotted the hose, so I grabbed it, pounced on him from behind, wrapped it around his neck and tied him up.'

'Wow!' John said, congratulating his friend.

'Ah, that's nothing,' Alicia piped in. 'I waited a couple of minutes after James had left then peeked round the bedroom door. I saw one of them going into the main bathroom, so I crept out and followed him. I peered round the bathroom door and saw him bent over the tub looking closely at the kitty litter. He picked a bit of it up and sniffed it. I grabbed a vase that was in the hallway then ran into the bathroom and smashed it over his head. Easy mate!' She high fived Beth.

'So, what about you?' John asked Beth.

'Oh, I wasn't nearly as brave. I stayed in the room. But then I heard something outside. I put my ear to the door and could hear someone opening the other doors in the corridor. I realised I only had seconds before whoever it was checked the room I was in, so I quickly grabbed a sheet off the bed and stood behind the door. Zhu Zhu was lying on the floor. The door burst open, and he came rushing in. I threw the sheet over his head. He tripped over Zhu Zhu and knocked himself out on the end of the bed.' The girls high fived once again.

'Okay, so what about the other guy?' John asked.

'That was an inadvertent team effort,' Jimmy said. 'We all pounced on the poor chap, including Zhu Zhu, from four angles. He didn't stand a chance. We quickly bound him up and pushed him out onto the terrace.'

'Wow! You guys are amazing although *very* stupid. You could have all been killed.'

'Yeah, but we weren't, were we, Johnny?' Beth said.

The captain came out onto the terrace. 'The media's been tipped off—there's news crews and reporters outside. They've been filming live for the last few minutes. It's like a circus down there. Now the bystanders are arriving.'

They went into the living room and turned on the TV.

'Damn!' John said, watching the crowds of people standing behind police barriers along the length of the street. 'You better do what you have to do, so we can get out of here,' he said to Beth.

Beth gave Zhu Zhu a preliminary check-up then announced that they were ready to leave.

Zhu Zhu stood in the middle of the elevator while John, Beth, Jimmy, Alicia, and Captain Williams squeezed in on either side.

They got off at the ground floor and made their way through the reception area. The deafening sound of the crowd cheering and

The Tiger Chase

shouting outside startled them. Journalists jostled near the entrance, taking pictures. The crowd began to clap and whistle when they caught sight of them.

Zhu Zhu gave a low roar and strode with her body close to the ground when they stepped outside and made their way down the cordoned-off walkway.

One reporter shouted, 'The eyes of the world are on you. Is there anything you want to say?'

'Yeah, mate. Save the South China tiger … NOW!' Alicia yelled back.

'You heard the lady,' John said.

Everyone laughed when John opened the cab door of the large racehorse transport, allowing Zhu Zhu to jump in and sit on the rear seat. Beth and Alicia climbed in and sat either side of her.

Two drivers had been allocated for the short journey to the zoo and, when they motioned for John and Jimmy to join the girls on the back seat, John strolled around the cab and opened the driver's door. 'Step down, son … this is a job for the GIs.'

Beth and Alicia looked at one another, shook their heads and smiled as if to say: 'Boys!'

With Jimmy by his side in the passenger seat, John turned the key and revved the engine loudly. He honked the horn and slowly pulled away from the sidewalk.

The crowd waved and cheered.

The convoy grew longer when twenty or so black and whites were joined by TV vans and curious motorists. Eager well-wishers lined the route, whistling and waving as they passed. Twenty minutes later, they pulled into the rear entrance of the LA Zoo where Doctor Malcolm Wilson and his team of specialists were waiting.

John stood by the enclosure while Beth conducted a complete medical examination of the LA Zoo's latest attraction, including an ultrasound test which showed four healthy cubs. For the next few weeks, Zhu Zhu would remain in quarantine before being introduced into her new enclosure.

Beth looked back and waved at Zhu Zhu through the bars when she and John walked away from the pen. They joined Jimmy and Alicia, who had been waiting outside. John, noticing a small tear in the corner of Beth's eye, put his arm around her and comforted her. A surge of energy suddenly raced through his veins. The pair flinched as if zapped by a static charge.

'Whoa ... what was that?' John said snatching his arm away.

'What was what?'

'Nothing.'

Later, when Jimmy and Alicia had gone home, John and Beth returned to the quarantine bay and stood against the enclosure watching Zhu Zhu sleep.

Beth looked up at John and smiled. 'I'm glad you're here.'

'I'm glad to be here. How is she?'

'She? Don't you mean *it*? She's fine. Healthy and safe.'

'Listen ... there's something I haven't told you ...' John paused awkwardly. 'Over the last few months ... I've been having the strangest dreams.'

'And I've been in them, right?'

'Yeah, how'd you know?'

'Because you've been in mine too!'

'Really?'

'Yep, but there's more,' Beth said, turning to look him in the eye. 'You've been in my dreams for longer than the last few months. Do you remember when we were kids, and you wouldn't let me play? I used to go up to my bedroom and watch you in your garden from my window. When I said Mrs Smith used to talk about you nonstop, well that was true, but I used to do a lot of talking too. You never knew it, but you had your very own fan club, John Dean, even though you were a bully.'

John blushed.

Beth stood on her tiptoes and kissed him. 'What do we do now, Johnny?'

63

Li and Yu trekked slowly through the forest holding hands. Yu was heavily pregnant and found the going hard. In the distance they could see the mighty blue monolith. Li smiled at Yu reassuringly.

When they reached the place of the secret entrance, Li carefully parted the enormous bamboo shoots for Yu to pass through. At the concealed entrance, Yu rested, while Li pulled the sliding rock open. Something startled them.

Lee Chong stepped through the bamboo, holding a rifle. 'At last, the secret entrance!'

'Lee Chong, I've been expecting you,' Li said.

Lee Chong lifted his rifle and aimed it at Li. 'You are a fool, Li Pang. You have defied the ancient code by leading me here.'

'True, but you are the fool, Lee Chong. You were given a great opportunity, but you didn't learn.'

Lee Chong looked round warily when a strange wind whipped up. 'What is happening?'

The wind grew steadily stronger, and a blue mist swirled around them.

'You didn't change, Lee Chong.' Li had to raise his voice to be heard. 'You were warned what would happen, but you didn't listen.'

The wind howled and bellowed. Suddenly, an enormous blue tiger pounced through the mist and knocked Lee Chong to the ground.

Li Pang put his arm around Yu and turned away, shielding her eyes and ears.

Lee Chong's screams were drowned by the sound of the wind and the ferocious snarling attack.

The wind dropped as quickly as it had started. The forest fell silent.

Li and Yu heard a long low growl, gradually growing in momentum. They slowly turned to find themselves staring into the eyes of a golden male tiger.

The tiger crouched and snarled. Its lips quivered over enormous fangs. *'GRRREARGH!'* It pounced and raced towards Li and Yu.

Li pushed Yu behind him and stood tall.

The tiger stopped right in front of them. It snarled and spat, baring its teeth. Then it turned and disappeared into the trees.

'Goodbye, cousin!' Li Pang called after it. 'Look after the forest.'

Li Pang stepped back from Huan Loh's grave, dusted the dirt from his hands and patted Wang on the head. He returned to where Yu stood holding their young son, and placed his arm around them both. *How lucky I am*, he thought. *A beautiful wife and son, a new home ... and a new job. Such responsibility.* The future of the world and mankind was in his hands and those of his beautiful wife. The child of Tao would be nurtured and taught the ways of the forest until it was time for him to leave and take his place in the real world. When that day finally came, people would learn to live in harmony with nature, or perish. There would be no blood sports or trophy hunts. Forests would no longer be plundered. Each creature would claim its right to what it needed for survival—no more, no less.

That night, in their dreams, Li and his family would fly on dragon's wings to the City of Angels to witness the joining of the Dragon and the Tigress. Li's gift to them would be eternal love, eternal happiness ... and eternal life.

64

'Silence, silence—be seated!' yelled the warden.

Anxious shouts and catcalls gradually lowered into excitable whispers while Robert Baker and three hundred men in orange uniforms took their seats.

A large clank echoed through the gymnasium followed moments later by an identical sound from the opposite side of the hall. Everyone rose to their feet, craning their necks for a better view.

Two figures, flanked by guards, made their way to the boxing ring in centre of the hall. The warden nodded to the short stocky referee then took his seat.

The two figures entered the ring and stood toe to toe while the referee read out a list of rules. Everyone took their seats. The room fell into silence.

The bell rang out. *DING DING!*

Tony Lee sucked hard on his gum shield and lifted his gloves until they almost hid his face. Then, dragging his right foot behind him, he shuffled towards the middle of the ring.

Raymond Brown stood without moving in the opposite corner. His head was raised slightly and his lips chattered as if he were arguing with himself.

Tony Lee beckoned with his gloved hands for him to approach.

Raymond suddenly marched towards him with his arms by his side.

Robert Baker's money was on Raymond Brown. He knew it should only take one punch, but something told him not to underestimate his old boss, Tony Lee.

The fighters were only an arm's length apart now and Raymond Brown was wide open. As if seeing his chance, Tony pulled his shoulder back as far as he could and let go with the most tremendous right Robert had ever seen. At that exact moment though Raymond Brown's enormous right fist rotated and exploded upwards like a mechanical piston.

SMACK!

The crowd erupted and rose to its feet when the two fighters made contact at exactly the same time.

A single lifeless body fell to the canvas.

Acknowledgments (2004)

I'd like to thank my wife, Jane, for her unquestioning love and support. My kids—who are no longer kids—Lucy and Lee, for keeping my feet planted firmly on the ground.

I'd like to thank my friends and family—Megan Hunt, Mark Gibbons, Tracy Parr, Jennie Price and Susan Clackett for reading an early draft of the original manuscript and giving valuable feedback and support. I'd also like to thank Sue Pearson for her advice and for making me a better writer.

My sincere thanks go to Ms Li Quan of the Save China's Tigers charity, who I am sure will be rightfully recognised one day soon as the saviour of the South China tiger, and to the Chinese government for their efforts in saving one of their most valuable treasures.

Thank you to Maxine Annabell of the Tiger Territory NZ for the very first blurb and to all those who have reviewed my work.

The following individuals unknowingly helped me by providing a wealth of information either in book form, video, or Internet: Dr Ronald Tilson and his team at the Minnesota Zoo; Peter Jackson, President of the IUCN; Michael Day, author of Fight for the Tiger; Colonel Jim Corbett; Billy Ardjan Singh; Fateh Singh Rathore; Kailash Sankhala; Valmik Thapor; Guy Mountfort; Dr Gary Koehler; The World Wildlife Fund, and The Tiger Foundation.

And finally to those people who for reasons of their own felt they couldn't contribute, and to those single-minded experts who have given up on the South China tiger, I'd like to thank them all for stirring up a passion in me to prove them wrong.

If you would like to learn more about the South China tiger's plight please visit: www.savechinastigers.org

ABOUT THE AUTHOR

ANDY M^CD (aka Andrew M^CDermott) lives on the glorious Gold Coast of Australia and is the CEO of Publicious Book Publishing. His first novel (*The Tiger Chase* - 1st edition) was published in the US in 2002, which was followed up with the launch in San Diego and a book tour of the US, including LA and Las Vegas. More titles followed.

2022 sees the unveiling of the new brand ANDY M^CD, and the launch of Andy's exciting new novel set entirely on the Gold Coast called *X*. This will be followed by the launch of three more titles throughout the year, with more to come in 2023 and beyond.

Andy was born in Nottingham, England. A naturalised Aussie he has lived on the Gold Coast for the last 32 years with his wife, Jane. He is a patron of the Gold Coast Writers Association, and currently resides at Kirra Beach.

SAMPLE CHAPTER FROM X BY ANDY McD

1

3 September
Unable to look at the victim, the ruddy-faced security guard watched me with industrious eyes as if awaiting instructions.

'Who found her?' I asked.

He nodded towards a group of students huddled close by.

'You know her?'

He shook his head. 'Seen her around the campus, that's about all …' The mints he'd recently consumed did little to mask the smell of cigarettes on his breath.

'Do any of you know her?' I called back to the group.

'Yes,' a tall, skinny guy with a beard said. 'Her name is Lisa … Lisa Wei.'

'Okay, I'm gonna get you guys to move back.' Pointing towards the edge of the building. 'Over there, please.'

Surveying the area where the killing had taken place. It was outside the entrance to Varsity Towers – privately owned student accommodation at the outer edge of the Bond University campus.

'And I'll get you to make sure no one comes out the exit,' I instructed the security guard.

He nodded, willingly taking up post in front of the glass doors, his back to the scene.

This would be the seventh murder in only three weeks. I'd only seen pictures of the previous crime scenes. The killings had been identical—all young women, their throats slashed in an X, jugular veins skilfully severed on either side, causing the victims to bleed out in a matter of minutes. On each occasion, the victim had been laid out with a large pool of blood at their feet.

Although I was the first on the scene, the wailing sirens in the distance meant I wouldn't be alone for long, so there wouldn't be much time to look around.

The victim was about twenty years old. Asian, possibly Chinese. Her body and clothing were saturated in blood from the gaping wounds on her neck, but her face was as white as chalk. Looking straight ahead as if startled, eyes that only moments before would have sparkled with the inquisitive energy of a carefree student, now dull and void of life.

Kneeling beside the blood, I could clearly see where she'd fallen to her knees, supported herself with one hand while probably clutching at her throat with the other. But there was no sign of her collapsing forwards. The killer must have grabbed her hair from behind, yanking her head backwards, increasing the dwindling blood flow. Then, once she'd lost consciousness, he'd laid her out.

With so much blood, there had to be footprints—or at least some sign of a struggle. Squatting, I followed the edges of what was two pools of blood combined as one, but I found nothing. All the marks appeared to be from the victim.

Suddenly, the whole area lit up as the first of a zillion squad cars came to a squealing halt.

'Step away please, sir,' a uniformed constable yelled as two of them jumped from the first of the cars.

I held up my detective's badge as more units arrived.

Detective Inspector Dion Gardner, the first detective to arrive, immediately took charge.

'What the hell are *you* doing here?' he asked, noticing me.

'Doing what a detective does, mate.' I had a problem with calling him 'sir.'

'Detective? Ha! I'll get you to step away.'

Reluctantly, I rose to my feet and moved to one side. Ignoring Gardner, I continued to scan the scene as if he wasn't there.

The ground floor of the building was a car park. Entry to the apartments was accessible via a double glass door leading to a small foyer and lifts. Looking up at the security camera, I realised that from the angle at which it was set the murder scene was out of shot—but only just. The killer had positioned the spot perfectly.

I imagined him waiting out of sight, and Lisa, possibly late from a class, marching back towards the dorm with her head down. The blood spray facing away from the door indicated he must have approached her from behind, making her turn. A tap on the shoulder perhaps?

'You still here, fuck face?' Gardner said loudly enough for all the uniforms present to hear. 'Why don't you go get us all a cup of coffee, eh?' he continued, clumsily stepping in the edge of the blood. 'Shit.'

I was about to reply when the detective in charge arrived— Detective Inspector Des Williams. By this time, the uniforms had cordoned off the area. Forensics personnel continued to arrive, and a white tent was erected over the scene.

'Who found her?' Des threw the question into the air, aiming it at everyone present.

Gardner shrugged, wiping his shoe on the ground.

'Over there,' I pointed to the group of students. A crowd was now forming on the other side of the police barrier.

'Scott? What are you doing here?'

'I was on my way home, sir. Picked up the call.'

'You the first here?'

'Yes, sir. I was heading along Bermuda Street.'

'Okay, come with me.'

Des was my boss. He was a good bloke. Already at the top of his game and having been so for some years, he had nothing to prove.

'Which one of you guys found her?' he asked the group.

A small Indian girl raised her hand. She was being comforted by the tall bearded guy.

'Did you see anybody else in the area? Anyone at all?'

'No.'

'Is there anything you can tell us?'

'No, I was just coming back to the dorm and … and she was lying there.' She turned into the tall guy's chest, sobbing.

'Do you all know the victim?'

The group nodded in unison.

'Okay. Detective Constable Stephens here is going to ask you some questions, but we'll need you to come down to Surfers Paradise Police Headquarters to make official statements.' He marched back towards the crime scene.

I pulled out my notebook.

X

It was after midnight when I finally returned to Surfers Paradise. Des had called the team together for a briefing. When I say 'team,' I mean the group of detectives and selected uniforms who had been brought together to form the catalyst of the investigation. All were privy to the more delicate details of the case. But in reality, every police officer on the coast was part of a much bigger team, canvassing the surrounding neighbourhoods and taking statements. There was also a 24/7 presence on the streets and in the air, ensuring a visible vigilance was maintained. Two floors of Police Headquarters had also been allocated to over a hundred officers and staff manning the phones and sifting through possible leads.

As usual, I sat at the back of the room. Jenny Radford, our newest detective, joined me.

'Hey.' She was friendly, a bit younger than me perhaps, but a fellow surfer. 'I hear you were first on the scene.'

'Yep.'

I was surprised to see Superintendent Andrew Ripley enter the room. He took his place by Des's side.

Des stepped towards a large whiteboard that displayed photographs of the previous victims. 'Okay, you all know why we're here.' He added another photograph to the board. 'Victim number seven. Twenty-year-old Lisa Wei, a Bond University student, was killed at approximately nine o'clock this evening.'

Without being prompted, Dion Gardner stood. 'As usual, there was no evidence at the scene—no prints, nothing, but I ...'

'Take a seat, detective.' Des cut him short, preventing him from showing off in front of Ripley.

Gardner slunk back into his chair like an ostracised schoolboy.

'We know very little about the victim at this time,' Des continued. 'Scott, perhaps you'd like to fill us in?'

I was listening but not comprehending. Was he talking to me?

'Scott?'

Shit, he was! I rose to my feet. 'Uhm ...' I'd never spoken in front of the team before.

'Tell us what you learned about the victim.'

I pulled out my notebook. The only information I had to add was that Lisa Wei was an overseas student from Hong Kong. She'd been studying social sciences at Bond University for two years. Her parents—the father, an eye specialist; and the mother, a clinical psychologist—had been notified. She had a small group of friends, whom she usually met on a Tuesday evening at Varsity Lakes Tavern for trivia night.

'Is that all you got?' Gardner sneered.

'You were first at the scene,' Des said, ignoring Gardner, 'notice anything out of the ordinary?'

'I did get the chance to have a bit of a look around before anyone else got there.'

Superintendent Ripley raised an eyebrow.

'This was a very cleverly planned operation. The attack took place literally millimetres out of shot of the entrance's security camera, and at the time of night when most students were either in their dorms studying or over at the tavern for the trivia.'

'So, you think the killer is carefully picking the locations?' Des questioned.

'Yes.'

'And the victims too?' Ripley threw in.

'It's obvious the victims have been preselected and watched in the days leading up to the killings,' Gardner said.

I was surprised when Des and Ripley looked to me for confirmation.

'I don't agree. I think the location is the important factor. A spider will build a web in a high-traffic location.'

'Right, so the victims are like flies. That makes sense,' Ripley said, glaring at Des as if to say, *Why the hell hadn't you thought of that?*

'Each crime scene has been in an area where young women come and go,' I continued. 'Look at tonight—student accommodation. Perfect!'

'Did you notice anything else about the scene before it was … contaminated?' Des asked, shooting an irritated glance at Gardner.

'I would have expected to see some tracks, but once again, this killer knows exactly what he's doing.'

I'd always liked Des. He was an honest cop who treated people with respect.

'What are your thoughts, detective?'

It felt good to be spoken to as an equal. 'With the amount of blood at the scene and the rate at which it would have sprayed from the victim, some had to have landed on the killer.'

'You think he was covered up?'

'Yes. Perhaps a coat of some kind, or an overall, but something he could arrive at the scene wearing without being too conspicuous, then remove and get away without being noticed.'

'Have all the bins in the area been checked?' Des asked Senior Detective Constable Dale Mason, who was seated at the front.

'Being done as we speak, sir.'

'Like on the previous occasions, I don't think you'll find anything,' I added. 'My guess is it would be something he could stuff into a backpack and take away with him.'

'Good work, detective,' Des said.

'Yes, good work indeed!' Ripley agreed, his gaze lingering in my direction.

'Wow. Look at you,' Jenny said in a hushed voice when I returned to my seat. 'You actually sounded like a detective!'

'Perhaps I *am* a detective.'

Available in paperback and ebook here:
andymcd.com.au

SAMPLE CHAPTER FROM FLIRTING WITH THE MOON BY ANDY McD

1

Detectives and uniformed police officers filed into the crime incident room and took their seats.

I glanced over my shoulder at the gruesome gallery of victims. Eleven young people each murdered and left in a public place, their bodies mutilated beyond recognition. Beside this, was a projector screen showing a map of LA, and next to that a whiteboard covered in newspaper clippings. A front-page headline of the *LA Times* blared: 'Is Detective Joe Dean Flirting with The Moon?' The press and I shared a mutual loathing. And it was they who had coined the phrase "The Moon" due to the killer's penchant for striking on the first night of the new moon.

My partner, Detective Jacqueline Sanchez, handed out copies of the latest profile report.

Being old-school, I had mixed feelings about the presence of Doctor Charles Dudley, aka 'Chuck,' our in-house FBI profiler. The fact that he looked like a freshman didn't help, but I figured he'd at least be able to field some of the questions.

When everyone was present, I began.

'As we know, tonight is the start of the new moon.' On the overhead projector, I drew a circle on the map, its diameter covering East LA to Santa Monica, North Hollywood to Inglewood. All the killings had occurred within this relatively small area, and all over the last eleven months.

A detective at the back of the room thrust his hand in the air.

'But it's New Year's Eve and we've got just about every cop this side of Texas in town, surely—'

Chuck stepped forward and stood beside me. 'We can't assume that he won't strike. The pattern is unlikely to change. If anything, I believe the added risk will spur the killer on.'

'We have to be extra vigilant,' I interjected. 'Look for anything out of the ordinary.

You all have your assigned areas; it's going to be a wild night.'

I placed a second slide on top of the one already on the projector lens. Sanchez had marked the position of the previous murder scenes. 'According to the profile, it's unlikely that the killer will return to any of these spots, but we also can't rule it out. Going by… shall we say … his past creativity, if a killing does take place tonight, it'll be staged in a way that'll be completely different to the others. Are there any questions?'

'Yes.' A burly, balding detective with the face of a prize-fighter lumbered to his feet. 'Can whoever gets to nail this bastard have some time off?'

I knew where he was coming from. Unshaven, red puffy eyes, shirt hanging out the back of his pants—all signs that he too had been working around the clock. The rest of us didn't look any better.

'How's a week in Vegas sound for the cop who catches The Moon?'

Sanchez raised a questioning eyebrow.

I needed to solve the case and put this psychopath behind bars. I needed to get my life back. At this point I'd promise anything to achieve this.

'Woo hoo!' the detective cried. 'Vegas here I come!'

The room erupted with applause.

After the briefing, Sanchez and I made our way to the communications room.

'I'm sure the LAPD won't be springing for no trips to Vegas, Joe.'

'I know. But I will, and gladly!' I stopped mid-stride as if I'd had a sudden thought. 'I'll catch you up, just got to get something from my office.'

The little crease between Sanchez's eyes, the clamping of her lips and the subtle shake of her head told me she knew exactly where I was going.

'It's okay, I'll just be a minute.'

Grateful that my office had no windows, I closed the door behind me, strode to my desk and pulled out a bottle of Jack Daniels from the bottom drawer. Once you've descended into the gutter of addiction, one of the first things you lose is a need for ceremony. I twisted off the bottle top and gulped down the bourbon like a marathon runner at the last water stop.

There was a knock and before I could answer, Sanchez was poking her head around the door.

I fumbled the bottle back into the drawer. 'What is it?' I snapped.

She gave me her usual knowing look. 'You got visitors.'

'What? Who?' I rustled among the piles of papers on the desk, found what I was looking for and scooped a mint into my mouth.

Sanchez opened the door fully and stepped aside. My wife swept into the room carrying Johnny, our three-year-old son.

'Kathy?'

'Seeing as you haven't been home since God knows when I thought I'd catch you here. I reckoned at least here we'd be able to talk while you were sober. She looked at my mouth working on the mint. 'I see I was wrong.'

Ignoring her, I reached out for my son. 'Hey Sport.'

Johnny frowned and pulled away as if he didn't know me.

'It's okay,' Kathy comforted him. 'Go with Aunty Jacky. I won't be long.'

Sanchez quietly took Johnny from his mother's arms and left the room.

Kathy closed the door behind her.

'What's going on?'

'What's going on?' She threw back her head and laughed. 'You're the big-shot detective, surely *you* can figure it out!'

I offered a searching shrug, but a feeling of dread was cooling the hot liquor in my belly.

'Okay, I'll spell it out for you, and I'll keep it short because I'm sure you're just dying for another drink.'

Part of me already knew what she was going to say but even so, when she said the words, they pierced my guts like a knife.

'It's over, Joe, I'm leaving you.'

The effects of the bourbon were now completely gone, and I began to shake. 'Seriously? You're telling me this here? Now? On tonight of all nights?'

'And there we have it ... Joe Dean the victim. How could *I* possibly do this to *you*? Especially when you've been working *so* hard. What a *heartless* bitch I am!'

'Not now, Kathy, please.' I glanced at the desk drawer longing for the comfort and escape that lay inside. 'You know what's been happening with the case and the pressure I've been under—'

'I don't know anything. You don't talk to me. I only learn what's happening from what I see on the news.'

'That's not true. Let's get tonight over with, then we can talk.'

'When was the last time we had a conversation? When was the last time you spent any time with your son?' Her voice rose with each word until she was screaming.

'Shhh ... keep it down.' I rushed to the door as if doing so would dampen the sound from the rest of the building.

'I just came to tell you it's over. You can pick up your things from the house, but you won't be staying. I've been a single parent for a long time now, may as well make it official. We *don't* need you anymore!'

'You can't just kick me out of my home and stop me from seeing my son.' Now *I* was yelling.

Kathy repeated that humourless laugh. It was as ugly as the scorn on her face. 'Your home? *This* is your home right here. Always has been. And as for your son, ha! He doesn't even know who you *are!*' She stormed out of the room.

I should've followed her. I should've begged her to reconsider and promised her I would change. I should've fought to save my marriage. But I didn't. Instead, I closed the door behind her, rushed to my desk and dived through the escape hatch.

Sanchez sat at one of the control panels in the communications room wearing headphones and a mic. She didn't look up as I entered.

There were two walls filled with monitors, each showing a close-up view of a specific area in the city. A row of uniformed officers worked in front of consoles, making the room look like NASA mission control.

I took the vacant seat next to Sanchez and put on a matching headset. Static and short radio bursts from the cruisers and mobile units on the streets filled my ears. On one of the monitors there was a view of Hollywood Boulevard. 'Unit Five, do you read me?' I said into the mouthpiece.

'Loud and clear.'

I watched as The Roosevelt Hotel appeared to driver's right, while the ever-present crowd from Grauman's Chinese Theatre spilled onto the road on his left. My God, what an impossible task this was going to be.

On another monitor, Santa Monica Boulevard and the entrance to the pier were also heaving, and it was only eight-thirty. 'Unit Nine, do you read me?'

'Copy that.'

I didn't need to ask them how things were going; the monitors showed me exactly what they were seeing. I felt useless here; I wanted to be out on the streets, I wanted to catch this bastard myself and nail him up on the nearest wall.

By eleven-thirty, the streets of LA were one big open-air party. I tried to remember the last time I had let loose and enjoyed myself. Being drunk and enjoying yourself are two completely different things—on the former I was an expert, the latter a novice.

Basically, all we had done for the last three and a half hours was watch the monitors, listen to radio transmissions and, in our minds, try to piece together the jigsaw that The Moon had created. When the City Hall clock struck midnight, I was damn right miserable.

'Happy New Year!' one of the young female cops cried out, snapping me out of my stupor.

The others rose from their seats and shook hands, slapped each other on the back, and hugged. I stayed put but Sanchez leaned across and wrapped her arms around me. 'Make a resolution, Joe,' she whispered in my ear.

'Already have.'

'I don't mean catching The Moon.'

I knew exactly which way the conversation was heading. I turned back to my console and was about to put on my headset when Sanchez grabbed my arm.

'I'm talking about the drinking.'

'I know you are. I'm okay, it's under control.'

'Is it?' Those arching eyebrows again, speaking a language all of their own. 'So, if you knew of a detective who was drinking while on duty would you say it's okay?'

'I said I'm okay, goddamn it!' I growled at her but instantly regretted it. Sanchez was tough, not the kind of woman who'd back down from a male outburst.

'Stop drinking, sort things out with Kathy, and spend some time with Johnny no matter the outcome of tonight.'

Well, that was easy because in my mind that's exactly what I'd decided to do. 'Okay, I promise!' It might have come out as a mutter, but it was a promise I desperately wanted to keep.

Over the next hour the festivities on the streets continued but were noticeably thinning out.

'Let's pray for a miracle, Joe.' Sanchez's voice was heartfelt. I suspected she still attended Catholic services, but she rarely spoke of her private life.

As we watched the monitors gradually grow quiet, the churning in my stomach was telling me it was *too* quiet.

'You hungry?' Sanchez said.

I realised I was and nodded.

'Mexican?' She was already rising to her feet.

'Speedy's still open?'

'Yep, all night.'

Sanchez didn't need to ask me for my order. We ate takeaway from Speedy's Casa de Mexico a lot. More adventurous than me, my partner liked to try different dishes, but mine was always the same—burritos and chilli. 'Anyone else want Mexican?' she yelled turning to the rest of the crew.

Her question was met by grunts and headshakes.

Most of the monitors were now showing street cleaners going about their work and a handful of drunken revellers here and there reluctant for the party to end. There had been the usual arrests but nothing serious, which was good but still my stomach churned, and the hunger wasn't helping. Sanchez had been gone a while. I checked my watch—3.00 am. I swung around to the room. 'Anyone see Sanchez come back?' I asked loud enough for everyone to hear.

There was a chorus of 'Nopes.'

I tried her cell phone. It rang until her message bank clicked on: 'This is Detective Jacqueline Sanchez of the LAPD. Leave a message. I'll get back to you.'

Speedy's could've been busy, but at three o'clock in the morning? Fresh air seemed like a good idea for me too. I'd sat at that console playing Big Brother all night. 'If anyone needs me, I've got my cell.' I grabbed my jacket, made a detour to my office, and downed a conservative estimate of two doubles—which in reality was probably more like four—then headed out of the building.

Speedy's was only a block away from the Parker Center off East 1st Street. It was the last establishment at the far end of a narrow alley that hosted a few other small businesses: a Chinese restaurant, a tattoo parlour and a gym. The light from Speedy's window barely illuminated the way. It was the only place still open. The rest of the storefronts were quiet and dark. The little, middle-aged hombre with the biggest smile this side of Tijuana was cleaning the counter tops.

'Hey Detective José,' he said with a tired grin when I leaned in through the door. 'You catch el bastardo?'

'No, not yet.'

'So, you steel hungry?'

As soon as he said that, I knew. In fact, if I'm honest, I'd known the last time I'd checked my watch back at headquarters.

I must've suddenly looked ill because Speedy stopped cleaning and rushed to my side. 'What's wrong, Mr Dean?'

'When was Detective Sanchez here?'

'About an hour ago. She buy usual burrito with chilli for you and special New Year rice for her.'

I don't remember leaving Speedy's and heading back to the Parker; I don't know if I ran or walked. When I entered the lobby, the duty officer called me over. 'It just arrived, sir. I was about to call up to you.' He handed me a Speedy's takeaway carton.

Looking down at the unopened box in my hand, I could feel its warmth.

'Everything all right, sir?'

'Who brought this in?'

'A young delivery guy.'

'Speedy doesn't deliver. No sign of Detective Sanchez?'

'Haven't seen her since she left earlier, sir.'

Flirting with The Moon

I went straight to my office, closed the door and placed the carton on my desk. 'Sonofabitch.' I paced the room, taking shots of bourbon, stealing glances at the carton, still pacing, pacing. In a matter of minutes, the bottle was empty. I tossed it into the waste paper bin then suddenly felt the need to busy myself. I checked my watch but didn't see the time. I glanced along the files on my shelves but didn't see a single one. I wanted to do anything but look inside that carton. I opened the bottom drawer of my filing cabinet, knelt on the floor, and reached into the back to where my stash was hidden. I was a prepared alcoholic.

When I finally sat at my desk with the now half-empty bottle of Jack Daniels, my life had changed forever. Detective Joseph Dean of the LAPD was no more. Joe Dean, husband and father was no more.

I slammed down the bottle, grabbed the carton, opened it, and looked inside.

Available in paperback and ebook here:
andymcd.com.au